Katia Lief is the author of several crime novels, including YOU ARE NEXT (Ebury Press). She teaches fiction writing as a part-time faculty member at the New School in Manhattan and lives with her family in Brooklyn, New York.

D0264146

Also by Katia Lief:

You Are Next

Hide
And
Seek

Katia Lief

EBURY
PRESS

3 5 7 9 10 8 6 4

"Family Tree" written by Tunde Adebimpe, Dave Sitek, Kyp Malone,
Jaleel Bunton & Gerard Smith, © 2008 Chrysalis Music and Stunzeed
Music. All rights administered by Chrysalis Music. International
Copyright Secured. Used by Permission. All rights Reserved.

First published in the US in 2010 as *Next Time You See Me*
by Avon Books, an imprint of HarperCollins Publishers

Published in the UK in 2011 by Ebury Press, an imprint of Ebury Publishing
A Random House Group Company

The Random House Group Limited Reg. No. 954009

Addresses for companies within the Random House Group can be found at
www.randomhouse.co.uk

A CIP catalogue record for this book is available from the British Library

The Random House Group Limited supports The Forest Stewardship Council
(FSC®), the leading international forest certification organisation. Our books
carrying the FSC label are printed on FSC® certified paper. FSC is the only
forest certification scheme endorsed by the leading environmental
organisations, including Greenpeace. Our paper procurement policy can be
found at www.randomhouse.co.uk/environment

Printed and bound by CPI Group (UK) Ltd, Croydon, CR0 4YY

ISBN 9780091937928

To buy books by your favourite authors and register for offers visit:
www.randomhouse.co.uk

For Eli

ACKNOWLEDGMENTS

I'd like to extend my gratitude to the people who have stood by me before and stand by me still as I strive to tell stories I hope will captivate readers. Matt Bialer, my longtime literary agent, continues to be a savvy early reader and booster of confidence. I would be remiss not to thank others who work alongside him at Sanford J. Greenburger Associates: Lindsay Ribar for her keen editorial eye and all-around smarts, and Stephanie Diaz for extending the reach of my books into other countries. I am grateful to my editor, Lucia Macro, whose clear-eyed yet always gentle editing brought this novel to a safe landing. And to Esi Sogah, Eleanor Mikucki, Thomas Egner, Pamela Spengler-Jaffee, Shawn Nichols, Christine Maddalena, and all the talented people at HarperCollins who turn a manuscript into a real book: *You* made it beautiful and readable, and I thank you.

To my children: You amaze me as you grow and transform beside me, book after book after book. You are in every single child I ever write, and in every thought a mother thinks on my pages.

And for Oliver, my husband . . . there aren't enough words. Tender man, expert editor: You are the net under the high wire, keeping me balanced and safe.

PART I

CHAPTER 1

I opened my eyes moments before Ben cried. It was the same every morning, as if our bodies were aligned with the sun. I would wake up just in time to see the first trickle of light seep around the edges of the blackout shades on our bedroom windows, banishing the gray from the white walls, revealing the gold bicycle and silver moon in the framed poster across from our bed, and I would hear it: a hum, at first, and then a moan that transformed into my name. Not my name, exactly—not Karin—but *Mommy*.

The first time he'd called me that, about six months ago, I burst into tears. Deluded by half sleep, I had thought for a split second that Cece was calling for me; and then I remembered that she had been gone for over five years. The memory of her small, murdered body, her bloody room, flashed at me. I had to shake my head to disperse the image.

As I moved to get up and go to Ben, Mac's fingertips ran lightly down my back. His touch startled me; I hadn't realized he was awake.

"I'll go," he said.

"I don't mind."

"Let me."

I lay back in bed and closed my eyes, listening as my husband's footsteps crossed our room into the hall, as the toilet flushed, as he walked into Ben's room across from ours, as a mournful "Mommy?" became a gleeful "Daddy!" Silence as the diaper was changed. And then Mac carried Ben to our bed, saying, "I have a present for you." Ben snuggled beside me, and I breathed in his sweet first-morning smell, and ran my fingers through his hair, dark brown like Mac's before it went half gray. We cuddled until Mac returned a few minutes later with two cups of coffee and the morning paper. Before heading into the bathroom to shower and shave, he turned on the TV and Ben crawled to the foot of our bed where he sat bolt upright watching *Sesame Street.*

"It's already hot out," Mac told me, having opened the door to retrieve the newspaper from the front stoop. "Want me to put on the AC?"

"Not yet." I hated the grind of the air conditioners as much as I liked how they dried up the spongy end-of-August heat. Soon it would be autumn and we'd have the respite of cool breezes. I sat up, sipped my coffee, opened the newspaper against bent knees. After fifteen minutes of browsing the front section I picked up the business section and was greeted by Mac's face. He had recently been interviewed by a reporter about his new job.

"Mac!"

"What?"

"They ran the article today."

I got out of bed with the newspaper and tapped on the locked bathroom door. "It's me. Open up." We still weren't ready to let Ben see the constellation of scars covering Mac's body, the vivid reminder of our former lives as detectives. Someday we would have to tell our son the story of what happened to us in our encounters with the Domino killer, the simplest way to think of the team of serial killers who brutally murdered my first husband and child, and nearly stole Mac's life as well. Someday, but not yet. Right now, Ben was an innocent toddler in what could possibly be the sweetest year of his life; at least that's how I remembered the year between one and two with my daughter, Cece, before the terrible twos struck with a vengeance. She barely made it to three. Eventually, gradually, the world would rob Ben of his innocence. And someday, when the time was right, we would fill in the details.

The bathroom door swung open and there was Mac, naked but for a towel wrapped around his lower half, his chest and back speckled with the tough little whitish scars. Just below his left collarbone was the nickel-sized tattoo of a lavender dahlia he'd gotten in a bout of adolescent rebellion when his father was pressuring him to go to college so he wouldn't end up in the family business, running the hardware store; in the end, he decided his father was right and gave up his resistance, but the tattoo remained. He'd once joked that he didn't need to explain his life to anyone, he could just lift his shirt and his history would be revealed in the ruinous alterations of his skin.

Half his face was slathered in foam (erasing the cleft in his chin) and the other half was cleanly shaven. I held up the newspaper for him to see the photograph of himself sitting behind his desk at the corporate headquarters of Quest Security, above a caption reading: *Seamus "Mac" MacLeary was recently promoted to senior vice president of Forensic Security,* and below the headline "MacLeary Replaces Stein in Sudden Shift at Quest."

"He said it would run sometime early this week and that he'd give me a heads-up."

"Which he didn't do."

"Who knows? I haven't checked my e-mail all weekend." He peered at himself in the newspaper. "I'm still not sure it was such a good idea."

"You're in the private sector now," I reminded him. "Fair game. And that kind of promotion always comes with scrutiny, especially since Deidre was well liked."

"True." He shook his head. "Did you read it? What does it say about her?"

I skimmed the article, looking for Deidre's name. "It says '. . . who was let go abruptly last week in an alleged pay-for-play corruption scandal involving an exchange of money for altered forensic testimony in a high-profile legal case.' That's all it says."

"Alleged," Mac said. "That's good. They'll have to *prove* she cheated. It makes me sick to get her job this way." It had been his mantra the entire week since Deidre had been forced out. His other mantra had been: "I hope she countersues for race discrimination or sex discrimination, take your pick."

I had met Deidre a few times, briefly. She was a light-skinned black woman in her middle thirties, with an impeccable educational pedigree and a reputation as an effective manager and a tough cookie. Mac had worked with her for over a year and had always thought highly of her. Watching her get the axe, seeing himself moved abruptly into her position, had pained him; but he was no wilting lily, having been a cop for two decades, and he dutifully took the job.

"Good news and bad news," he had said upon returning home one night a week ago. "What do you want first?"

I had stared at him, unwilling to answer. He knew I didn't want it if it was bad news.

"Okay," he plunged in, "good news first: I got a huge

raise. Bad news is they went through with it. Deidre's out. I'm the boss now."

I had to remind him to focus on the positive: A promotion of that caliber was an honor, not to mention that his pay raise would be a boon to us as I was bringing in nothing at the moment besides my disability income (those checks were another sad reminder of how my life and work had fatefully collided). Motherhood had slowed my progress toward a college degree but I was still plugging along, taking courses in forensic psychology at John Jay College of Criminal Justice, in slow preparation for my second career. After a couple of margaritas at the local Mexican restaurant over the weekend, Mac had joked that we should both ditch our last names and call ourselves Mr. and Mrs. Forensic. I laughed, but couldn't help wondering if the comment betrayed disappointment that I had stayed Karin Schaeffer, holding on to my first husband's last name, especially since Mac's first wife, Val, gave up MacLeary to become Ng when she remarried.

He patted dry his face and kissed me. His skin carried the spicy scent of the aftershave I'd given him for Father's Day as a kind of joke. Next year maybe he'd get a tie. The year after, a golf ball paperweight. For Mother's Day, so far, he hadn't risked a silly gift but had taken the challenge to please me seriously: beautiful earrings, a lush silk scarf.

"Have time for breakfast?" I asked him.

"I do."

The phone rang and on his way back into the bedroom to get dressed, he answered it, repeating "Hello?" twice before hanging up.

"Who was that?"

"Unknown caller."

"I hate that guy."

We laughed.

A minute later the phone rang again, caller ID announcing NYPD—New York Police Department. I answered.

"Karin, it's Billy. So Mac's famous now!" Detective Billy Staples, from Brooklyn's Eighty-fourth Precinct— our very own—had become Mac's closest friend since he'd quit the Maplewood Police, moved here, married me, and started a new life. "How's it feel to be hitched to a big shot?"

"You'll have to convince him he's a big shot yourself." I passed the phone to Mac, who took it between shoulder and ear as he finished buckling his belt.

Sesame Street went into a sketch change and I used the opportunity to switch off the TV and transition Ben to breakfast time.

"Can't tonight," I heard Mac say. "Karin's got a class." He listened, then looked at me and asked, "Friday? He's busy every other night."

"Friday we have our dinner at the Union Square Café!" My tone reminded him how important it was: Our second wedding anniversary was less than a week away. Accustomed to doing things out of sync (I was five months' pregnant when we got married), we had settled for a Friday night reservation when we couldn't get one for our actual anniversary on Saturday. We'd had the reservation for over a month.

Mac cringed, embarrassed he'd forgotten, and whispered to me, "Wants to take me out for a drink to celebrate."

"Go tonight," I said. "I'll ask Mom to babysit."

"You sure?"

"Positive."

They arranged to meet after work at a bar on Smith Street called Boat.

I handed Ben to Mac—handsome in his crisp gray suit, white shirt, and blue paisley tie—and he carried our little boy upstairs while I scrolled open both window shades, flooding the bedroom with light.

I had served in the army. Been a cop and a detective. Had my life, heart, soul, and mind eviscerated by a madman and his muse. And yet here I was, alive and well, on a bright summer morning. If happiness was possible for a person like me, this was it.

It was past eleven that night when I got off the subway after my first class of the new semester, The Psychopath in Criminology and Drama. It was what they called a psychology ISP course, meaning interdisciplinary studies, and though I found it odd to be studying psychopathology in the context of, basically, TV and movies—because they usually got it so badly wrong, aggrandizing and blundering through situations that in real life were always awful and never had an ounce of redemption of any kind; for real cops and real victims, the idea of poetic justice was a really bad joke—the professor had made it interesting, and anyway, it was a required course.

I turned down my block, yawning, and hoped Mom had set herself up in the spare room and called it a night. Ben would have been asleep for hours by now, and I hadn't realized how late eleven would feel when I'd asked her to sit. Our block was dark and quiet but there were a few people out, which made me feel safe; having lived in the city for a few years now, I'd grown more fearful of the isolation and stillness of suburbia, exurbia, and countryside than the urban reality of living with every variety of stranger. The way I saw it, most strangers would help you in a pinch.

When I got to my house, I paused to retrieve my keys from my purse, and noticed that I had left my phone on silent mode. I turned on the sound and it immediately beeped seven times. My mother, it seemed, had repeatedly tried to reach me. My pulse accelerated at the thought of all the things that might have happened to Ben: falling down a flight of stairs, choking on his dinner, drowning in his bath.

I hurried up the stoop and opened the front door into

the parlor level where our living room, dining room, and kitchen shared a large, high-ceilinged space replete with ornate architectural details that had survived innumerable paint jobs since the nineteenth century. All the lights were on and it was way too quiet.

"Mom?"

She came running up the stairs when she heard my voice. I could tell she had been lying down because her short rust-red hair was squished on one side. But she hadn't been sleeping; her eyes looked weirdly awake for this time of night.

"Is Ben okay?"

"He's fine. Sleeping." She burst into tears and pulled me into a tight hug.

"What's wrong? Why did you call me so many times?"

"Why didn't you answer?"

"I turned off the sound so it wouldn't disturb the class. What's going on?"

"And Mac, I've been calling him, too, but he left his cell phone here when he stopped in earlier to change. I called him and I heard it ringing. How can both of you be unavailable when you leave your child with someone else?"

"Didn't you do that before cell phones?"

"We always left an itinerary with phone numbers of the restaurant, the movie theater, a friend's house, wherever we were."

"You could have called the school."

"I *did*. The switchboard answered with voice mail. You had to have an extension to dial in, and I didn't." Her tone had turned almost angry.

I pulled away and looked at her, half a foot from me, crying. She had grown lonelier and more sensitive since my father passed away and Jon, my only sibling, moved his family across the country to Los Angeles. I wouldn't have called her neurotic and yet she was behaving strangely.

"What happened, Mom?"

"The Bronxville Police called here tonight . . ."

Bronxville was the Westchester town, just outside the city, where Mac had grown up.

"Why?"

"Hugh and Aileen"—Mac's parents—"were found in their home."

"Found?"

"Murdered," she whispered, as if the word could infiltrate Ben's innocence, all the way downstairs, in his sleep. "A home invasion. Botched, they said."

It sounded unreal, wouldn't penetrate. *"They're both dead?"*

Staring at me, she nodded. Her eyes were bloodshot; she had been crying a long time.

"I don't believe it." I walked in a daze to the couch and sat down.

"I know." She sat beside me. "I know."

"Hugh and Aileen? Both of them?"

"They think it happened late in the afternoon. What I don't understand is why they were home in the afternoon. Don't they work in the store all day?"

"It's closed on Mondays."

"Closed on Mondays," Mom repeated. "Why?"

"It was their day off—a holdover from the old European ways. It's always been like that at the store."

"The thieves must have thought they'd be out."

"Probably. I don't believe it. Hugh and Aileen?"

"Poor Mac," Mom said—and suddenly I realized that I would have to tell him.

CHAPTER 2

Even this late on a Monday night the bars along Smith Street were buzzing. There seemed to be at least one on every block, spilling intoxicated hipsters clustered on the sidewalks in clouds of cigarette smoke. It had been a hot day and the air now was pleasantly cool. I walked slowly in the direction of Boat, the bar where Mac had said he and Billy were going to meet, in no rush to get there. In no rush to turn Mac's world inside-out. I had called the Bronxville Police Department to confirm my mother's report about Hugh and Aileen, and the cop's words were still ringing in my head.

It was a bloodbath, from what I heard.

And the cruel silence that followed.

They didn't teach sensitivity training in cop school, that was for sure.

After walking five or six blocks, I wondered if I had gone too far.

"Excuse me?"

A girl in a spaghetti-strap minidress, her right arm covered wrist-to-shoulder in a flower show of a tattoo, pulled her attention from her chattering group and looked at me.

"Do you know where Boat is?"

"Three blocks up. It's got no sign so look for the red phone booth."

I thanked her. She eyed me a moment—trying to classify me, too young to be her mother, too old to be trolling the bars—before turning back to her friends.

I backtracked three blocks and passed a group of smokers to make my way inside. The walls were red, and a bittersweet song sent a fragment of lyrics straight to my heart: . . . *in the shadow of the gallows of your family tree . . .*

Why? Why wouldn't that shadow stop growing?

I breathed. Moved forward.

I had to tell Mac.

Didn't want to.

Couldn't bear to.

But had to.

It was dark and moderately crowded, a glittering collection of bottles tiered in front of a mirror behind the bar. My gaze tripped along the barstool faces, looking for Mac. I continued into the back room, where I was not surprised to find him and Billy hunkered at a table in a far corner: a white guy and a black guy, alone in a crowd, absorbed in conversation like they were in a business meeting. Even though Mac was as retired as I was from the police force, cops never could give up the brotherhood when they found themselves with someone still on the job.

Mac smiled when he saw me. Billy stood and came right at me for a hug. He was wearing jeans, cowboy boots, and a brown plaid shirt with abalone snaps. I had never seen him dressed for a night out on the town with the boys— or in this case, the boy—but wasn't that surprised by his Wild West motif. I knew he liked country music and had once noticed a ten-gallon hat in the back of his car.

"Hey, Karin!" This close, I could smell his pungent beer breath. "Good to see you! What're you drinking?"

"Nothing, thanks."

The way he looked at me, the way he paused, showed me he read trouble. He glanced at his watch. "Yeah, well, it's getting late. Congratulations again, man!" He held out a hand and Mac grasped it. "I'm proud of you."

"Billy," I said. "You don't have to go." Maybe it would help if he stayed. Unless Mac wouldn't want another man to see him cry.

"Thanks, but I'm on the early shift again tomorrow. You be good now." He kissed my cheek and walked through the dim red room, past the bar and out the door.

I took Billy's seat and faced Mac. He leaned forward and touched the back of my hand. "What's wrong?"

"Let's go."

He stared at me, saw that I meant it, and we got up to leave. Everything my eyes fell upon—the round shining edge of the mahogany bar, the reflection of a kissing couple in the mirror, a Band-Aid on a woman's manicured thumb—hit me like a snapshot, images I would always remember. Outside, a young man wearing blue eyeliner and a nostril ring, talking to a chubby woman in a tight lace dress. The quietness of Smith Street between each bar, at midnight, as the rest of the neighborhood slept. The bitter lozenge of regret caught in my throat for what I was about to do to Mac.

"You okay?" He put his arm around my back and pulled us together. "How was class?"

"Fine."

"Have you been home?"

I nodded. "Mom's there with Ben. Everything's fine."

"Good."

And then I realized that I had lied. "I mean, everything's fine with Mom and Ben."

He stopped walking. We had turned onto our block and, standing in the hushed darkness, I took him in my arms and whispered the news about his parents into his ear. I felt him melt away. He didn't fall but it was as if he was falling. Every muscle in his body seemed to lose its shape and intention; and though he wasn't leaning on me, I felt as if any movement would cause his collapse. We might have stood like that, our arms around each other in stunned silence, for five minutes, or ten, or fifteen. I knew that, for Mac, time had stopped. I knew it because I remembered how it had felt when I'd learned that Jackson and Cece were dead, murdered: The shock jolted you into a nether zone between the living and the dead, a place of pure hurt, in a nanosecond. You wanted to get out of it but couldn't see how you ever would.

Mac pulled away and touched his front pants pocket, the way he always did, to feel for his wallet and listen for the jangle of his keys. He wasn't crying but his eyes were red and his face had transformed, pinched in like a prune by the unbearable pain. When he started to walk in the opposite direction from our house, I followed.

Three blocks later, we were unlocking the gate to the lot where Mac parked his car. I waited while he got the green MINI Cooper he'd had since before we were married—the little car that was unexpectedly comfortable for two tall people like us. The motor rumbled in the sleepy quiet as he drove out of the lot and onto the sidewalk. I shut and locked the gate, then went around to the driver's side.

"You've been drinking."

"Right."

I got behind the wheel and he sat in the passenger seat as we made our way along the lonely early morning roads to Westchester. We hardly spoke until we arrived at his parents' house in Bronxville—not the rich part of town where the power brokers lived a very commutable distance from Manhattan, but the more modest part of town that edged the highway, the decent but unfancy neighborhood where working people like Mac's family lived.

His parents were both Irish; they had married in Dublin at the age of eighteen and immigrated to America together the following year. Theirs was the typical story of the successful immigrant: years of hard work seeding a family business, in their case a local hardware store that thrived. They became not only citizens but enthusiastic patriots, painting the window frames of their two-story white stucco house blue and the front door red. Aileen had planted pale blue hydrangea bushes on either side of the front door, and seamed the bottom of the white picket fence with alternating clusters of red and white impatiens. Now yellow police tape was strung across the top of the fence and the lawn hummed with crime scene investigators who looked like they were finishing up. Two ambulances waited with their red-and-white lights rotating and back doors gaping. As soon as we pulled up, Mac's eyes nervously skimmed the scene before settling on his childhood window; his room had been above the garage. A uniformed cop noticed us and immediately headed our way, his irritated expression implying that we were rubbernecking.

"Move along, please."

"I'll explain," I told Mac.

"No. Drive around the block."

The cop shrank in the rearview mirror, standing by the fence, watching us drive away. I saw him shake his head and turn back toward the house. I drove slowly in a large circle that bordered the highway and a main road before returning to the house. Not knowing what else to do, I was going to keep driving when Mac told me to stop.

"I have to go in." He looked at me, his blue eyes beseeching mine.

I shut the ignition and took his hand. In my peripheral vision I saw the cop approaching again, determined to shoo us away.

"Let me deal with him."

Mac stayed in the car while I got out and faced the officer: He was shorter than I was, his blond hair crew-cut close to his scalp. His name tag read *Renfrew*.

"Ma'am, you can't—"

"My husband's parents live here."

The cop stared at me, and I wondered if he was struggling to believe me or correct me: *lived* here. They lived here, past tense; they were dead.

"We're both former detectives—New Jersey." I put out my hand and waited another awkward pulse for him to reach out and shake it. "Karin Schaeffer. My husband is Mac MacLeary."

Officer Renfrew's eyes roamed my face for what felt like a moment too long. My fame was sticky, infamous, uncomfortable; it dogged me like a recurring illness I wished would finally capitulate. Every now and then, someone would seem to recognize me without knowing why. At the time of my family's murder, and later, during the prolonged and complicated hunt for a madman the press have tagged the Domino killer, my story bubbled into the news with disconcerting frequency. I was *one of those faces* that looked familiar. *One of those names* you might have seen or read about somewhere. I never helped people clarify their confusion when they met me; if they wanted to know, they'd have to ask me outright, but no one ever did.

Renfrew peered into the car at Mac, who took the cue to open the door and step out.

"Who's in charge?" I asked Renfrew.

"Detective Arnie Pawtusky, over there." Renfrew pointed to a tall baldheaded man in brown slacks and an orange-and-green striped polo shirt, with a cigarette parked between his scalp and one ear.

We crossed the lawn and introduced ourselves. Pawtusky eyed us cautiously at first, caution that moved swiftly through reservation into what felt like a kind of sad respect.

"I'm sorry for your loss," he said, looking right into Mac's eyes in a way that made me instantly like the man. And then he turned to me, looked into *my* eyes, and said, "And I'm sorry for your loss, as well."

That floored me. I wasn't sure what he meant. My first loss? Or this one?

"Thank you," I said.

"Am I clear to go inside?" Mac asked.

"Sure you want to?"

"If I don't, I'll never—" He couldn't finish but I knew what he would have said: . . . *never stop rearranging the furniture in my head*. The *furniture* being the facts. He had investigated too many crime scenes to be comfortable not knowing the details of his parents' last moments.

Pawtusky glanced at the house. "Give me a minute." He went inside and as we stood there waiting I remembered our last visit here: the Fourth of July, the MacLearys' annual late afternoon barbecue to which they invited every neighbor, friend, and acquaintance. The fourth was also my niece Susanna's birthday—this year she'd turned seven— and normally Mac and I spent the day traveling a loop from Brooklyn to New Jersey to Westchester, unwilling to miss either event. But since my brother Jon and his family had moved to Los Angeles, this year we'd had to settle for singing "Happy Birthday" to Susanna over the phone, and had come early to help Hugh and Aileen prepare. They had welcomed me into their family without missing a beat, never belaboring the fact that they'd adored Mac's first wife, Val.

"Almost ready." Pawtusky strode toward us across the lawn.

A pair of emergency workers came out of the house carrying a stretcher upon which a zipped body bag lay with lumpen stillness. It could have been either Aileen or Hugh; they had been more or less the same size. A second stretcher and a second body bag followed. We stood there with Pawtusky and watched as Mac's parents were loaded into the ambulances and driven away. For the second time that day, I wept uncontrollably. Mac's eyes grew redder, but still he didn't cry.

"Whenever you're ready," Pawtusky said.

After a moment, we followed the detective into the house. Pawtusky stood back and didn't speak while we took it all in.

A glistening pool of blood at the foot of the stairs, emanating rays across the front hall tiles like a giant starburst.

A pink terry-cloth slipper—Aileen's—half soaked with blood; the other slipper across the room by an umbrella stand.

A dozen family photographs on the wall, three frames on the right severely disarranged.

I held Mac's hand and led him away, arbitrarily turning left into the living room. And immediately regretted it.

Another pool of blood by the smashed-in sliding glass doors that led from the living room to the back porch.

Hugh's favorite armchair was in its recline position, footrest levered up, next to the side table upon which a glass was overturned but not broken. The smell of spilled whiskey.

And the butcher smell of fresh blood: metallic, sharp.

Across the room, red splatter on the white living room wall. Drips of it now dried mid-path on its way down the glass of a framed Norman Rockwell poster: a man and a boy at the counter of a soda fountain on a sepia afternoon.

Blood on the blue twill couch beneath the poster.

In front of the couch, under the coffee table, Aileen's knitting basket was undisturbed, needles jabbed into a ball of green yarn, the neat rows and cables of something nearly finished. I remembered now: She had called me last month for Ben's size; she was knitting him a sweater for the fall.

Mac pulled away and walked out of the living room. I followed him through the foyer, the dining room, and kitchen—all weirdly serene considering the mayhem in the other part of the house—and up the narrow back staircase.

The first room at the top of the stairs had been Rosie's. Her real name was Siobhan but, like Seamus, forty years ago difficult names like that had been jettisoned for easy nicknames. By the time Hugh and Aileen had had their third American child they'd wised up and named him Daniel since it came with a ready-made nickname, Danny, that was still essentially his given name. Rosie's room was now a guest room fitted out with a double bed and two sets of bunk beds to accommodate her family when they visited. Danny's room was last, closest to the master

bedroom at the far end of the hall, and still had just the
one twin bed. Mac's room was in the middle, with a door
at either end to access both the back and front stairways.
He was sitting on the edge of the double bed that had
been installed at the time of his first marriage. There was
a crib for Ben in the corner of the room. Aileen and Hugh
had been avid grandparents, gathering the entire family
together as often as possible.

I sat beside my husband and put my arms around him,
aware of the soft heaves of his chest. There was absolutely
nothing I could say to make him feel better. And so we sat
there in silence, locked in each other's arms, while wave
after wave of grief barreled through him.

Finally his breathing slowed. He lifted his head and
looked at me. "I have to call Rosie and Danny."

"I can do that."

"No. I need to."

He had left his cell phone at home so I handed him mine.
He called Rosie first, not only because she was the oldest
but because by nature she was far steadier than Danny.

I heard the first wail of Rosie weeping, and then listened
while they discussed her now inevitable travels from Long
Island to Westchester. The entire family would come,
Larry taking off from work and the children missing their
first days of school. Mac and Rosie agreed that everyone
would stay together at a local hotel.

The call to Danny, next, turned out to be easier simply

because he didn't answer.

"Probably passed out," Mac said, handing me back my phone.

On our way out, Mac stopped to look at one of the framed photos hanging on the foyer wall: a Sears portrait circa 1979, showing Hugh and Aileen posed in a tight cluster with their three children in front of a hazy blue backdrop that suggested a warm spring afternoon.

Outside, sleepless neighbors huddled, watching the investigators go about their work. Pawtusky stood near the curb, talking with someone. Chilly wisps now laced the middle-of-the-night air. Grasshoppers sawed mercilessly. I wanted to get out of there, wanted to take Mac home and put him to bed so in the morning we could wake up and realize this nightmare was just a dream. But before we could reach the car, Pawtusky stopped us.

"We'll need someone to ID the bodies," he told Mac, "and we'll want to interview you."

"Of course."

"Mind if I ask you one question now?"

Mac paused. Waited.

"Your mother, did she wear any rings?"

"Just her wedding and engagement rings."

"Expensive diamond—that kind of engagement ring?"

"Wasn't she wearing it when . . ." He couldn't finish. "She's worn her rings for forty-five years. Hasn't been able to take them off for twenty."

Pawtusky said nothing; he didn't need to. There was only one reason you would ask that question. And there was only one answer.

"How did they get the rings off?" Mac ground his jaw. His face grew red.

"Sorry," Pawtusky said.

"Did you find her finger?"

Pawtusky nodded, his Adam's apple moving slowly up and slowly down. "And the wedding band. But not the diamond."

Three days later, we buried them. In the interim, I had returned to Brooklyn to collect Ben and my mother and pack a few things, while Mac stayed in Bronxville to arrange the funeral. Meanwhile evidence was collected but there was almost nothing, just a single unidentified fingerprint that didn't match any entries in any database. Their killers were either seasoned or lucky. The randomness of the crime— that it appeared to be a botched robbery, with the thieves hastily severing Aileen's finger and taking her diamond ring so they would reap some reward for their trouble— was particularly excruciating. When my family had been murdered, we knew who we were looking for; this time, there were no suspects, not even a person of interest. The MacLearys had been exemplary citizens, consummate parents and grandparents, and had had no enemies. No one could think of a single reason anyone would want to kill them and yet they had been attacked by someone who had been intent on leaving them dead.

As we waited by two gaping holes side by side on the cemetery lawn, the only conversation anyone seemed capable of sustaining was about how lucky we were that the weather had cooperated. It was a beautiful day, balmy and breezy. Mourners had excavated their summer closets for dark clothing: men buttoned up in their suits, women in their pantsuits and dresses and hats.

Mac stood at the head of the graves with Rosie, Larry, and their kids fingering rosary beads while the priest read a poetic eulogy to Hugh and Aileen, who he called "two truly beloved people" as if he had known them personally, which he probably did. I stood at the front edge of a large crowd with my mother, Ben, Billy Staples, Mac's ex-wife, Val, and her husband, Paul. Behind and around us gathered what seemed like innumerable friends, neighbors, and customers from the MacLearys' hardware store. Detective Arnie Pawtusky was also there, representing the local precinct, and if I knew detectives also keeping his eyes open, working the case. Only after the caskets had been lowered into the ground, Mac had shoveled a dollop of earth over each parent and was handing the spade to Rosie, did Danny MacLeary finally show up.

Drunk. Unsteady on his sneakered feet. Loudly bawling. Wearing jeans and a T-shirt with an ironic—inappropriate—retro logo from a bowling alley.

Rage flashed across Rosie's face and she raised the shovel as if she might strike him. Mac touched her arm and she froze a moment, then shook her head and drove the spade into the ground to dig up some of the preloosened soil, which she tossed atop one buried coffin and then the other. Rosie was a tall woman like the rest of the family, slender but thickened at the middle from childbearing; she had given birth to five children, one stillborn, the oldest now in college and the youngest in kindergarten. She suffered no nonsense, like the kind Danny always seemed to bring with him. She handed the shovel to Larry, her husband, and turned her attention to the yawning holes that were about to swallow her parents.

Danny lurched past us, smelling of whiskey, the same brand drunk by his father. But Hugh had controlled his drinking and had openly reprimanded Danny for his lack of discipline with alcohol and everything else.

"Who did this?" Danny shouted. He grabbed the shovel from Larry and flung dirt into the air, hard chips of ground that fell partially into the graves but also sent dust into the eyes of the nearest mourners. "*Who fucking did this?*"

Mac pulled the shovel out of his younger brother's hands and Danny buckled to his knees, sobbing. Looking at the back of his head, I noticed new strands of gray in his thick black hair. He might never grow up, but even Danny would age.

We waited, and soon enough the usual narcissistic drama

that Danny tended to serve up at family occasions subsided enough for the priest to finish the service. I could tell that Mac and Rosie were thinking about Danny, though, the way Mac's jaw was clenched and Rosie's eyes were narrowed.

Afterward everyone was invited to a local tavern for food and drink. Mac and Rosie stood together, stoically accepting condolences from the line of people streaming in. Mom; Rosie's husband, Larry; and I sat at a table feeding the kids. The large back room allotted to our reception had two windows but they were covered with heavy drapes, erasing the bright day outside.

Across the room, Val greeted a blossoming group of people she seemed pleased to see, people she had assumedly met on parental visits during her long marriage to Mac, people I didn't know. After a while, she came over and squeezed in a chair between me and my mother. I had had dinner with Mac and Val once when they were married, and had liked her. She smiled, sending a spray of tiny wrinkles upward beside both eyes. Her hair was longer now, styled to accentuate her pretty cheekbones, and colored a lighter shade of brown. When she leaned in to whisper in my ear, I smelled her sweet perfume.

"Everyone thinks you stole Mac from me." She pulled away so I could see her wink.

"Is that why no one's talking to me?"

"I straightened them out. They'll come around. Of course . . ." She trailed off, not wanting, I supposed, to state the still undigested fact that there was now little reason for us to visit Bronxville. "You hanging in there?"

"More or less."

"And Mac—dark side grab him yet?"

"What do you mean?"

She looked at me, decided something and didn't elaborate. I looked over and saw Mac watching us with a frozen expression that was broken by a tentative smile. He had slept little in the last three nights and his eyes were badly bloodshot. Every time I looked at him lately, I felt helpless, uncertain how to ease his pain. Is that what she meant? Was Mac prone to depression in a way I had never seen in him?

Val patted my shoulder and went looking for her husband, Paul.

"So that's Mac's wife," Mom said.

"No, I'm his wife."

"You know what I meant. She seems nice."

"She is."

"It's a good thing they didn't have children."

I nodded. It *was* a good thing. Though maybe children would have held them together when the accumulation of years couldn't.

"Speaking of children," Mom whispered as Danny's voice rose above the din. Danny, the eternal child. Beggar of attention. Breaker of hearts and wallets.

"I was out of town; I don't know why no one could find me!"

Detective Pawtusky seemed surprised by the outburst, but he had never met Danny before let alone tried talking with him about a subject he wasn't interested in pursuing—such as why it had taken forty-eight hours to locate him even after his parents' murders had been splashed across the headlines.

"Let's go outside," Pawtusky said.

Danny raised his hand to the bartender, who didn't have to ask his order, just handed him another whiskey. He took a long drink before gracing Pawtusky with a response.

"No way."

Pawtusky stared at him a moment before handing him a business card. "Give me a call when you're sober." He turned around and made a path through the crowd—and didn't flinch at what Danny said next as he ripped up the card and tossed it on the floor.

"Fuck you."

But I knew Pawtusky heard him, because everyone did. After a brief lull, subdued chatter filled the dark space again.

By the end of the afternoon, when most everyone had gone home, a small group stood outside in the parking lot saying our exhausted good-byes. Billy Staples had lingered and took the opportunity to hold Mac in a long, tight embrace.

"I'll give you a call tomorrow," Billy said.

"I'll probably be at the office."

"Take another day off."

"We'll see."

"Stop trying to hold it all together. I mean it. Karin?"

"I'll take care of him," I stroked Mac's back; his tension felt steely beneath the dark suit jacket. "I won't let him go to work until next week. I'll make him take some time for himself."

Mac nodded; he wasn't going to argue with me in front of people. But I knew him: His impulse was to take action against his emotions. Fight them off. Stay in control. But I had other plans for him tomorrow. I would send Ben out with Mom and keep Mac home with me, give him a back rub, a neck rub, make love to him, whatever it took to help him know that love had not abandoned him despite the tragedy. Tomorrow night was our long-planned anniversary dinner, and more and more I thought we should keep the reservation, even if just to honor the strong marriage his parents had sustained for nearly fifty years. A quiet celebration, just the two of us, with wine and candlelight . . . it wouldn't hurt him and maybe it would even help a little.

"You hear that?" Billy said. "She's the boss, so you listen to her."

Half Mac's mouth rose up in a sort of smile, satisfying Billy that he had broken through a bit. "Okay. Talk tomorrow. I love you, man."

"So"—Mac turned to Rosie as Billy walked to his

car—"I was thinking I'd stop by Mom and Dad's house to get one last look at the scene."

"I haven't been there yet," she said. "I've been afraid to face the damage."

"It's up to you."

Rosie looked at me, and I said what I thought: "It *is* hard to see."

"I don't think I can."

"We'll have to deal with the house," Mac said. "But it can wait a bit."

"Meantime, what do we do about Danny?" Rosie asked.

"Danny . . ." Mac shook his head.

"Did the lawyer find you before?"

"No."

"He said Mom and Dad were in the process of changing their will. They were at his office just last week."

"Changing it how?"

"They were cutting Danny out. They should have done that a long time ago, as far as I'm concerned. But they didn't get it done in time so now we're going to have to deal with him when we make decisions about the house and the business."

Mac took in the news, betraying little reaction. Hugh and Aileen had always been fair with their three children, never showing favoritism or making judgments beyond Hugh's occasional harsh comments to Danny about his drinking and his lifestyle. Danny had never developed a career and frequently changed jobs, apartments, and girlfriends. He had recently turned forty and I wondered if Hugh had finally lost patience.

"You heard him in there," Rosie went on, "cursing at that detective?"

"I heard it."

"You know what I think? I think *he* thinks that Danny—"

"Don't go there," Mac said. "He's our brother."

"Oh, come on, Mac, don't tell me it hasn't crossed your mind. Especially with what we know now about their intentions for their will. And the ring"—her voice rose—"was going to *me* and I was going to pass it on to *one of my girls*. Danny knew that. He's always been a jealous, good-for-nothing, son-of-a—" She stopped herself as jaws dropped all around her.

Mac stood there staring at his older sister. He was the middle child, the peacemaker, and though I had never known him to disrespect the bottom line of truth, I could see in the way he winced that the possibility of this one was too harsh even for him, despite what his years as a cop had shown him of unimaginable cruelty.

"Rosie," he said, "Danny didn't do it."

"How do you know that?"

He sighed, didn't answer.

"We *have* to consider it."

"No we don't. Not today."

CHAPTER 3

As soon as my eyes opened I felt that Mac wasn't there. His side of the bed was rumpled, but barely. I had woken briefly in the middle of the night and heard sounds in the kitchen. My guess was he hadn't slept at all.

I waited for Ben's morning cry . . . and waited. Finally I got up and went to his room: His crib was empty. I went to find them, a hook of nervousness catching in my stomach. Something felt off about today, a strange foreboding I couldn't pinpoint. As I went upstairs to our parlor level my mind dialed through today's agenda, or what today's agenda would have been had Mac's parents not been murdered four days ago and buried just yesterday. Nothing would be the same for a long time; Mac would have to adjust and I would have to figure out how to help him. I had already decided, for starters, that his own behavior toward me when Jackson and Cece were killed would be my guide: vigilant caring and attention but most of all *being there*. He had stuck by me through the thick and thin of my own depression and insanity. I would stick by him.

As soon as I saw Mac and Ben sprawled on the living room floor stacking multicolored blocks and knocking them down (Mac stacking, Ben knocking) in a flood of peachy sunlight, my feeling of apprehension melted away. Through the doorless archway into the kitchen I saw breakfast dishes scattered on the counter and the newspaper open on the table. Mac looked up at me from the floor with weary eyes—but he smiled.

"Morning."

"Morning." I crouched down to kiss him.

Ben toppled the latest tower, shouting, "Down!"

"Down!" Mac and I said in chorus to our son.

"Thought I'd let you sleep in," Mac said.

"Did you sleep at all?"

"Couldn't."

"Take a sleeping pill tonight."

"Maybe."

"You can't go on not sleeping."

"You're probably right. I will."

"And you have to stop thinking about Danny."

Mac sighed and got up. I watched him walk into the kitchen, his robe hanging open over his boxers and T-shirt. While he refilled his coffee, Ben thrust a green block into my hand.

"More!"

I built Ben another tower while he eagerly waited for it to get as high as it could without falling on its own. Every now and then I looked over at Mac, pacing the kitchen, shaking his head. Beyond him, I saw that our late summer garden, which had been neglected all week, was browning from lack of water. The thought of having to care for the garden and the house and the new semester and Ben *and Mac* made me feel suddenly overwhelmed. Mac, who walked our kitchen like a courtroom, considering a maze of possibilities, all of which were awful. Mac, who emanated an energy of desperation I recognized all too well . . . standing on the precipice of a day that appeared mercilessly bottomless. His suffering over his parents' deaths was bad enough. But adding to it the gathering cloud of suspicions of Danny was unbearable.

The phone rang, startling all of us.

Mac walked to the counter and looked at caller ID. "Rosie."

"Don't answer it."

He picked up. "It isn't even seven o'clock yet" was his hello. Her greeting must have been similarly blunt because he dove right into listening. When his eyes locked on mine, I knew something had happened. "I'm calling Pawtusky and telling him he's making a mistake." He hung up.

"Danny?" I asked.

"He has an alibi for Monday—he was with some woman

at the Seventy-ninth Street Boat Basin in Manhattan, holed up in her boat—but Rosie said Pawtusky's not buying it."

"I didn't know Danny had a new girlfriend."

"He can't remember her name, just that her boat was called *Party On*."

We shared a look of disbelief about something that was all too believable, when it came to Danny.

"This has to be stopped before it starts." Mac carried the phone through the living room and into the front hall, where I heard him rifling through something—yesterday's suit jacket—looking for Detective Pawtusky's business card.

"Don't call Pawtusky," I said. "Let him do his job."

"Danny might be an asshole but he didn't kill our parents."

I couldn't tell if it was Mac's harsh tone or his actual words that got Ben's attention, but his face screwed up and I hugged him to circumvent tears. From the front hall I heard eleven dialing bleeps and the tense beginning of what turned out to be a short conversation, ending with Mac's declaration, "It isn't right!"

He stood in the doorway between the front hall and living room with an expression of helplessness that made him look like he was on his way down a slippery slope with no chance of a foothold. I had never seen him this way before—desolate. Not even when we were hunting JPP. Or when he thought I might try to take my own life again. Or when his own life had hung, literally, in the balance. Val's words of yesterday rang through me: *Did the dark side grab him yet?* If she asked me that now, a mere fourteen hours later, I would have answered unequivocally yes, without even knowing what that meant.

"The *Party On* set sail Tuesday evening," Mac said, "without Danny. The boat hasn't been back since and they can't find any witnesses seeing him at the boat basin."

"What was her name?"

"The woman?"

I nodded.

"Connie, I think."

"Is it her boat?"

"Does it matter?" Mac's face tightened with derision. "Pawtusky said they found Danny's DNA all over our parents' house. Well, what did they expect? He grew up in that house. Visited all the time."

"DNA from?" I asked, knowing as well as Mac did that the source mattered.

"Hair, skin. Not blood."

"They won't be able to prove anything without something more concrete—a good witness, a weapon, your mother's ring. Someone else's DNA."

"They didn't find anyone else's, that's the problem. And that fingerprint doesn't amount to anything if they can't identify it. They've got nothing, so what do they do? They get a warrant on Danny's apartment."

It didn't look good for Danny. But Mac was my husband and I decided, then and there, that I would support him by sharing his opinion about his brother's inherent guilt-lessness. I knew that in time Mac would be able to separate emotion from logic; but for now, he was too blinded by grief to see anything clearly. I set Ben down in front of the blocks, got up, went over to Mac, and put my arms around him.

"Danny didn't do it," I whispered. "They'll find that out."

When he reciprocated my embrace, I knew my agreement had done its job, at least for the moment.

"Mom's coming over at eight-thirty to take Ben to the park. She doesn't have to be at work until one o'clock. We'll have the whole morning alone together." I kissed his neck, behind his ear, the side of his face. "I love you."

"I love you, too."

As soon as I had installed Ben in his stroller and Mom had pushed him down the block, Mac and I headed to our bedroom. It was both exciting and frightening the way we couldn't wait to get each other naked: the way he yanked off my nightgown, the way I pulled off his robe. You could feel that it was going to be a humid day, and a sheen of perspiration coated us before our skin even touched. He felt sticky and tasted salty; and the way he kissed me—it was as if he couldn't drink in enough of me. We lowered ourselves onto the bed and made love with an intensity we hadn't experienced for a long time, since the beginning. I wrapped him in my arms and legs, turned him over and slowed him down, my fingers splayed across his collarbones. He gripped my forearms, closed his eyes, lifted his chin. I watched his eyeballs move like metronomes beneath his lids, as if he couldn't stop thinking. Leaning down, I touched his dahlia tattoo with the tip of my tongue . . . and all at once his eyes stopped moving, his head skewed back, and my body joined his completely.

After, I lay on top of him for a long time. He held me loosely with one arm and the other hand gently stroked my back. I listened as our breathing came into sync, and would have sworn he was asleep until he sighed and said, "Well . . ."

I rolled off him. "Let yourself sleep."

"Can't. It's like jet lag: better to wait until tonight."

"Why? Honestly—you're exhausted."

"I have to get into the office."

"*No.*"

He looked at me, half smiled. "You think I'm fragile."

"It's been a hellish week for you. You can take off another day."

"One more day won't make any difference." He sat up.

"Let's go out for coffee and then maybe we can see an early movie—"

"I'm going to work." He got out of bed and headed into the bathroom.

I lay there, frustrated, thinking. It didn't seem as if my wisdom was going to prevail. Finally I followed him into the bathroom and said loudly, above the rush of his shower, "What about our anniversary dinner tonight? I think it would be good for you." I didn't expect a yes, but thought it was worth a try: anything to help him feel even an iota removed from the horrific events of Monday. His answer was slow in coming, which told me he hadn't completely ruled it out.

"Maybe . . . I don't know."

"Think about it?"

"I will."

I got into the shower with him and soaped the damaged skin of his back, the constellation of hard whitish scars reminding me that deep down Mac was as tough as they came. It would just be a matter of time before he steadied himself. I felt his muscles relax under my hands and turned the washing into a massage, kneading deep under his shoulder blades with my thumbs, pressing upward along the tight muscles of his neck, raking my fingertips up and over his scalp. He sighed, turned around, kissed me in the streaming water, and whispered, "I have to go."

He left me alone in the shower. By the time I finished and was all dried off, he was dressed for work. I threw on shorts and a T-shirt and followed him upstairs to the front door.

"Call me when you get there." I kissed him.

"I'm sorry—"

"Don't apologize for anything. None of this is your fault."

"I'm burdening you with my crappy mood."

"Oh, *please*. I think I owe you big-time in that department." What I'd put him through a few years ago when I was more or less in his position could have filled a book.

"You owe me nothing." He leaned forward and tenderly kissed me again. "I promise, next time you see me I'll be—"

I stopped his guilty apologies with a third kiss. "Go. And let me know about dinner. I'll leave the reservation in place until the last minute, but whatever you want to do is fine with me."

Standing on our front stoop, I watched him walk up our leafy block toward Smith Street and the subway. He moved slowly, as if he was in no rush to leave despite his urgency to get to work today. A wave of love for him came over me. I couldn't take my eyes off him until he was at the end of the block.

And then, just as I was turning to go back inside, he pivoted, looked for me, and threw me a kiss. I pretended to catch it and affix it to my heart.

Just before one o'clock I rendezvoused with my mother at BookCourt, the bookstore on Court Street where she worked part-time as an inventory manager, and took Ben off her hands. I had hoped to get him home for lunch and a nap in his crib—and to use the time to get some homework done—but he had fallen asleep in his stroller.

"I tuckered him out." Mom smiled; she didn't have to tell me how much she loved spending time with her grandson, particularly since her other two grandchildren had moved three thousand miles away. "He *loves* the swings at the playground."

"You're telling me. I pushed him for at least an hour the other day."

"Do you still need me tonight? How is Mac?"

"Not good. I don't think he'll be up for going out."

"I'm flexible." She glanced at her watch. "Just let me know."

I watched through the plate-glass window full of books as she entered her workplace, greeting the young woman behind the counter and a man, the owner, who smiled and said something as she passed him on her way to the office in back.

Since Ben was already asleep and it was a lovely summer day, I decided to run errands. After an hour the stroller handles were festooned with plastic bags. I was tired, and stopped in at One Girl Cookies for an iced espresso to go. Waiting my turn, I saw a strikingly decorated cake—turquoise frosting encircled with bright yellow starbursts—and when I reached the counter asked if it was too late to order one for tomorrow.

"Not at all," the girl said, and passed me a book of choices.

I ordered a pumpkin cake with cream cheese frosting and requested red decorations: two linked hearts, for our two years of marriage, and the succinct but fitting platitude *Happy Anniversary*.

I pretty much figured Mac would cancel our dinner reservation tonight but refused to let his sorrow deny him any celebration at all. I truly felt that remembering an event that was happy might remind him that *all* was not lost. Tomorrow, Saturday—which was the date of our actual anniversary, anyway, and not just the day we were able to get a reservation at a popular restaurant—I would order our favorite sushi (I was not much of a cook) and we could celebrate quietly. On my way home, I picked up a bottle of champagne, already comfortable with the assumed change of plans.

Halfway down our block, I saw that there was something on our front stoop: a rectangular box. As I got closer it became clear that it was a delivery from a florist—Mac had been receiving a steady stream of condolences all week, numerous cards as well as two bouquets and a flowering plant. I parked the stroller (with Ben still asleep) on the sidewalk and climbed the stoop to see who this one was from. Sitting on the top step, I placed the box on my knees and opened it.

A dozen lavender dahlias were nestled in white tissue paper. An unsigned note card read: *I will be waiting*.

I knew they were from Mac, a romantic gesture and a confirmation, if cryptic, of our dinner plans. He wasn't much of a poet but his note was one of the sweetest things I'd ever read.

First I called my mother and told her we were on for babysitting that evening.

Then I called Mac and reached his voice mail. "I got the dahlias. They're beautiful. I'm glad you decided to go— see you at seven at the restaurant."

This was even better: Now we would celebrate two nights in a row.

Married couples seldom sweat the details, especially when you have children; you communicate in a kind of relay, passing information back and forth in broad strokes. It hadn't concerned me that I never heard back after leaving my message on Mac's voice mail. I knew him: knew that he checked messages frequently; and he was not someone who failed to show up when expected.

It didn't worry me that I was the first to arrive at the Union Square Café in Manhattan. In fact, I was five minutes early and thought nothing of it. The maître d' led me past the bar to a small square table in the central part of the restaurant, which was packed, bubbling with conversation.

I ordered a glass of wine and resisted the bread basket

until Mac arrived. I wanted him to see how pretty the table looked: the white linen tablecloth, the tiny yellow orchid in a small glass vase, the offering of artisanal breads. Behind our table was a framed still life of fruit done in watercolors, and as it happened the pale green dress I was wearing matched a trio of pears in the painting. It was all too perfect. Here we were—or would soon be—sharing two hours of culinary bliss in a beautiful, if temporary, bubble. When he arrived I was going to set some ground rules: no talking about anything serious or important, including his parents' murders, including Danny.

I waited, slowly sipping my wine. When it seemed Mac was running late, I checked my voice mail—nothing. I tried his cell and left a message letting him know I was at the restaurant.

At seven-thirty I read the menu. And then I called my mother to find out if Mac had phoned the house. He hadn't.

"Don't worry," she said. "He's preoccupied. He lost track of time."

She was right, of course. The shock from a violent loss of loved ones didn't go away for a long time; it skewed your thinking on many levels. Basic things you took for granted, like measurements of time, evaporated. The only thing you were really aware of was a burning ache at your core.

At seven forty-five I picked at a piece of bread. Checked for messages again. Nothing.

By eight-thirty I had left Mac four messages, drunk
two glasses of wine, and grown too embarrassed to face
eating dinner alone at a fancy restaurant. Because they
couldn't possibly know the circumstances of our lives,
to my neighboring diners and the hovering waitstaff I
looked like a woman stood up on a date. I wasn't brave
enough to ignore the growing feeling of humiliation and
so, finally, I paid for my wine, apologized to the waiter—
who pretended it was all in a day's work; in thanks for
his graciousness I left him an outsized tip—and unsteadily
made my way through the packed restaurant and bar and
onto the sidewalk where reality was waiting.

Why had I even thought he could come out tonight?
It had been delusional of me. I had been unfair to even
suggest it.

On my way to the subway on Sixth Avenue, I called Mac
twice.

"I'm heading home now. See you later. I love you."

And the second call, in afterthought: "Don't worry about
this, okay? It doesn't matter. *I love you*."

By the time I got home at twenty past nine I was more
tired than intoxicated. And I was hungry. I changed from
my dress into a nightgown, then peeked at Ben asleep in
his room, curled on his side, breathing heavily. Mom sat
with me in the kitchen while I ate some leftover pasta.
Normally when she babysat at night Mac would walk her
home; she lived seven blocks away and was uncomfortable

alone in the city in the dark, having lived in the suburbs her entire life until recently.

"He'll be home soon," she assured me not once, not twice, but three times.

But after two hours, he still wasn't home, and he still wasn't answering his phone.

"Could he be with Detective Staples?" Mom asked.

"Good idea." I tried Billy but he hadn't heard from Mac at all today.

"He could be at his sister's," Mom suggested.

So I called Rosie, too, but she said she hadn't spoken with him since their early morning phone conversation.

Finally, at midnight, still no Mac. I put Mom to bed in the spare room next to Ben's, and went to my room to get ready for bed . . . and wait. Worry would never let me sleep, not until I heard his key in the door, his footsteps, the weight of his body in bed next to me.

And then, before I knew it, it was morning. I had lain there all night, drifting in the shallow space between sleep and wakefulness, until the first grains of sunlight infiltrated the room, vanquishing the darkness, replacing night with day. Mac's side of the bed was untouched. And still, despite the plain fact that he had not come home at all last night, I wondered if somehow he would make it before Ben's wakeup cry. He was a devoted father, and missing the family's routines would bother him.

Ben cried. I waited a minute, wondering if Mac was

somewhere else in the house, if he would go to Ben. Waited another minute, and another, as Ben's cries escalated.

"Shall I get him?" my mother called.

"That's okay. I'm up."

Ben was standing in his crib, holding on to the bars so tightly his knuckles were almost white, tears streaming down his little face.

"I'm sorry, baby." I kissed his wet doughy cheek. "Shh, Mommy's here, it's all right, it's all right."

On weekdays the plaza at Metrotech bustled with corporate workers, but this morning, a Saturday, it was almost deserted. Other than me, there was an older couple resting on a bench and a homeless man picking through an overflowing garbage can, occasionally putting something into his mouth. Since becoming a mother, I no longer turned away from the derelict and down-and-out; instead, their invisibility had taken form and substance and now the mere sight of one filled me with an aching reminder that a woman had given birth to him or her. The man eating garbage in the plaza on this quiet morning had been someone's baby, someone's child, and somehow during the journey of his life he had become lost. I handed him a five-dollar bill on my way past and made a point of making eye contact before continuing on.

Out of the plaza, I crossed the street to the entrance

of the Eighty-fourth Precinct. I hadn't wanted to do this on the phone, with my mother in the house, because her nervousness made me nervous. Coming right out and saying, "Mac is missing," might make it true before Billy Staples, a seasoned cop, would have the chance to reel off all the statistics about how usually people who didn't come home weren't missing so much as AWOL for some other, understandable reason that had not yet made itself apparent.

I found Billy in the second-floor detectives unit, feet up on his desk, tapping his iPhone with both thumbs. Half of a greasy-looking egg-on-bagel sat on a crinkled piece of wax paper.

"How old is that sandwich?" I pulled a chair from a neighboring desk, straightened it beside Billy's, and sat down.

"Karin!"

He sat up swiftly, like a child caught goofing off though it was quiet in the unit. Assumedly all the action had taken place last night, and being Saturday even more would be expected tonight—this was the standard lull between the storms. A single perp sat listlessly in a holding cell against the far wall; the others would have already been processed and moved to the Brooklyn House of Detention, known as the House, for safekeeping.

"Still haven't heard from him?"

"I'm so worried."

He set his iPhone down amid a mess of paperwork, and I saw that he had been playing a Sudoku game. "Yeah," he said, "I don't like it, either."

I was almost disappointed that Billy wasn't going to try to talk me out of feeling alarmed, but why would he? I knew the drill. And he knew as well as I did that disappearing without a word was not like Mac.

"I called his sister, his brother, his friends," I said. "No one's heard from him since yesterday morning. He didn't tell anyone anything about going somewhere that wasn't home."

"Did you try his ex-wife? They were married a long time." Billy kept his expression bland in the way you did when you knew something you said might not go over well. "You never know."

"I don't have her number in my phone."

He turned to his computer and looked it up. "You want to call or should I?"

I read the number off his screen and dialed my phone. Val answered after five rings, sounding groggy.

"Val, it's Karin Schaeffer. Sorry I woke you." I heard something rustling on her end of the phone and the sound of something falling. "I can call back."

"No, it's fine. My glasses fell. Give me a minute." The phone clunked when she set it down and a few moments later she was back on the line. "Okay."

"I'm sorry to call so early on a weekend—"

"No problem. What's up?"

"Mac . . . is he there?"

"No. Why?"

"Did you hear from him yesterday at all?"

"I haven't spoken to him since the funeral." She paused again. "He's depressed, isn't he?"

"To say the least. Is that what you meant about 'the dark side'?"

"It gobbles him up, but just for a couple days at the most. It's like he digests it and lets it out. It's scary when it happens, Karin, but he always gets over it."

"Why didn't I know this?"

"I didn't see it until we were married five years. I'm sorry."

"No. Really. It's okay." But I felt like such a fool, having to be counseled by my husband's former wife about his emotional habits.

"Did you call his friend Stan? They used to spend a lot of time together."

"The sculptor with the shack—"

"—behind his house. Yes. Do you have his number?"

I wrote down Stan's phone number, feeling a ray of hope.

"Thanks, Val. I appreciate it."

"Anytime. You heard about Danny?"

"Not since Mac was home yesterday morning."

"Oh boy. Not that you'll be surprised, but he was

arrested in Westchester last night. The old grapevine lit up and called me."

"Did they find Aileen's ring?" My stomach turned, asking that.

"The police aren't saying. But they must have, or why arrest him?"

"If they haven't said they found it, I wouldn't assume anything."

Val had been married to a cop for nearly two decades; she knew I was right.

"Poor Danny," she said.

"I can't believe I didn't hear about this. I guess I've had my head in the sand. I—"

"You were waiting for Mac. I understand."

I could tell by the weight of her tone that she did understand, and that it made her sad.

"Mac was always protective of Danny," she said. "This probably upset him a lot. Did you call that detective from Bronxville?"

"I didn't think of it, but I will. Thanks."

"Call me and let me know how Mac is when he turns up, okay?" Her tone was tentative, as if she didn't know whether this was a reasonable request between generations of spouses.

"I will." And I would. Why not? The more I encountered Val, the more I liked her, and she and Mac had loved each other once.

As soon as the call was over, I phoned Stan. He sounded happy enough to hear from "Mac's new wife" but hadn't seen or heard from him since the funeral, either.

"I'm sorry I didn't get a chance to meet you the other day," Stan said.

"Another time."

The awkwardness was so thick you could have sliced off a chunk. I had phoned someone I didn't know looking for my husband—what were the chances a marriage that required *that* would last long enough for another opportunity to meet?

I ended the call and told Billy about Danny. He immediately picked up his desk phone and dialed Pawtusky's number from the card he had lying on his desk, which he must have gotten at the funeral.

I listened to Billy's end of the brief conversation with the Bronxville detective, just as I had listened to Mac's yesterday. He hung up, shaking his head. "He's stuck on Danny, just doesn't buy the boat thing. And they did *not* find your mother-in-law's ring at Danny's or anywhere else. But the main thing: He hasn't heard from or seen Mac."

"So where is he?"

"Question of the hour," Billy said, and got to work. Mac was his close friend and he wasn't going to wait the usual twenty-four hours before launching a missing persons investigation.

On my way home I called my mother's cell and found out that she and Ben were at the playground near the hospital, so I joined them there. He was settled into one of the low-slung baby swings, careening back and forth, happy as could be. Mom watched me intently as I crossed over to them. I kissed her cheek and took over pushing Ben for a while.

So that was it. Mac was gone. And no one knew where he was.

But I couldn't stop hoping he would appear at any moment. He loved me and he loved Ben. I knew he did. And today was our second wedding anniversary. I *knew* he would come home soon.

At six o'clock that evening, as I sat in my kitchen watching my mother cook dinner—sustaining the vigil with me, refusing to leave me alone until we knew something—my cell phone rang.

I hopped over Ben, who was playing on the kitchen floor with a couple of small pots and a wooden cooking spoon, and ran to my purse in the front hall. I answered quickly, without looking to see who it was, my heart beating fast.

"Mac?"

"Mrs. Schaeffer?"

I never liked hearing that. It was *Ms*. Schaeffer, Karin Schaeffer. *Mrs*. Schaeffer was Jackson's wife, and both of them were gone.

"Who's this?"

"Your cake is ready any time you want to come get it. We're open until nine. I thought maybe you forgot."

"Nope, just running late." A lie; I had totally forgotten. I left Mom with Ben for fifteen minutes to go pick up the cake. And then, waiting on line at the bakery, my cell phone rang again.

"Karin."

"Hi Billy. Anything?"

"Yeah, but I don't get it."

"Just tell me."

"He rented a car in midtown at about three o'clock yesterday afternoon, and it hasn't been returned."

"Why would he rent a car? We have a car."

"Exactly."

I reached the counter and pulled a twenty-dollar bill out of my wallet, having already left a five-dollar deposit, and whispered to the young woman, "Picking up a cake for Schaeffer." She went to the back and returned with a brown cake box.

"E-ZPass had him going through a toll on the Triborough Bridge at four-eleven P.M.," Billy said. "So it looks like he left the city, heading north."

"What did he do between renting the car at three and going through the toll? It isn't that long a distance."

"A Friday afternoon in the summer? Probably sat in traffic."

"Right." The bakery door dinged as I exited. "Any E-ZPass after that?"

"Nothing. And no credit card use."

"He must have gone up to Westchester to see Danny, maybe get him a lawyer. That would make sense."

"It *would* make sense, Karin, except that he didn't do any of that. I talked to Pawtusky again, called the jail, gave Rosie another call. Nothing."

"What now?" But even as I asked that I knew it was a useless question; it was what frustrated family members always asked the detective when they had hit a dead end.

"We hang in there." Billy summoned an authoritative confidence to his tone, having shifted gears from friend to detective.

"Call me the minute you know something. *Anything*."

"I promise."

"Day or night."

"You're in my speed dial, trust me."

I knew Billy wouldn't rest until he had found out where Mac was. He loved Mac and wanted him safely home almost as much as I did.

Back at the house, I slipped the cake box into the refrigerator and sat down for dinner with my mother. Gave Ben his bath and put him to bed. And then night descended with its menacing stillness and quiet. Mom and I played cards at the kitchen table while the wall clock ticked off time.

Eight o'clock.

Nine.

Ten.

Eleven.

Midnight.

Another night passed. And the phone didn't ring again. And the door didn't open. I moved the cake from the fridge to the freezer and went to bed.

CHAPTER 4

On a perfect September morning—a Friday two weeks to the day since Mac disappeared—I returned home from an early class to find Billy Staples running up and down the sidewalk on my block, laughing like I had never seen him laugh. He was chasing Ben, who loved to run and hated to fall but always picked himself back up and kept going. We dressed him in blue jeans, never shorts, to protect his knees. Billy caught up with Ben and lifted him into an aerial spin that made him shriek with joy. My mother, who sat on the bottom step of my stoop, smiled watching them. It was a beautiful, happy moment to stumble into, a temporary bubble that popped the moment Billy saw me coming down the block.

He set Ben down, crouched by his ear, and said, "Go on, go to Grandma."

Ben ran off as instructed, turning twice to make sure Billy was running after him.

"Come!" Ben shouted to Billy, his tiny fingers clawing at the air as if he could draw Billy onward.

"Gimme a minute, little man!"

Ben scrambled into my mother's lap.

"That kid's going to outrun me any day now." Billy breathed heavily. "Gotta get into better shape."

It was an odd statement because Billy, of all the middle-aged men I knew, looked like he was in excellent condition. Actually, watching him play and let loose like this, for the first time I really noticed how handsome he was . . . and quickly chased the thought away. In the two long weeks Mac had been gone, my mind had been a hive of unexpected and usually unwelcome thoughts:

He had left me.

He had sunk into a horrible depression and was alone somewhere, eating what he could find from a garbage can.

He was on a beach in the Caribbean sipping margaritas under a palm tree with another woman, a wealthy woman who paid his way, as nothing had been charged on his credit cards since the unaccounted-for rental car.

He was dead.

No. I still *felt* him. He *wasn't* dead; he was just gone.

The Sturm und Drang of all those thoughts and more, in discord with the rationale that in fact I knew nothing except that Mac wasn't nere with us, crashed through my mind as I walked toward Billy. It was how my days were now: skirting premonitions, refusing dark fears, grasping for facts. But so far, in two weeks, no facts other than the rental car had presented themselves. All anyone knew was a timeline: Mac's parents were dead; his brother Danny had been arrested for their murder and was sitting in jail while the prosecution struggled to build a case against him; and Mac had rented a car and vanished, swallowed, presumably, by an onslaught of depression.

I stopped in front of Billy and we stood there looking into each other's eyes. His were dark, lush brown. He didn't smile. After a moment he took the book bag off my shoulder, the release of its weight instantly lightening me. He slung the bag over his own shoulder and said, "Let's go inside."

"No."

"Karin—"

"Tell me here. Right now."

One side of his mouth pinched in defeat. He knew how stubborn I could be.

"They found the rental car."

"And Mac?"

"Just the car."

"Where?"

"Long Island Sound. A lady saw it from her house in Stony Creek. She's got a private boat launch and they're thinking he drove right into the water, probably in the middle of the night when all the neighbors were sleeping and she was out of town."

"*No.*"

"It's a long drive. Why don't you come with me? See for yourself."

But I had dissolved and couldn't answer. Tears flowed uncontrollably as my brain tried to shore up against a tidal flood with imbecilic rationalizations for why Mac's rental car would turn up in an ocean:

He had taken a wrong turn onto a private launch and jumped out at the last minute, delirious from grief, possibly drunk, and was wandering Connecticut.

Someone else had driven into the sound: a carjacker. Mac had been mugged at a rest stop heading north and suffered amnesia. He was out there, trying to remember who he was, trying to remember who loved him.

The car rental company had mixed up Mac's credit card information with someone else's. *Someone else* had driven into the sound. Not Mac. Mac was alive and well somewhere else, nursing his grief, stealing time until he was ready to come back.

But Mac hadn't drowned. He wasn't dead. He was alive. I felt it. I had been a widow once. I knew the difference.

"But they didn't find him?" I asked Billy again.

"Not yet." His soft tone masked the awful probability that Mac's body had floated into the depths of the ocean by now.

"So there's no evidence he was even in the car?"

Billy shook his head. "They're just pulling it out now."

I sat beside Billy in his gray sedan as we drove north on Interstate 95. After a while he put on a CD for distraction: bluegrass; he was a country music fan, which seemed odd for a black guy born and bred in Brooklyn, New York. I stared out the window as we drove through the knotted arteries of New Haven and farther north where suburban sprawl gave way to pockets of the seafaring countryside that snaked up the coast. Billy took the Branford exit and drove us through a neighborhood that grew more affluent the closer we came to the shore.

Once we turned onto Flying Point Road, it was easy to find the house because of the cluster of emergency vehicles from seemingly every department: police, fire, medical. The sight of an ambulance parked by the curb jump-started my pulse. I got out of Billy's car and walked straight to two medics standing there talking with a fully uniformed fireman.

"Was there a body?" I asked.

All three stared at me, obviously stunned by the interruption.

"A body. In the car. *Was there a body?*"

"Who are you?"

"I'm the wife."

"Whose wife?"

Billy then appeared at my side, got a firm hold of my elbow, and guided me away.

"Karin, cool it. They don't know who you are. They don't even know what they're doing here. They're just waiting."

"Right," I said, though more than anything I was confused. If all these emergency workers were gathered, wasn't it to save someone? To save Mac? But a voice from the dormant police officer and detective buried deep inside me rose with a strong reminder to get my bearings and look at the facts.

The facts. I reminded myself of the litany of facts as we knew them:

Murder.

Arrest.

Disappearance.

Discovery of car.

There had been three facts; now there were four. In two weeks, we had come one step forward.

Billy led me across a vast lawn toward the house, freshly painted white, with a veranda that wrapped from front to back and three chimneys. An overtanned, fiftyish woman in a turquoise floral dashiki stood on the veranda with a small, skinny woman in khaki pants, a bright pink shirt, and a matching silk scarf tied around her head, its long ends floating on a breeze I couldn't feel in the air. The shorter woman was talking and listening like a cop but wasn't in uniform, and the scarf seemed too dramatic . . . unless she was sick. In the seconds it took to walk up the veranda steps onto the porch, all the signs jumped out: emaciated, bald, tired. She was a cancer patient, in chemo. Billy went right up to her and introduced himself.

"Detective Billy Staples, Brooklyn Eight-four."

"Patrol Sergeant Eleanor Jones, Troop G, Connecticut State Police."

They shook hands.

"You've got the missing persons of the guy who rented the car." She didn't ask it as a question; it was obvious why Billy was here.

"That's me."

Jones's eyes—small, pale brown, and lashless—strayed over to me, standing beside Billy. But before she could say anything the other woman spoke in a surprisingly high, childish-sounding voice.

"I'm Sally Owen, this is my house."

Billy acknowledged her with a nod.

"Are you . . . ?" she asked me, not finishing the question because she knew the answer.

"When did you see it?"

"The car? This morning. I was sitting on the back porch having my coffee. Just looking out at the water, you know? And I saw something floating, some kind of raft. Then I realized it was the top of a car. I didn't believe it at first, but I called a neighbor and she saw it, too. It wasn't there yesterday."

"Could have drifted," Sergeant Jones said, "or surfaced for some reason."

"I couldn't believe it," Sally Owen said, "a car, floating right in my backyard."

She led us through the front door of her house, into an opulent foyer and out again through a set of glass French doors that led directly onto what she called the back porch. It was a massive veranda with a broad awning providing shade for expensive outdoor furniture, facing her own private sliver of the sea. A small marble table sat between two chairs near a swath of dripping honeysuckle.

"There." She pointed at the table. "I was sitting right there when I saw it."

My eyes fled from the veranda and the table to the emerald lawn whose hand-laid stone edge met the gently splashing water. Perfect. This place was *perfect*. It must have made Mrs. Owen's day, her week, her *life* to have sat there in her beautiful bounteous solitude, spotted a car in the ocean, and now, *now*, have her own house the center of an investigation that might have been something right out of a movie. You could see how excited she was by all this. Now, no matter how awkward a situation might be, she would always have this trump card of a conversation piece.

I hated her.

I hated this place.

Because the first thing I saw when I looked past the luxury was a dark blue two-door Honda Civic sitting on the asphalt boat launch that led directly into the water. Sitting there—not just a car but *the* car, the last car Mac drove— baked dry in the hot sun. Half a dozen investigators went about their work, looking as if they had been at it for a while and were finishing up.

"When they pulled it out," Sally Owen said, "*blankets* of water just *cascaded* off. And one of the doors was hanging off *like a broken wing*. What you *imagine* when you see something like that . . ."

Sergeant Jones sighed. Nodded. "Could have been open when the car drove in. Can't be sure."

How long had she been here, listening to the dramatic rendition of a house, a yard, a car? If she was like every other cop I had ever known, she had seen too much to be swept away with the kind of fluffy interpretation of events that had entranced Mrs. Owen.

"Is that always there?" I pointed to a boat sitting on a trailer on the grass near the blue car. Two squad cars were parked behind it.

"Usually the boat's parked on the launch near the shore," Jones said. "They had to get it moved off to the side before the tow truck could get into the water."

"How could anyone drive into the water with a boat parked there?" I asked, pointing out the obvious . . . one more reason it wasn't possible that Mac had driven himself into the ocean.

"It wasn't there two weeks ago," Sally Owen said. "I was gone most of August and early September, sailing off Bermuda with my boyfriend."

As we descended from the porch and crossed the back lawn, I saw that the boat was named *Free at Last*. The money here—fancy neighborhood, big house, nice boat, lady living alone—reeked of high-priced divorce. Not that I cared. I wanted only one thing. One person.

Billy, Sergeant Jones, Mrs. Owen, and I stood about twenty feet from the car. I wanted to move forward and touch it but didn't dare. So this was it: the car Mac rented two weeks ago. The car he paid for with his credit card. The car he drove north in the hours before I even went to the restaurant to wait for him. Had he already reached Flying Point Road by the time I ordered my first glass of wine? I felt sick at the thought of it.

Billy and Sergeant Jones approached the car to get a closer took, while I stood back with Sally Owen and watched as investigators finished up. The trunk and hood were open. Obviously the car had been thoroughly searched and no body had been found. I didn't know if not finding Mac in the car was good news or bad news, and took a step forward. Sally grabbed my arm to stop me.

"Maybe you shouldn't," she said.

I pulled away and joined Sergeant Jones and Billy, who

put his arm around me as soon as I came close. His warmth startled me; I hadn't realized how cold I felt until his skin touched mine. I looked at him: He didn't appear any more relieved than I was that Mac had not been found in the car.

"The driver's side door was open when they hauled it out," Jones reminded us, as if reading our minds. She didn't have to say it: The body could have floated out, dragged by currents into the greater ocean.

"Maybe he wasn't in the car to begin with," I ventured.

Jones looked at me and didn't say anything. I wondered what her illness made her feel about death: if something as vague as a body-less car hauled out of the ocean qualified as a definitive event. I wondered if she was able to care about anyone else's demise when she was staring right at her own.

"No sign of him in two whole weeks," Billy said. "It doesn't look good."

"Billy, you don't have to—" But before I could regret my strident tone as it sought to tamp down his pessimism, an investigator picked something up from behind the opposite side of the car and came around to us. He was holding a paper bag.

"Go ahead," Jones told him.

He stood in front of me and opened the bag. I looked in and saw a brown leather shoe. Part of the sole had come unglued and flapped down.

I recognized it immediately. "Oh God," I muttered,

hoping no one had heard me, because if no one heard me, maybe it wouldn't be true. Maybe I would blink my eyes and the wet shoe dangling from the man's hand would not be Mac's.

A hush fell, a stillness. It was as if I had screamed: *My husband is dead*. As if I had just realized something everyone already knew.

"Where was it?" I asked.

"Wedged under the driver's seat," Jones said.

I felt dizzy and suddenly knew I was going to faint. Billy pivoted to get both his arms around me in time to catch me. I was aware of his size and strength as he took all my weight at once, preventing me from crashing to the ground. I was not a small woman but he was able to lever me gently down and maneuver me so that the next thing I knew, I was lying with my legs outstretched in the grass and my head in Sergeant Jones's lap. Her dry, thin hand stroked my forehead, and in my delirium I thought, actually believed, that it was death touching me. My mind wove between a dream state, in which I saw Mac waving good-bye at the end of our block, blowing a kiss, wearing the brown shoes, and reality, in which I felt the physical presences of Jones and Billy and saw the car on the sloping asphalt drive.

Mac's shoe.

Wouldn't have been in the car.

If Mac hadn't been in the car, too.

When it drove into the Sound.

Sally Owen fed me some sweet tea and a brownie on her shady veranda. And then Billy loaded me back into his car and drove me home through rush hour traffic, straight into a blinding orange sunset.

"He didn't kill himself."

"Karin—" Billy glanced at Mom.

"Sweetheart, *please*."

I pulled my hand out from under hers as soon as she touched me. "No, I can't bring myself to believe that. I just can't."

"We may think we know someone," Mom said, "but there are always surprises."

"Anyone could have buckled under that kind of pressure." Billy meant Aileen and Hugh's murders. Danny's arrest.

"*He sent me flowers that day. He confirmed our date.*"

They glanced at each other but otherwise kept still. Finally Mom got up from the kitchen table and topped off Billy's coffee. She replaced the coffeepot and fussed with something at the counter before finally, reluctantly, returning to the table, where it seemed we had sat without end for two straight days and nights since I had come back home from Connecticut. If I had slept, I couldn't remember; if I had eaten, I had no idea. There was only one thing I could think about, and that was my conviction that without a body there was no proof of death.

"Did you know Detective Pawtusky called me yester-day?" I asked Billy, staring at him hard so I wouldn't miss an iota of reaction. Everyone was treating me like thin glass lately, trying to be strong so they could catch all my pieces when I broke. Trying to wait out my stubborn certainty that Mac was still alive. Trying to make me believe the unbelievable.

Billy sighed. "No, I didn't know he called you."

"Have *you* spoken with him recently?"

"A couple of times."

"He *asked* me, he *actually asked* me if Mac had been unfaithful. He said there was gossip in Bronxville that Mac was unfaithful to Val, that he cheated on her with me, and that he cheated on me as well. *What goes around comes around*, Pawtusky said to me. I told him that Mac was not that kind of man. I told him that Mac and I didn't get together until well after he and Val had separated. He sounded like he didn't believe me."

"I'll talk to him," Billy said.

"It's like Pawtusky thinks if he can prove Mac was unfaithful, he can prove I didn't know him as well as I thought, and he can prove they're a family of liars and cheaters and killers—*and Danny is guilty as charged*. It's character assassination."

"The detective does seem to be awfully insensitive," Mom agreed.

"Like I said, I'll talk to him."

I could have gone on all day like that, railing against everyone, the injustice of all the false accusations against Mac—infidelity, abandonment, suicide—but Ben woke up from his nap. Mom went downstairs and returned with my groggy little boy who had his father's eyes and smiled just like him, too. I took him on my lap, in my arms, breathed in his sweetness.

"*Mac isn't . . .*" I said to Mom and Billy, shaking my head in place of saying the final word, *dead*, to spare Ben's innocent ears.

Mom and Billy traded another one of their awful, knowing glances. And then Billy stood up.

"I have to get going."

"Will you keep looking for him?" I said. "Please?"

"Sure, Karin. I'll keep looking for him."

He patted my shoulder and then walked away. Mom showed him out. I heard them talking in low voices at the front door and though I couldn't hear what they were saying, I could imagine it. *It's just a temporary insanity. She'll come around. Give it time.*

The next morning the doorbell rang with a delivery from a messenger: a large cardboard box from Mac's office. Even they had decided he was never coming back and had cleaned out his desk for its next occupant. He had only been senior vice president of Forensic Security at Quest for a week before his parents died, two weeks before *he* died. Every time I thought that, a lump caught in my throat; no matter how hard I tried to swallow the un-fact of his suicide it wouldn't quite go down.

But I was trying. Going through the paces of my second widowhood. This time around was different from when I'd lost Jackson and Cece because I still had Ben. I would devote myself to him, we would live our lives day to day and just take it from there. Meanwhile I would finish school and start my new career; no more Mr. and Mrs. Forensic, as Mac had joked (a thought that made my eyes water) but Ms. Forensic, single mother. It wasn't exactly what I'd expected but if you think life is going to turn out the way you plan it, you're a fool. At the ripe age of thirty-seven, I knew that lesson by heart.

I carried the box to the living room, put it on the floor, sat down near Ben—who was coloring madly with washable markers on newspapers I had spread out for him—and proceeded to unpack Mac's workaday personal belongings. There weren't many things.

An extra charger for his personal cell phone; he had left his employer-supplied BlackBerry on his desk and presumably they had reassigned it.

A brand-new white shirt still in its packaging, a pair of clean black socks, and a small toiletry kit; he was prepared for the occasional unanticipated business trip.

A gym bag with sweatpants, an old T-shirt, white athletic socks, and battered once-white now-gray sneakers; he was

ready for a lunchtime visit to the midtown branch of his
gym. He had stuck by that pair of sneakers like an old
school friend who no longer fit into his life, refusing to
replace them. I had planned to surprise him with a new
state-of-the-art pair for Christmas this year.

A worn paperback of Emile Zola's *Germinal*; someone
must have loaned it to him, knowing how much he liked
to read classic novels. I hadn't learned this about him until
after we became lovers and I got to know him well: Mostly
he used the library, which was why his bookshelf at home
wasn't crammed with the detritus of his reading life. Mac
had not worn his true self on his sleeve; he was layered,
and if you had the patience to slowly peel back his layers
he only got better and better . . . and more complicated . . .
depression . . . why hadn't I learned about it before it led
him off a cliff . . . not off a cliff but into the water . . . a
drowning death . . . *how horrible.*

How had I not known?

I put the book down and removed the last thing from
the cardboard box: a slip of white paper, clearly a receipt.
I unfolded it, expecting it to be for the flowers Mac had
sent me the last day I saw him (he always used the florist
in the lobby of his office building, and he always paid in
cash), but I was wrong. The receipt was from a jewelry
store in midtown Manhattan for a necklace described in
neat script as *Diamond and ruby cluster pendant on 18k
gold chain*, costing twelve hundred dollars and dated three

weeks ago. It must have been a receipt for a gift Mac
planned to give me for our anniversary. Its price stunned
me; we had never had the money for extravagant presents.
But his promotion had come with a substantial raise. I
looked again at the date on the receipt: four days after his
promotion, and three days before his parents were killed.
I wondered where he had put the necklace. It would have
been imprudent to hide something of this value at work,
but at home I might have found it. Where would he have
decided was the safest place to squirrel it away? Had he
planned to give it to me at our dinner on Friday night, or
on our actual anniversary on Saturday? What would he
have done? How would he have thought? As I considered
it, nothing seemed clear or obvious—yet one more thing
to feel distressed about since I had never second-guessed
Mac before he vanished.

I picked up Ben, hoisted him onto my hip, and carried
him downstairs to his bedroom, where I changed his
diaper and took his favorite cuddly, a floppy brown
bunny, out of his crib. He grabbed it to him and squealed.
Then, in my room, I set him down on the floor and started
searching through my husband's things: dresser drawers,
closet, jacket pockets, small secretary desk where I paid
our bills, two-drawer file cabinet. I looked under the
bed and even between the frame and mattress. Then the
spare room, especially the closet where we kept our small
locked safe that was crammed with our few things that

were too valuable or dangerous to leave out: I removed the envelopes containing our birth certificates, our wills, our life insurance policies, and finally picked up the licensed gun we kept mostly out of habit—a Ruger P85 9mm handgun Mac had chosen with my blessing—and stared into the empty safe. Next I checked through Ben's room. Upstairs, I looked everywhere in the coat closet, including inside shoes and boots. and went through every kitchen cabinet. The more I looked, the more agitated I became. *Where was it?* And then I remembered that there was a safe at Quest for expensive electronics sometimes used on security assignments.

I picked up the phone and dialed Mac's office number from memory. His secretary, Tina, answered on the second ring.

"Sigrid Albert's office."

Good, I thought: *They gave the promotion to a woman.* I had never met Sigrid Albert but Mac had spoken highly of her. She had been at Quest about as long as he had and had been Deidre Stein's other protégé.

"Tina, it's Karin."

"Oh! Hi!"

"Thanks for sending over the box of Mac's stuff."

"You're welcome."

"But I have a question about something. Do you have a minute?"

"Shoot."

"There was a receipt at the bottom."

"The folded-up little paper? I didn't look at it; it was in his personal drawer."

"It was a receipt for a necklace—our anniversary was coming up—but I can't find it anywhere."

"I went through the whole office and I didn't see any necklace."

A note of tension had entered her tone but it was unnecessary; I didn't suspect her of having taken the necklace. Her fiancé was a wealthy young man and the engagement ring on her finger had to be five times as valuable as the necklace. She wouldn't have had any reason to steal it. Besides, she seemed like a nice young woman and it hadn't even occurred to me.

"I just thought he might have put it in the office safe."

"Oh *right*. Maybe he did. I'll check and get back to you."

While I waited, I started making lunch: a grilled cheese sandwich that Ben and I would share. Half would be enough to fill him up along with part of a banana on the side. The other half would be about all I'd be able to manage eating, as I'd lost my appetite since Mac disappeared. Before the sandwich was finished cooking, the phone rang.

"Hi Tina," I answered.

"Nothing in the safe, and I looked really carefully."

"That's strange." I flipped the grilled cheese and replaced the lid on the pan.

"Maybe a friend's holding it for him?"

"Could be." I thought of Billy, who lived near enough that it wouldn't have been an inconvenience getting the gift from him on the day of our anniversary. But why wouldn't Billy have said something? I knew he would have—he would have, in fact, given me the necklace. He wouldn't have held that back.

"I'm really sorry about Mac," Tina said. "I really liked him. I couldn't stop crying for like two days."

"I know."

"Everyone around here is really upset about it. Sigrid hates that this is how she got the job, you know?"

"I do—Mac hated getting the job for the wrong reasons, too. He always believed in Deidre."

"Yeah, I know, and then how they started dragging *him* into the investigation, like he *and* Deidre would *both* do something like *that*."

She was referring to the pay-to-play scandal, the accusation that Deidre's testimony as an expert forensic witness was for sale, that had cost her her job. But I had never before heard anything about Mac also being implicated; if he had been, he had never told me.

"I'm a little confused."

"Who isn't?" Her voice fell to a whisper. "I mean, why would they give him her job one day and then say he didn't deserve it the next day? Personally, it makes me sick. I would look for a new job if I wasn't about to get married."

"Mac never mentioned any of this to me."

"It just started like a couple of days before his parents—" She cut herself off, then shifted directions. "I mean talk about a case of bad timing."

"What exactly are they saying about Mac?"

"Same stuff they were saying about Deidre, more or less. Hardly anyone around here believes it, though. Mac? *No way.*"

"Where is Deidre working now?"

"I heard she went back to Florida—that's where she's from. There are a couple of big security firms down there."

So she had resuscitated her career closer to home, and in better weather. Not a bad move given what Quest had put her through, according to the stories Mac had been bringing home in the weeks before her ouster.

There was a loud sizzle from the stove and only now did I notice the acrid smell of the sandwich starting to burn.

"Thanks, Tina."

"Good luck finding the necklace."

"I'll have to look harder at home."

"I guess he was good at hiding stuff."

"I guess so."

I hung up and lifted the top off the pan in a blast of smoke. Loosened the sandwich with a spatula and dropped it onto one of the plates I had set out. After it cooled a moment, I scraped off charred bits, cut it in half, and set Ben up at the table in his high chair. I sat with him but couldn't bring myself to eat my half just yet.

To hear that Mac himself might have been facing similar pressure to what Deidre had suffered in her final weeks at Quest was an upsetting surprise. I could only assume that he hadn't told me about it so as not to worry me. My semester had been about to start, and we were always busy with Ben. We were *always* overtired. He wouldn't have wanted to cause me anxiety unless he had to. But to learn that he had seen a dark cloud moving in at work just days before the tempest of his parents' murder and his brother's arrest, and knowing now about his history of debilitating depression . . . well, it sent my head spinning. Mac the stoic and Mac the depressive must have coexisted uneasily; it must have taken a lot of energy for him to maintain his balance while juggling mounting anxieties with his sense of himself, and the image he projected of himself, as a man who was supercompetent.

Why hadn't he told me about his troubles at work?

Opened up to me. Talked to me; told me *everything*.

I could have helped him.

I might have saved him.

CHAPTER 5

The air had lost any warm note of a lingering summer and today had its first real bite. As I walked up West Fifty-eighth Street on my way to the subway at Columbus Circle, I buttoned my sweater all the way up. It was late afternoon and the sun was slanting down, making way for the evenings that seemed to arrive earlier every day.

Summer was gone.

Autumn was here.

Winter would come soon.

The wheel turned, seasons shifted, and still Mac wasn't home. One by one over the past seven weeks the cases had slapped shut: Pawtusky in Bronxville had his killer locked up, Staples in Brooklyn had found his missing person, and Jones in Stony Creek had her suicide. Turn the page. End the chapter. Close the book. Move on.

But how?

And why did this ending feel so incomplete? Or was that just how it was when someone blew you a see-you-later kiss and evaporated into thin air?

I ducked into a Duane Reade drugstore on the corner of Eighth Avenue to see if they had any Halloween costumes for Ben. This morning my mother had asked me what he was going to be this year and I'd admitted I hadn't even thought about it. She gave me a look; Halloween was tomorrow. When we had last discussed it, two weeks ago, I had told her that I would take care of his costume. How had the holiday come so fast? Lately it was as if time was melting; it was as if loneliness was engulfing me, drowning me, the more Mac's absence sank in. It was awful: the coldness of it. The repetition of days, how they became weeks then months and you were still without him. Another thing I recognized in her look was just how badly I was doing. Along with forgetting appointments and wearing clothes too long before putting them in the laundry, I had been unable to concentrate on doing my homework and so, because I was unprepared, I had skipped most of my classes. A minute after my mother's look, I decided something I had been contemplating for days: I would drop out of school for the time being, get my bearings, and then figure out what to do next. I had just come from the John Jay enrollment office, where I had made it official: I was a thirty-seven-year-old dropout.

I browsed through the little costumes hanging on rods

that protruded from a pegboard under a sign reading *Seasonal*. A Tigger costume looked like it would fit Ben, and I bought it. Back on the street, it was already darker than when I had gone into the store. Forty-five minutes later, when I emerged from the subway onto Smith Street, night had fallen.

The first thing I smelled upon opening my front door was roasting chicken. If I knew my mother, she was also making the diced potatoes, onions, and carrots mélange she liked to cook alongside the chicken. She had made dinner every night since she had moved in with me two weeks ago, and not just to help me care for Ben; she had given up her rental apartment (not too difficult, as she had no lease) so that we could join our financial resources. Now that I was living on disability from my interrupted career with the Maplewood Police and nothing else, I couldn't afford the duplex on my own.

After Mac had been gone three weeks, and I had mustered enough focus and energy to pay my first round of bills, the reality of his lost income really hit me. After two weeks, his paychecks had stopped. Because the police had deemed his so-called death a suicide, his life insurance policy was considered forfeited. His pension and my disability weren't enough to cover our mortgage. But because we co-owned our co-op apartment, I couldn't sell it without either Mac's signature, a power of attorney, or a death certificate. None of which I had. I soon learned that, without a body, it would take seven years to produce a death certificate, unless you obtained a court order, which I wasn't prepared to do because I still had trouble believing my husband was really dead. I told everyone I knew that I accepted Mac's presumed death, and I *tried* to accept it, but maybe it was the cop in me: I needed the body to be sure. More and more, I understood why in some cultures viewing the body at a funeral was so important: It convinced you the person was truly gone, that the remains were just a shell, a leftover. You couldn't argue with a dead body. And while hope may spring eternal, it never survived a face-to-face encounter with a corpse. I had learned, and was learning, so much more than I'd ever known about how cultural and legal definitions of death were sometimes at odds with each other. And that for people like me—for families left behind when the primary breadwinner vanished—there was a vast gray area that extended from the emotional to the financial. A miasma you fought for a while and then sank into.

"Like it?" I held up the costume.

"Adorable. I gave him his bath early. Hope you don't mind."

"Thanks."

"He seemed tired, and I thought an early night would be good since tomorrow's a big day." Mom opened the oven, lifted out the pan of golden chicken and roasted potatoes, and set it on the stove. Steam burst upward and then diminished.

"He won't really understand trick-or-treating, Mom."

"No, but he'll be there, and we'll take pictures. When he's older it will mean a lot to him. You'll see."

"Where is he?"

"In bed."

"Oh, I thought—"

"I bathed him *and* fed him. Is that okay?"

"Whatever you do is okay, Mom."

She stared at me.

"I mean that." And I did. How could I dispute a bedtime with someone who had altered her life to take care of my child?

"Do you know what time it is?" she asked me.

"Six, six-thirty."

"It's *seven*-thirty."

I looked at the wall clock: It was seven thirty-five.

Mom had already set the table and we sat down to eat. I still hadn't regained my appetite so ate what I could manage of the delicious dinner, but not much. The chicken and potatoes seemed to naturally lead to the topic of turkey and of course Thanksgiving, which was just around the corner.

"Jon and Andrea have decided to stay in California," Mom told me, "so it will just be us."

"That's fine," I said, though the thought of Thanksgiving, my favorite holiday, without Jon, Andrea, their kids, *or Mac* made me very, very sad.

"We'll take pictures."

"Mom, why are you so determined to photograph everything lately? Ben won't remember any of this."

"So that he'll *know*."

She leaned over her plate and caught my eye when she said that, and I understood. She wanted to document every milestone so that one day Ben would know about his life before his own memory kicked in, since clearly *my* memory of this time was going to be fairly skewed. My mother wanted to make sure that Ben would know that nothing important had been neglected, that *he* had not been neglected, in the wake of Mac's death.

"Mom, I've been meaning to ask you."

"Yes?"

"How can you be so sure?"

She put down her fork and nodded. She knew I meant *sure* about Mac being dead and not just missing. We had discussed it enough times.

"Because it's easier."

Of course it was. *Not* being convinced of it was exhausting to sustain, like when you're dreaming that you're flying and you stay up by dint of the *belief* that you're flying, a belief predicated on the power of suspended disbelief that dissipates as soon as you begin to wake up.

Halloween was weird and fun and depressing and exciting. Tigger sat strapped in his stroller holding a round plastic pumpkin with a light-up face, while I pushed him and Mom walked beside us with her little digital camera. We had deliberately come out in daylight so as to ease Ben into this peculiar holiday that gained intensity as darkness fell; but even now, at four o'clock in the afternoon, costumed children, teenagers, and even adults were everywhere and merriment was high. There were witches and goblins and ghosts and skeletons and princesses and storybook characters and ghoulish creatures with fake blood hard-dried down green-glowing faces. Every now and then someone would lean over from a stoop and drop a candy into Ben's bucket. He would glance over, baffled. He wasn't officially trick-or-treating but he was fully equipped, as my mother believed it was important that he was seen to be holding a candy bucket *in the pictures*.

We turned onto Court Street, where many of the local merchants stood outside their shops handing out candy. When we came to the bookstore, Mom stopped.

"Let's go in. I want you to meet Jasmine."

"The new girl you told me about?"

"I think she's working this afternoon."

We went inside. Jasmine was not only working but she was fully costumed for the occasion, and she was not a girl. She was a woman of thirty or so, a slight and very pretty Hispanic woman dressed up as Peter Pan. She danced over to us when she saw my mother.

"Pam, Pamela, Paminsky!"

"Not everyone can wear green tights like that," Mom told her.

"Not bad, huh?" Jasmine raised her arms and turned so we could view her from varying angles. "At first I was going to be a Lost Boy, but nobody would've recognized me. My husband's the lost boy, anyway, if you want to split hairs." She rolled her dark brown eyes. "*Ex*-husband, I mean."

"Hi." I extended a hand, which she shook with surprising force. "I'm Pam's daughter, Karin."

"I figured."

"It's slow in the store," my mother noted.

"Yeah. He's putting me on candy duty."

She detoured to the front counter where she picked up a large bowl of assorted candy, and we followed her outside. Walking straight to the middle of the sidewalk, she wasted not a moment actively soliciting takers.

"Who wants candy? Trick or treat! Candy right here! Happy Halloween!"

"Wow," I whispered to Mom.

"She's fun, isn't she?"

I nodded, though I wasn't sure if Jasmine was fun or borderline.

"Trick or treat!" A boy in a Batman costume raised a plastic bag with two hands.

"What do you want, a trick or a treat?"

The boy contemplated the unexpected question, and answered, "Treat?"

Jasmine dropped in two candies and the boy walked away.

"Tell Robin we got candy!" she shouted after him.

He glanced back, nodded, and picked up his pace until he rejoined his group.

"Cute," she said. "But I'm glad I never had kids, considering."

"How long have you been divorced?" I asked her.

"Separated three months ago, divorce is in the works."

"So it's still fresh." She was so cheerful, I was sure she had left him; but she swiftly corrected my assumption.

"You bet it's fresh—bastard left me for another woman. You there! Angel kid—candy! Get over here and bring your friends!" After the throng of kids moved along, she said, "That's why I moved down here, to start over."

"Sometimes I wonder if my husband left me for another woman," I ventured.

She looked at me, speechless. Obviously Mom had filled her in about Mac's suicide. I didn't know what had inspired me to say that to someone I had just met—a desire to voice it, maybe, as I'd ruminated so hard and long over all the reasons Mac might have had to take his life or possibly just flee. I quickly changed the subject.

"Where are you from?" I asked.

But before she could answer, a teenager wearing a head-to-toe Darth Vader outfit passed too close and Ben burst into tears.

"Nice to meet you," I told Jasmine.

"You too."

I could hear her summoning another group of children as Mom and I walked away, pushing the stroller.

"I invited her to Thanksgiving," Mom said. "I hope you don't mind."

"When? I didn't hear you."

"I asked her earlier today. She said yes."

I looked at her and shook my head. A stranger at our family's holiday meal? The prospect of it was painful.

"She's all alone here, she doesn't know anyone, and honestly, Karin, I thought we could use a little levity."

"Okay," I said, because maybe Mom was right, and what did it matter, anyway? I could almost hear her sigh as we turned the corner onto our street, which was quieter than the main drag, and thus a big relief. "I guess she'll be in all the pictures, so it'll look like we had a party." And someday Ben would glance back in time and feel convinced that his mother and grandmother had managed well in a crisis and never let him down.

By the time Thanksgiving rolled around, Jasmine Alvarez was no longer a stranger. I had run into her at the bookstore one day when I was dropping Ben off with Mom—she was about to finish up and planned to take him to the park—and Jasmine was just leaving her shift. It was the first time I'd seen her without her Peter

Pan makeup; now, instead of green from head to toe, she was dressed in tight jeans, cowboy boots, a close-fitting red shirt, and dangling feather earrings. She threw on a leather jacket, slung her oversized purse over her shoulder, and we walked out the front door together into the chilly November afternoon.

"Come on, let's get a drink," she said.

"It's only three o'clock."

"So what?"

"I'm on my way to a yoga class."

"Yoga?" She tilted her head and stared at me.

"It's part of my therapy plan."

"I thought you were some kind of ass-kicking cop."

"Former cop. My therapist thought it would be good for me."

"I see." She wove her arm through mine and turned me away from the YMCA on Atlantic Avenue that my mother and I had recently joined. Ben was taking a Tumbling Toddlers class and Mom sometimes went for exer-robics in the pool. "Ever had a Blue Devil?"

My mind did a back bend over that, instantly picturing an actual *blue* devil hovering over me in bed. Then I realized it was some kind of drink.

"Nope."

She steered me left on Dean Street and right onto Smith Street, which at this time of day was busy with backpack-slung kids coming home from school. I admit I didn't argue or fight; yoga was okay, but I ached for two days after every class, and in truth I felt more like drinking than down-dogging my way through the afternoon. Walking along Smith, she seemed to have a comment about every bar we passed.

Snack: "The tapas aren't as good as they look."

Ceol: "Good crowd but stinks of beer."

Bar Great Harry: "*Really* stinks of beer once you get over the fancy-schmancy."

Boat: "So *red*."

Angry Wade: "Regular barfly there got murdered by some teenage sex psycho."

"Yikes! At the bar?"

"In his home, but still. They set up a shrine at the bar where he sat. Gives me the creeps to think about it."

And then we came to Camp, which earned Jasmine's rating of approval: "Now *this* place I like."

The bar's storefront had an outdoorsy theme that really took hold once you stepped inside. The first thing I noticed was the deer's head mounted on the wall, then the kayak and the light fixtures that were actually buckets. Behind the bar was a huge photograph of a lake. A wood-burning fireplace crackled and glowed and sent out a welcome wave of warmth. Despite the early hour, there were five people posted on barstools and a couple of men at a table in the far corner of the smallish space. Jasmine plunked herself down on an overstuffed armchair facing another one that was artfully mismatched, but when sat in was very comfortable. My body sank in so deeply I knew it would be a while before I had the will to get up.

"Smell that?" she asked.

I sniffed. Mingled with the woodsy scent of the burning fire was something else: chocolate and marshmallow. "It smells like s'mores."

She pointed to a dark corner where a young man sat at a butcher block table building the treat I had loved as a child at sleepaway camp.

"How long have you been in Brooklyn?" I asked Jasmine.

"Two months, more or less."

"And you know *all* these places?"

"I get out. Don't believe in sitting home complaining to myself."

I could hear her saying that to my mother at work, and my mother recognizing my polar opposite—just what I needed. When times got tough, I dug in; apparently when times got tough for Jasmine, she burst out. I envied her.

In the end I didn't try a Blue Devil but the specialty of the house, a Dirty Girl Scout—heavy on the vodka and white crème de menthe—because Jasmine was trying one for the first time and she made it sound like an adventure.

"Sitting in here," I said, "it's like night."

"Doesn't matter the time of day, here it's always campfire time. That's one reason I like it."

"How often do you go out?"

"Five, six nights a week."

"I don't think I'd have it in me. Even when I was single, I stayed home a lot when I wasn't working."

"You were a cop—you didn't need to go out for excitement."

"What did you do in—?" I didn't know where she was from.

"Maine."

I stared at her.

"Yep, we're way up in Maine. We're *everywhere*."

"I didn't mean—"

"Whatever. Everybody thinks you'll only find Dominicans in the cities or down south. I don't take it personally."

"So what did you do before—in Maine?"

She shrugged. "This and that. Stores. Restaurants. You know—service jobs."

"And your husband?"

"*Ex*. Ski bum. Instructor." She made a shivering gesture with her shoulders. "I get cold thinking about it—the place, *him*. Next subject?"

So we talked about something else, anything other than our husbands and the lives we had lived before September. We had that in common: We were refugees from a past that was still so close you could almost touch it.

We were on our second round of drinks, concentrating on deconstructing a Jenga tower—we had fished as many pieces as we could find from a basket of games near the fire—when the front door swung open, revealing a purplish slice of late afternoon. In walked Billy Staples, wearing his out-on-the-town plaid shirt and cowboy boots—and jarring me out of the sweet, warm cocoon Jasmine had lured me into.

"Hey, Karin!" When he leaned down to kiss my cheek I smelled a whiff of cologne mixed with the snap of cold November air he'd brought in with him. My heart started beating quickly, which surprised me; and then I remembered this past September when I'd noticed how attractive he was. Again, I forced my mind away from that thought. Feeling attracted to another man was an acknowledgment that Mac was never coming back, an acceptance of his death, and I still wasn't quite ready for that.

"Jazz, babe." Billy's voice turned gooier than the s'more I'd eaten. He leaned down and kissed her.

"You know Karin?" she asked him.

"Long time." He winked at me. "Didn't know you knew Jazz."

"We just met recently. She works with my mother at the bookstore. I'm so confused!" I smiled foolishly, feeling as tipsy as I probably looked. It was then that I noticed that their cowboy boots actually matched, and that hers were stiff and new.

"I found this little lady sitting right here about—what?"

"Twenty-seven days ago." When Jasmine blushed, her mocha skin turned almost russet and made her even prettier. Of course Billy would want her.

He sat on the arm of her chair and she put a hand on his back.

"Can I take a turn?" he asked.

"No way," she said. "You'll knock it down in two seconds."

"So you guys are a *couple*," I said, looking at them, smiling now for real.

"I'm through with men." She blinked her eyes at him. "But this one here? He's more like a god, you know what I mean?"

"Okay—spare me the details, please." I pulled a piece from the middle of the Jenga tower, which didn't shift even slightly. "Your turn."

She sat forward, her back board-straight. I saw Billy glance down into her cleavage while she considered her move. She ignored him and used the tips of her long fingernails to edge out a piece. As I watched her I found myself wishing her move would fail and the tower would come crashing down. An irrational impulse swept through me.

It wasn't fair.

I wanted to *be* Jasmine.

I wanted Billy to want me—and I wanted to not care that Mac was gone.

I sat back in my comfy chair, closed my eyes, and forcibly banished the foolish thoughts.

"You okay?" Billy asked me.

"Fine. Just a little woozy. What time is it?"

"About five-thirty."

I fished around the floor for my purse and found it partway under the chair. Stood up. "I should really go."

"Stay," Jasmine said. "Get lost, cowboy. This is girls' night."

"No, really. I want to see Ben before he goes to bed."

"Yeah, well"—she glanced at Billy, who rested a hand on her shoulder—"I guess you can't argue with motherhood."

"Karin's a great mom," Billy said.

"I bet she is."

"Walk you home?" Billy offered.

"I'll be fine. Thanks anyway."

As I made my way through the nose-ringed multi-tattooed patrons who had filled the space when I wasn't looking, I heard Jasmine ask Billy, "How do you know her?"

"Friend of her late husband's."

"Ouch."

And then I was out the door, passing through the cluster of sidewalk smokers and walking along Smith Street amid teenagers listening to iPods, workers heading home, mothers pushing strollers and holding older children's hands as they crossed the street. It was a relief to be out of the faux comfort of Camp and back to the real, grown-up world where my mother and son waited for me in our quiet house—where I could remember Mac to my heart's content, smell him in our closet, sense him in our bed, and mourn him properly.

On Thanksgiving, Jasmine came early to help. As she stood at the kitchen counter, wearing my mother's favorite cow-print apron and chopping celery, she filled us in on details before we asked for them.

"My parents died when I was sixteen, same year, Mom first of cancer and then Pop of heartbreak. I mean it, he died of heartbreak just like they say. After that I stayed with my granny but she wasn't up for having a kid around, and anyway like I said I was sixteen, so whatever." *Chop chop chop.* "And then before you knew it I met Jesus who thought he was *God* and I made my first big mistake by moving in with him. Two years. Then I met Ricky who thought *he* was God and big mistake number two, four years. Then here comes Joe-on-skis the biggest God of them all and I really go for it this time, I *marry* him after knowing him three and a half weeks. Six years later, ladies, here I stand. Ready to start anew. Where do you want all this celery, Pam?"

"In that big bowl. Thanks."

"Next?"

"Read the package of bread crumbs over there and just do what it says."

"You got it."

"Are you serious about Billy?" Concentrating on peeling a potato in a perfect spiral, I didn't look up.

"Serious? Who said I was ever serious?" Jasmine's laugh was like glass bells.

"I think he's a lovely man," Mom offered, "and *handsome*."

"Mom!"

"Just because I'm old doesn't mean I'm blind."

"I never really noticed if he was handsome." I picked up another potato. "Billy's just . . . Billy."

"Well, take a good look," Jasmine said. "Get an eyeful. But he's a good man, too, I think. And generous: He bought me these boots after our third date." She tapped one pointy toe three times.

A cry came from the baby monitor.

"Ben's awake," I said.

"I can go." Mom emptied some rinsed lettuce leaves into a salad bowl and dried her hands on the dishtowel slung over her shoulder.

"That's okay," I said. "I've got it."

As I hurried through the living room I accidentally knocked over Jasmine's purse, which she had left on the edge of a chair, upending it and all its contents onto the floor. I bent down to clean up the mess as Ben's cries escalated.

"Don't worry about it." Jasmine came over, crouched down, and started scooping up lipsticks, a hairbrush, a notepad, a toothbrush case.

I handed her some slips of paper and her cell phone, then picked up a partially open envelope spilling an airline ticket. The date caught my eye, because it was tomorrow.

"Are you taking a trip?" I looked more closely at the ticket. "To Miami?"

She grabbed the ticket out of my hand and tossed it into her bag. "Maybe."

"With Billy? That's so romantic."

"Nothing doing. I'm going *alone*."

"Why?"

Resting her elbows on her knees, still in her crouch, she looked at me. "Because it's my birthday Saturday and I want to spend it under a palm tree in the best company I can think of: myself." She stood up.

"I always wanted to do that!" Mom called out from the kitchen. "Good for you, Jasmine."

I hurried downstairs to Ben, who was standing in his crib, holding on to the bars. The instant he saw me his tears dissolved and he laughed and jumped. As I changed his diaper, I thought about Jasmine's birthday, the plane ticket, her plans—why hadn't she told us about any of that? It confirmed something I had long thought about very extroverted people: Deep down they're lonely, possibly lonelier than the rest of us, which accounted for their need for constant companionship. I wondered if Jasmine's plan to spend her birthday all alone was some kind of challenge. If it was, it didn't sit right.

All through dinner, while Jasmine peppered us with stories of her parents' arrival in Bangor, Maine thirty-five years ago and the locals' gradual embrace of this family that was so unlike most of them and that brought "spice to their plain vanilla," as she put it, I thought about her lonely birthday plans. *If I were Jasmine*, I found myself thinking, *I would throw myself a party. If I were Jasmine, I would get Billy to take me dancing. If I were Jasmine, I would go to Paris on the spur of the moment.*

But I wasn't Jasmine.

I was me, and when I did something impulsive it tended to beg the kind of danger I was sure Jasmine had never entertained in her life. If my life had invited darkness, hers had been filled with sparks of light. Which was probably why I had come to like her so much and why so many men fell in love with her.

After dinner, we refused to let Jasmine help with the dishes and sent her home. Standing beside me, drying as I washed, Mom caught my eye and asked, "So? Are you thinking what I'm thinking?"

"Depends."

"Jasmine doesn't want to spend her birthday alone."

"No, she doesn't."

"So do it—surprise her. You could really use a vacation, anyway, Karin. I'll be here with Ben."

I rested my rubber-gloved hands on the edge of the sink and looked at my mother. The same thing had occurred to me, and she was right: I could use a few days away from the day-to-day world that was filled with reminders of Mac. And I was convinced that Jasmine, of all people, didn't want to celebrate all by herself, beneath a palm tree or not.

By the time I went to bed I had an electronic ticket folded in my purse and a weekend bag all ready to go.

CHAPTER 6

The next day, my plane landed at Miami International Airport an hour before Jasmine's flight was due—when I had spied her ticket, I'd taken note of the airline and time her flight was leaving New York, and finding out her arrival details had been easy. I dragged my carry-on bag off the plane and past the luggage carousel (I hadn't checked anything), thinking that the post-holiday traffic would get worse by Sunday when I was due to fly home. I hadn't seen when Jasmine was leaving but decided that two nights would be about as long as I could bear to be away from Ben.

I walked the long corridors to the central part of the airport. There didn't appear to be much to do to entertain yourself while you were waiting, unless you liked fast food, or unless I had missed something. I bought a Styrofoam cup of burned coffee at a snack bar called Miami Express, parked myself at a table near its outer edge, and people-watched. Jackson and I used to love doing this back when we traveled pre-Cece; we would sit and notice things, like the higher the heel the shorter the step, or the deeper the tan the lower the cleavage, or the balder the head the hairier the chest.

I still missed Jackson. And *yearned* for Cece, my darling little daughter.

And I still loved Mac.

I tried not to think of him but instead to concentrate on the flow of travelers passing through the airport, coming and going to and from cities and countries all over the world: all the men and women and children I had never seen before and would never see again, each of whom was a universe unto him- or herself. It was amazing how many people there were. And humbling. I felt diminished, and my load felt lightened, to recognize my own insignificance in the flow of so much humanity. The longer I looked, the more I recognized common traits ranging from individual eccentricities to complete personas: There was the way this man walked with a kind of waddle that reminded me of a neighbor of my parents' old house in Montclair, there was the way a girl wore her sunhat that brought back a girl I'd known when I was about ten. And there were the broader categories people fell into as if we were all a certain type of doll: the short, stout, middle-aged mother in casual-expensive clothes; the lanky young dad dressed like his son in jeans, T-shirt, and sneakers; the well-groomed businessman who walked at a brisk pace. I looked for *my* type, wondering if I could force myself to see how I appeared to others, and found the first example in less than a minute: the tall, thin, semiattractive woman somewhere in her thirties, hair a shaggy mess, no makeup except for the slightest trace of lipstick, and dressed in shorts, T-shirt, and sandals as if she still thought she was on summer vacation from high school. One of my own type passed, then another. And then I spotted what I would have called the Jasmine: a pulled-together woman in her late twenties or early thirties, tight sundress, legs waxed to a shine, fingernails and toenails newly polished red, broad true smile.

When I looked at my watch and saw that only twenty minutes had passed since my flight had landed, I couldn't believe it. Well then, back to my game.

I saw four women who matched my mother, six elderly men who matched my late father, a dozen brothers Jon and three Andreas, his wife. There were at least nine families just like theirs, with two parents, a daughter about seven, and a son about four. Eleven families like mine and Jackson's and mine and Mac's, with two parents and a toddler, either a girl or a boy. I noted single parents of both genders tagged by groups of children varying in number and size. And then I saw a Danny—a man-boy with graying stubble, tight jeans, and a faux retro T-shirt—and was jolted out of my playful mood. The real Danny was still sitting in jail; Rosie had refused to post bail or hire him a private lawyer; a trial date had been set for January. Even I had started believing he had killed his parents . . . and for what? A cut of their modest will? A diamond ring (which, to my knowledge, still had not been found)?

Suddenly exhausted, I bought a second cup of coffee and sat back down at the same table. As I was prying off the plastic lid, some of the scorching hot liquid splashed onto my fingers and I reacted with a loud "Ow!" When I looked up, I saw that a man dragging a small black wheelie suitcase had paused briefly to look at me.

Mac.

I stood up, accidentally pushing the table and upending the entire cup of coffee. Hot brown liquid seeped onto the floor, just missing my suitcase.

Or a man who looked just like Mac.

"Wait!" I left my suitcase and jogged after him.

A man who looked so much like Mac it was uncanny, walking the way he walked, bracing his shoulders the same way, wearing just the kind of clothes he would wear: jeans, sneakers, button-down shirt, a digital watch. He picked up his pace and I started to run.

"Mac! Wait!"

I couldn't tell if he knew I was following him or if he even heard me. He kept moving, pressing his way through a swinging glass door and heading directly to a taxi stand at the curb.

"*Mac!*"

His face was obscured as he sidled into a waiting cab, leaned forward to direct the driver, and drove away.

I had caught only the quickest glimpse of him when he paused to note my spill. But it was him. I knew it: *It was him.*

Was it him?

I stood at the curb watching the car drive down the palm tree–lined road, shrink into a distance of hazy sun, and evaporate like a mirage. How long did I stand there before someone's suitcase bumped against my leg?

"Sorry," a woman said as she rolled past.

"That's okay." But she didn't hear me.

"Jasmine!" I ran at her as soon as I saw her coming out of her gate wearing a bright yellow halter dress. "*I saw him.* Mac, my husband, *he was here.*"

In front of her now, her up-close expression—astounded —startled me as much as my appearance at the Miami airport obviously startled her.

"Whoa, girl! What are you doing here?"

"I came to surprise you, so you wouldn't have to spend your birthday weekend alone."

She smiled. "You really *are* my friend."

"Listen, Jasmine, listen to me—"

"Did you say you just saw your husband?" Her tone was too calm; it was clear she didn't believe me. Why would she believe me? Why would anyone? The case was closed: Mac was dead.

"I was killing time waiting for your flight to arrive and *there he was—Mac—walking through the airport*."

"That's *crazy*."

"You think I'm crazy?"

"No! *It's* crazy—crazy good. Where is he?"

"He got in a taxi. Drove away."

"He didn't see you?"

"He did see me; at least I think he saw me. I called his name. I followed him."

"And then?"

"He kept walking."

Her eyes mirrored the deflation I felt when I heard myself saying that: *He kept walking*.

"So maybe it wasn't him," she said cautiously. "Maybe it just looked like him."

"I don't think so." But my certainty was already draining away.

She put her hands on my shoulders, bracing me. "He looked at you. You said his name. And he kept walking." She pulled me into a hug. "Listen, baby—"

"He looked so much like Mac," I said, dissolving into tears.

"You ever read that book *The Year of Magical Thinking*?"

"Joan Didion?"

"Good book, huh?"

I nodded. Cried.

"She saw her husband everywhere she went for like a year after he passed. And he had a heart attack right in front of her, eating dinner at the table."

I nodded again. Cried some more. The first time I was a widow, I used to see Jackson all over the place. And Cece. And the two of them together.

"And she still believed she saw him. She kept on seeing him even though she *knew* he was gone."

The word she kept avoiding was *dead*. Didion's husband was *dead*. And my husband was *dead*.

"I'm sorry." I pulled away so I could wipe my wet face with the palms of my hands. "I promise I won't ruin your birthday."

She smiled the way a mother would when she didn't believe a word that came out of her kid's mouth but didn't want to say so.

"You know what?" she said. "Let's just turn around and head back to New York, okay? It was so sweet that you wanted to surprise me but maybe it wasn't the greatest idea after all. And now that I think about it, I'd rather be in New York for my birthday."

"Liar."

"Like *you* know what's going through my mind."

"But we're here."

"No biggie." She forced a smile. "We'll go back."

But it seemed pretty obvious to me that she was offering to sacrifice her birthday trip to get me back onto safer ground.

"No."

"*Karin*."

"If I were you, I'd definitely want to spend my birthday under a palm tree with a Blue Devil in my hand, *not* pretending I was at sleepaway camp—even if there was a cute guy involved."

Her eyes rolled up, mock thinking, and she held flattened palms toward the ceiling, pretending to weigh the two options against each other. "Hmm . . . palm tree and Blue Devil . . . hot guy in cold New York." Her hands went up and down until finally the palm tree won. "Okay, but no crazy talk."

"I promise."

She insisted on calling her hotel to change the reservation from a single to a double instead of waiting until we got there. That was another thing that surprised me about her: She could be just as fussy about details as she could be spontaneous and toss them all to the wind.

Half an hour later we pulled up in front of the Marriott hotel in downtown Miami. The hotel was a tower that stood straight and tall beside Biscayne Bay like an uptight tourist too zipped up to undress and get into the water. We checked into our room on the twenty-first floor. Jasmine chose the double bed nearer the bathroom and I got the one by the window. When I opened the drapes I was surprised to see that we had lucked out and gotten a sweeping view of the bay instead of the city. Sailboats drifted on sparkling blue water as if it wasn't a frigid day back in New York.

When I turned around, Jasmine had already thrown open her suitcase and put on a black string bikini. A tiny diamond sparkled at the edge of her belly button, and every inch of her perfect skin was smooth as a peach. I was putting on my bathing suit—a two-piece that didn't qualify as a bikini compared to what Jasmine was wearing—when I felt something hit me. I looked up: Jasmine has tossed over her spare bikini, gold with metal hoops at the hips holding meager front to meager back.

"Thanks, but this is so not me," I said.

"Put it on or we're heading back to New York."

I stripped off my blue spandex and pulled on Jasmine's bathing suit, which more or less fit.

Jasmine surveyed me with a smile. "You are one hundred percent Miami, like you were born here!"

I found my sunglasses buried under my nightgown, put them on, and opened my arms. "Ta da! Ready to hit the beach?"

"Just be yourself, okay? Don't try to be happy and fun. That's my department."

"Then why am I wearing this?"

"Looking the part is half the battle, that's why."

We rode the elevator down to the lobby and found our

way to the nearest public beach. It was cooler near the water, and crowded. We spread out our hotel towels, dug in our hotel beach umbrella, lay down—and that was it. Hours melted away. It was lovely. Jasmine either read or talked in bursts—"I like working in the bookstore but I'm not much of a reader; I'd rather watch TV". . . "My ex used to take food right off my plate; talk about annoying". . . "Billy's perfect except for one thing: He's got no money"—as I listened and otherwise let my mind detour to thoughts I couldn't share with her.

I would plan something special for tomorrow, her birth-day; make a reservation at a nice restaurant and order a cake. I would ask at the hotel's front desk for a recommendation.

And I would look for Mac. I had to.

What if it *had* been him I'd seen at the airport? What if he was right here in Miami? What were the odds of that? I propped myself up on my elbows and gazed back and forth across the teeming beach. If Mac was here, he'd be wearing a T-shirt to cover his scars—at first glance I saw half a dozen men wearing T-shirts with their bathing suits. What if one of them was my husband? What if he *was* here in this city, right now? What if everywhere I went for a full year, I saw him? Haunted, insane, every sighting an unrequitable yearning to have him back. I lay down on my lumpy towel, closed my eyes, and let the heat of the sun soak into my skin.

* * *

I waited until almost midnight for Jasmine to fall asleep. And then, when I was sure, I brought my clothes into the bathroom and changed out of my nightgown. I took a room key and my purse and quietly let myself out.

There was a business center off the hotel lobby, a windowless room with six cubicles stocked with computers, faxes, scanners, whatever you'd need to conduct business away from home base. The center was empty except for me. I chose a cubicle in the farthest corner of the room and went online.

Finding a local private investigator turned out to be incredibly easy. In fact, the area had an embarrassment of riches when it came to resources for nailing cheating husbands, bolstering your case in a custody battle, finding out if your business partner was embezzling, or whatever else you wanted to know but couldn't find out yourself. One elaborate Web site after another offered an array of electronic and hands-on surveillance, and all you had to do was initiate a case and offer up your credit card number. It was that simple. As a former detective, I found the whole enterprise dubious; but on the other hand, I wanted someone to help me without letting Jasmine or anyone else know what I was doing. If she or my mother or Billy Staples or *anyone* knew that I wanted to make sure it wasn't Mac who had evaded me at the Miami airport, they would invoke magical thinking, outright delusion, or worse. Too much crazy; but that didn't mean I couldn't satisfy my own curiosity.

I dialed the 800 number on the screen and in moments my call was answered by a man with an Indian accent.

"Hello! My name is Peter! You have reached Miami Investigation Services! How may I help you?"

He pronounced it *Meeami*, confirming my guess that I was talking to someone in a call center in India. No matter. In the morning, when an investigator picked up his roster of late night calls, he'd find my request.

I shared only the essentials with Peter, skipping the complications about Aileen and Hugh's murders, Danny's arrest, and Mac's disappearance and presumed death. All he needed to know was that my husband had gone AWOL and I thought he might be in Miami.

"Do you have a photograph of your husband, ma'am? Of course it would much aid in the investigation."

"I think I have some in my phone."

I put the call on hold and scrolled through the pictures I'd snapped on impulse and forgotten about, each one inciting a poignant memory: Mac sitting on our couch, gazing down at Ben who slept in his arms; Ben gleefully throwing banana slices from his high chair to the floor while Mac grinned at me (at my phone, that every-ready surreptitious camera); Mac in front of our brownstone last winter, looking thoughtful and relaxed and very much like himself, less than a year before his life had come crashing down. That was the one. Peter gave me his e-mail address, I zapped the picture into the ether, and within moments

Peter confirmed he'd received it. Next he asked for my credit card and a contact phone number, and Project Find Mac Alive was under way. Before I let Peter go, I made sure someone would call me tomorrow, *someone from Miami*, I specified. His answer, "Yes indeed, ma'am," wasn't all that reassuring, considering that I'd just agreed to a five-hundred-dollar retainer charged to my credit card, and I had no real idea who I was talking to or where exactly he was. Still, I slept well that night knowing that finally I had done something, or at least believed I had done something. Crazy or not, it felt right.

The next day, Saturday, was Jasmine's birthday. We passed the morning at the beach, had lunch at a bayside café, and chartered a sailboat for the afternoon. I periodically checked my cell phone to make sure it was working. It was. As the hours passed I feared that I had thrown away five hundred dollars and also duped myself on a deeper level by tempting the impossible. It would serve me right for being such a fool. I was dying to discuss it with Jasmine but kept my lips sealed; I had promised not to ruin her birthday with *crazy*, and hiring a private eye over the Internet was certifiably nuts. I had been a cop; I definitely should have known better.

By the time we returned from our sail, feeling gorged on too much sun and heat and thoroughly exhausted, I had convinced myself that I would never hear from Miami Investigation Services Ltd., or Late Night Internet Rip-Off

Inc., whatever you called it. But then, as we walked along
the boardwalk on our way to our hotel, my cell phone rang.
I was dying to answer but couldn't in front of Jasmine, so
I ignored it. Later, back at the hotel while she was in the
shower cleaning up for dinner, I ducked into the hallway
outside our room and returned the call.

"Lucky Herman here, you left me a message?" He had a
voice that sounded as if it had survived too many cigarettes
and too much booze, the private eye voice that was so classic
it seemed like a put-on. But then I detected a faint operatic
crescendo on his end of the phone and my assumptions
readjusted themselves, smoothed out his edges. He was an
opera buff, or he lived with an opera buff; either way, I
knew nothing about him and it felt better that way.

"We have to speak quickly."

He chuckled. Apparently he'd heard that before.

I repeated the basic information I'd told Peter last night.
Lucky had the photo of Mac in front of him.

"Can I just ask you, Mr. Herman, what your experience
is?"

"Detective with the Miami Police, twenty-two years,
retired. If you met me in person you'd find out I don't look
anything like I sound. That's what they tell me."

"They."

"People. Everyone. You know what I mean."

"I'd like to meet you in person but I'm leaving for New
York in the morning."

"It's up to you." He coughed.

I wondered if he was telling the truth. If I met him in person, would he appear other than a broken husk of a former cop . . . who liked opera? I had known so many, and half of them sounded just like him.

"Find him if you can."

"If he's findable, I will. I've got your number if I have any questions or if your retainer runs out. If I locate him fast or decide it's a lost cause, you'll get the rest of your money back on your credit card. That's how it works."

Ten hours at fifty dollars an hour would go quickly, but what other choices did I have?

"Thank you."

"I wish you luck."

Was that how Lucky Herman always signed off at the end of a conversation? It was corny but effective. As I dressed for dinner, I found myself feeling optimistic that Lucky was a fitting name for the investigation I had just launched. If Mac was alive, and if he was in Miami, and if Lucky Herman was any good at his job, maybe I would find him.

But as the night progressed, and I treated Jasmine to a birthday meal at Le Bouchon de Grove, a French bistro recommended by the hotel concierge, my mind drifted in another unexpected direction. On the off chance that Mac actually *was* alive, and if he was here—why would he hide from me?

CHAPTER 7

It was the coldest January on record. The duplex apartment in the hundred-year-old brownstone seemed to leak heat from every window and door. The cost of oil was sky-high, and money was tight, so my mother and I kept the temperature as low as we could stand it. But on the morning of Ben's second birthday, on a quiet Saturday, we cranked up the heat to make sure our home felt comfortable for all the visitors we'd invited to help celebrate over lunch.

Today marked another event, as well, at least in my mind: It was the final deadline I had set for any remaining shred of hope that Mac was out there somewhere, alive. All the holidays had passed without a word or sign that he was still in this world, that he remembered us. And I hadn't heard anything from Lucky Herman since the one time we'd spoken on the phone. I had told myself that if Mac didn't miraculously reappear today, if he failed to remember our son's birthday, he *had* to be dead. It really *was* over. I would acquiesce to the obvious and embrace my second widowhood. Mac had now been gone more than four months.

The party was set for noon, but at eleven-fifteen the doorbell rang. Mom answered it. After a quick burst of animated chatter, Mac's sister, Rosie, and her brood streamed in, pink-cheeked from the frigid cold outside. The three younger kids instantly dispersed in the directions of Ben, toys, and TV while the eldest, Dave, who was on winter break from college, joined his parents in greeting the adults.

"We came early to help out." Rosie bear-hugged me with her husband, Larry, grinning behind her, and Dave, behind *him*, looking like a twenty-year time warp version of his father.

I kissed Larry hello and then looked over at the sudden activity that had filled the living room. "The kids are *huge*," I remarked; thinking, *If only Mac was here, if he could see how his nieces and nephews had grown in so short a time*. "What are you feeding them?"

"I tried not feeding them at all, but they grew anyway," Rosie said.

Larry emitted a bark of laughter.

Rosie winked. Then she squinted her eyes, assessing me. "You look good, Karin."

"That's bullsh—" I slapped a hand over my own mouth.

Larry laughed again. I even caught my mother snickering behind me at the kitchen counter, where she was frosting cupcakes.

"I can't believe he's two years old." Rosie shook her head, sighed, and plugged any chance of mournful feelings hijacking Ben's birthday by issuing an order: "Put us to work! How many people do you have coming?"

"Around fifty."

"Wow," Larry muttered.

"Dad, that's like what a party *is*." Dave shook his head at his pathetically out-of-touch father.

"It's snowballed a little out of proportion," I admitted. "We invited family, plus all the kids from Ben's tumbling class, and they're *all* bringing their parents and siblings."

Rosie followed me into the kitchen, saying, "The parties get more manageable when you can do drop-offs." My mother handed her an apron, which she tied over her blue sweater.

In the bright kitchen, I noticed that it wasn't just Rosie's children who had grown these past months; Rosie herself had visibly aged. Her skin looked paler and drier, and the bags under her eyes had an ingrained, permanent quality they'd never had before. We had last seen each other in person at her parents' funeral, and since then she had suffered the domino-like losses of her only siblings as well. She had remarked to me on the phone one time that she was "a real orphan now," and "thank God I have

Larry and the kids." I'd reminded her that Danny was still alive and it was possible he would be acquitted for lack of evidence—an assumption I clung to. At that, she had snorted loudly and changed the subject. I wondered what she knew that I didn't.

By noon, Rosie and my mother had finished frosting sixty-two cupcakes, chocolate and vanilla. Eight-year-old Alice had decorated them generously with rainbow sprinkles. The vegetarian chili Mom had made yesterday was heating on the stovetop, and the cornbread I had made from a mix that morning was keeping warm in the oven. A big pot of water was readied to boil hot dogs, and a heap of buns was laid out on a platter. Meanwhile, as Larry and I carried stacks of paper plates and bowls and plastic cutlery to the table, twelve-year-old Lindsay believed she had succeeded in teaching Ben how to send text messages, and five-year-old John had lost three Wiffle balls under various low-slung pieces of furniture.

By twelve-thirty the house was teeming with families, and the sheer force of so much innocence in one place created an infectious gaiety. There were so many children living in the moment you couldn't help following them even a little bit through that looking glass of wonderment, of forgetting what came before and worrying about what might come after. It was a good party. A happy few hours. When I spotted Billy and Jasmine sitting together on the floor in the living room, playing jacks with Alice and two other littler girls, my heart swelled: I felt I saw their future in that moment; a marriage, a family, the turning of the eternal wheel.

And then, just as quickly as the party had come together, it was over. By four o'clock, everyone was gone. Ben was wired from exhaustion and so was Mom. They went downstairs to share a late nap on my bed.

I poured myself a cup of coffee and was busy cleaning up when I heard what sounded like Rosie shouting, "Lindsay, answer the phone! Lindsay, answer the phone!" over and over again. But they had left almost half an hour ago for the ride back to Long Island.

"Hello?" I answered into mid-air, confused.

"Lindsay, answer the phone! Lindsay, answer the phone!"

Just as I realized that Rosie's voice sounded tinny and each repeated phrase was identical, I picked up a pile of scrunched-up SpongeBob napkins and unearthed Lindsay's silvery pink cell phone, flashing with a picture of her mother.

"Okay," I answered the call, "that scared the hell out of me."

"That's Mom's special ring," Lindsay said. "Like how she's always yelling at me to do stuff?"

"You forgot your phone."

"Gee you're smart, Aunt Karin." Her tone oozed with tween sarcasm.

"I'll send it to you."

"That would take *days*. Dad already turned the car around."

"See you when you get here."

As soon as I slipped the phone into my pocket, the doorbell rang.

"No way," I muttered to myself, unless Lindsay was being clever and had called from just outside the door. Grinning, I simultaneously swung open the door and held out the pink phone.

It wasn't Lindsay.

Instead, I was face to face with a man so short I had to look down to really see him. He was Indian, in his middle fifties, I guessed, with a halo of short white hair. Under a puffy red jacket he wore a suit and tie.

"Karin Schaeffer?"

That voice; I had heard it before. It took just a moment to place it.

"Lucky Herman?"

"I've got something for you." He handed me an envelope.

A taxi idled on the sidewalk in front of the brownstone. Sitting in the back was an Indian woman with short black hair wearing red lipstick and big pearl earrings.

"You said you wanted to meet me in person." His smile was tight and ironic but somehow friendly. A cop's smile. The kind of smile that wanted the last word.

"Don't tell me you came all the way here to—"

"*No*." He chuckled. "My wife gave me tickets to the Metropolitan Opera for Christmas. This is the big weekend. *Carmen* with Angela Gheorghiu and Roberto Alagna. Looking forward to it." He glanced at his watch. "Had plenty of time after the flight and this was on the way."

"You brought me the balance of the retainer?" But even as I said it, I knew that wasn't why he'd come.

My heart pounded as I opened the envelope. Lucky Herman stood there and watched me pull out a four-by-six glossy print of a man and a woman in conversation at a bar. The woman was perched on a barstool; I couldn't see her face, just her slender curved back leaning toward the bar on which her elbow was propped. Her sleeveless white shirt was bright against her toffee skin, and you could see that she was wearing a necklace by the thin chain hugging the back of her neck. Something about her looked familiar, though I couldn't place it. But she wasn't the reason Lucky had brought this photograph all the way from Florida.

The man faced her, and this was what Lucky was really delivering to me: the clear, straight-on image of his face.

Mac.

Sitting on a bar stool. His eyes fixed on the woman's eyes. A half smile taking in something she had just said.

Was it Mac?

He looked so much like Mac. But thinner. His face more heavily lined. And tan.

The longer I looked at the picture, the less certain I became.

I felt dumbstruck and confused. I had sought this out, paid for it, demanded it. But now I wasn't sure I really wanted it, because this image of a man who might or might not be Mac, this man sitting on a bar stool, did not solve anything. I tried to hand the photo back to Lucky but he refused.

"That's what I hate about this line of work," he said. "You give people what they ask for and then they argue with you."

"My husband is dead."

"That's for you to decide."

I looked again at the photo. "Do you think it's possible for two people to look really alike—two people who aren't twins and aren't related?"

"Anything's possible."

"Lucky?" his wife called to him from the taxi.

"There's a check in the envelope for unused time. Truth is, I found him when I wasn't looking. Had my assistant Peter pound the pavement at first—he costs half what I cost, by the hour—and I went out once or twice myself but it was a needle-in-a-haystack situation and I didn't really think we'd find him. Then I went to meet a client at that bar and bingo. One picture."

"When?"

"Yesterday. That's why I thought I'd hand deliver the

job, because I was coming to New York anyway. And that way, you could meet me." He smiled.

"Lucky!" An unmistakable note of irritation now in his wife's voice.

He turned and waved a one-minute finger at her. "She wants to get the most out of the weekend."

"What bar is this?" I turned the photograph over as I asked and found the answer handwritten on the back: Hotel Collins, on Collins Avenue in South Beach, Miami.

"Not the kind of place I usually go," he said. "Trendy. Drinks are expensive."

"Thank you."

"Nice to meet you, Ms. Schaeffer. Just give me a call if you need anything else. And don't worry: That's the only print and I erased the digital image."

"I appreciate that."

"It's what we do." He turned to leave.

"Wait! The necklace the woman's wearing, did you see it?"

"No. She never faced the camera."

"Did you notice if the chain was gold or silver? I can't see it well enough in the picture."

He came back up the stoop, took out his reading glasses, and looked closely. "Gold."

A terrible sensation rattled through me. I stood there, thinking of Mac, the necklace, another woman—a slim, dark woman who from the back very much resembled his disgraced boss, Deidre—as Lucky Herman joined his wife in the back of the taxi and they drove away. Just then, Larry pulled up in the family minivan. The side door opened and Lindsay hopped out. I came down the stoop with the phone and handed it to her, but instead of saying good-bye I followed her to the van.

"Rosie." I stuck my head in the driver's window, looking past Larry. "Take a look at this."

She stared hard at the photograph, then handed it back at me. "It's a picture of Mac."

"Are you sure?"

"Yes." And then her eyes brightened. "He looks a little different, though. When was this taken?"

"Yesterday."

Larry grabbed the photo and studied it. "That's not him."

"It *is* him," Rosie said.

Before the argument gathered steam, they all got out of the car and came back into the house. Hearing the commotion, my mother got up from her nap and joined us upstairs. For the first time I told them all about seeing Mac (or not) at the Miami airport in November and hiring Lucky Herman.

"Jasmine thought I was insane. *I* thought I was insane. I didn't want all of you to think I just wasn't accepting that he was dead."

Mom took a close look at the photograph and concluded, "I don't know. I'm just not sure."

"I'm with her," Larry said. "It looks like Mac, I'll give you that, but it isn't him."

"I think it is him," Rosie said.

"Honey," Larry's voice became syrupy, pleading, "he wouldn't just disappear, not Mac."

"But this picture," she said in a tone that sounded as desperately hopeful, as delusional, as magically wishful as me on my worst days. And I knew: Rosie had suffered badly, too. She also wanted Mac resurrected enough to believe almost anything.

Mom gently touched my arm. "Call Billy. See if he's free to come over."

I did. He was. Twenty minutes later, he was sitting on my couch looking at Lucky's photograph. When he looked back up at me, he shook his head decisively.

"It isn't him."

"How can you be so sure?" I asked.

Rosie agreed: "Look again."

Billy took another long look. "No way. I know you two are hurting, but you can't go on trying to bring back the dead. Everywhere you go for a while, you're going to spot him. I've seen it so many times. That's just how it works." He stood up, looked from me to Rosie and back to me. "I'm sorry."

Rosie and I gazed at each other, trying to will everyone else's pessimism out of the room. But it didn't work. As Billy headed out the door, back to his precinct, Larry looked at the picture another time.

"Yeah, I've got to agree with Billy. This guy sure looks like Mac, but it isn't him."

"Karin?" Mom said in a tone I recognized from my girlhood, when I would stubbornly refuse to relinquish a lost argument.

I looked at her and didn't say anything. I had already made up my mind. The hot, angry feeling was rattling through me again.

All this time I had refused to believe that Mac was dead. Now, if he *was* alive, if this *was* him, if *she* was wearing the expensive necklace I had never been able to track down—then, if I found him, I would kill him myself.

CHAPTER 8

I shoved the plastic key card into the slot of my hotel room lock so fast and hard that it snapped in half. Another shot of adrenaline fountained into my brain—I had been living on it since meeting Lucky Herman and seeing that photo of *Mac and his girlfriend*. I kicked the door three times, hard. The neighboring door swung open and a man with messy brown hair looked at me.

"It's three A.M.!"

"The card broke!"

"Well, don't make the rest of us suffer!" He slammed his door shut.

I dragged my suitcase back to the elevator and down to the lobby, a masterpiece of Art Deco symmetries and sleek designs with, in the case of the Hotel Collins, dashes of signature blue glass. The middle-of-the-night hushed silence was overwhelming when I wanted so badly to make noise and trouble, to shout and scream: *Where the hell is my husband and how could he do this to me?*

I dinged the bell at the front desk and in a moment the night attendant who had checked me in minutes ago appeared. Nate—according to the name tag he wore on the floral shirt that appeared to be the uniform of this South Beach hotel, as the door attendant had worn it, too— looked, by his creased, flushed face, as if he had caught a power nap in the minutes I'd been jamming my lock on the seventh floor.

"The card broke in my lock."

"That never happens."

"Well, it does now."

He eked out a weary smile. I still hadn't gotten over the sticker shock of the price of a room for a single night and felt no guilt in holding the hotel to high expectations. Like providing sturdier key cards. Or not harboring errant husbands.

"Look, can you just give me another room?"

He consulted the computer and presented me with a key card to a single room on the fourth floor. Good. I wouldn't have to face my angry neighbor on seven. I didn't think I could muster an iota of diplomacy.

I had to keep reminding myself that it wasn't anyone's fault but Mac's if he had left me for another woman. If he had abandoned me and Ben without warning. If he had spent the family money on jewelry for *her* that was more expensive than anything he had ever given *me*. But I didn't care about a necklace—*he had left us*.

I had to keep reminding myself that while my anger was legitimate, the only person who deserved to bear its brunt was Mac.

Not the flight attendant who had told me I couldn't stretch out on a double seat, even if it was unoccupied, because I had paid for only one seat. How many curses had I hurled at her before reeling myself back in? "My husband left me for another woman!" I told her. She glared at me anyway.

Not the cabdriver who drove too slowly and charged too much. Whose door I had slammed really hard, and who I didn't tip.

Or the lock that had greedily chewed my key card. Or the people on the seventh floor I had awoken.

Not front-desk Nate who couldn't have conjured Mac out of thin air even if he'd wanted to.

No one deserved my rage but Mac. And he was going to get it. If I could only find him.

"Are you sure you don't have a Seamus MacLeary or a Mac MacLeary registered here?" I asked Nate one more time before leaving the desk.

"Positive."

"And you're *sure* you've never seen this man." I whipped the photograph out of my purse. So far, I had shown everyone I'd encountered: three workers at the airport, the taxi driver, the hotel's front-door attendant, Nate.

"Positive." He didn't bother glancing at it this time.

I slid the photo back into my purse and rode the elevator up to the fourth floor. Carefully slid the key card in and opened the door onto my bottom-of-the-line-but-still-very-nice room.

How could Mac have done this to me? To us? Because when a husband runs away, he breaks his children's hearts, too. And if you break a child's heart, you *shatter* a mother's.

I stripped off my New York winter clothes and lay on the bed in my underwear, cooling off. After flipping television channels and accepting that there was no hope I'd ever concentrate on anything, I called room service for a bottle of wine. A soft knock on the door came a few minutes later, and I answered wearing a hotel robe, deliberately avoiding eye contact, hoping to spare at least one person tonight who had the misfortune to encounter me. Shame was starting to settle in. I handed the guy a big tip and locked the door behind me, thinking that I knew what he was thinking, what they *all* were thinking: *You work the night shift, you get the crazies, it's just part of the job.* And he was right, too.

I poured myself a first glass of wine. Drank it. Poured a second, and the stuck engine of my brain started to slow down.

What was I doing in Miami Beach in the middle of the night?

I still had no actual proof that Mac was alive. Rosie was the only one who had agreed with me that the man in the photograph was him.

I got my cell phone from my purse and lay down on my bed, thinking I should probably let someone know where I was. My mother had presumably heard the suitcase wheels rumble overhead toward the front door, the sound of me rushing out of the house—she was used to my impulsivity and knew that my training as a soldier and a cop tended to keep me safe even alone in the dark—but in my haste I hadn't left a note or told her where I was going. My guess was that she'd figured it out. She would understand that I had to follow this through, and she knew I trusted her to watch over Ben. I poured a third glass of wine, drank half, and closed my eyes.

Next thing I knew, it was morning. I woke feeling tired and embarrassed. The dark cloud had drifted away, leaving hurt and determination but not rage.

First, I called Mom. She withheld opinions and judgments and, as I'd expected, told me she understood. Then I opened the drapes to a bright Florida day and got dressed for summer.

Downstairs in the lobby, families, couples, and a few loners floated in and out of the off-lobby Palm Restaurant that was fronted with a sign boasting the delights of its brunch. But I wasn't hungry; I was on a quest. I started with the woman who had evidently replaced Nate at the front desk. Her name tag informed me that she was Tara.

"Excuse me, Tara." I slid the photo across the counter. "Do you recognize this man?"

She glanced at it and shook her head. "But I haven't worked here very long. Is he a regular?"

"I'm not really sure."

"I'll ask in the office. May I?"

She took the photo, disappearing through a door behind her. Although it was Sunday and quiet, it was *day*, and I felt hopeful that with more people around I might have some luck. But she returned moments later shaking her head.

"Sorry."

Next I spoke with the Palm Restaurant's maître d', an older man who stood at a podium near the door and greeted guests. His name tag read *Raul*.

"Table for?"

"Just a question." I showed him the photo. "I'm wondering if you've seen this man here. If you know who he is."

Raul's friendliness vanished and he looked at me with unveiled suspicion.

"And you are?"

"Karin. My husband went missing four months ago. I'm looking for him."

His entire face appeared to scowl. "Do you think I remember everyone who passes through here?"

"He looks a little different in the photo," I tried to win Raul over, get him to really look at the photo, "and there's been disagreement in my family. They say he killed himself but without a body how can you—?"

"Table for?" Raul addressed a couple who had walked into the restaurant. I stood aside and waited.

"Two."

Raul snapped two oversized menus out of a nearby stand and led the couple to their table. I noticed that he carried his body with stiff rectitude yet walked with a leftward tilt he appeared unable to control. When he came back he took another look at the photo.

"This was taken at the bar," he handed back the photo, "so shouldn't you ask *at the bar*?"

"It's nine-thirty in the morning."

"Your point being?"

I thanked him and crossed the lobby to a frosted glass door with words etched in jazzy lettering: *The Collins Bar* and below that *always open*. The door was ajar and the lights were on, but the place was empty aside from a bartender who smiled the moment I walked in.

"What can I get you?"

I showed him the photograph. Went through my routine.

Bill, according to his name tag, stroked his black mustache while he carefully looked at the picture. Then he sighed. "I don't know him, but I can tell you that this was taken after five o'clock. That's when we dim the lighting, bring on the mood." Smiling, he handed me back the photo. "I usually work days. Come back later and try the night shift on for size."

"Thanks."

I went to sit in the lobby and figure out what to do now. There was a *ding* from the elevator and a couple with their two teenage daughters passed through the lobby, dressed for the beach. I didn't know why but something about their easygoing chatter pulled me over a hump of resistance that had made me hesitate to take the next obvious step.

If Mac wasn't here, and he didn't appear to be, maybe he was at his girlfriend's. At Deidre's. A quick Google before I'd left New York had armed me with her Florida address.

Without any more rethinking or second guessing, I got up and went to the front desk.

"Tara, can you help me rent a car?"

"Of course."

Half an hour later, I was driving out of Miami Beach onto Route 934, on my way to the interstate and Rio Vista in Fort Lauderdale.

I stood in front of the cream stucco house beneath dripping magenta bougainvillea and waited for someone to answer the door. It was gearing up to be a hot day, and I was grateful for the sliver of shade provided by an overhang above the entrance.

The moment I heard footsteps I started to tremble with

what was becoming a familiar rush of adrenaline: a toxic mix of anger and shame. I wanted to reap vengeance and at the same time I wanted to run away, get back into the car, and return to the relative safety of the hotel.

But it was too late: The door swung open.

"Karin!"

Deidre Stein looked different: Instead of the business suits or tailored dresses she had worn to her and Mac's office, where I had met her several times, she was barefoot in white linen shorts and braless in a blue camisole. Her mocha skin was darker than it had been in New York and she had let her hair digress into its natural full-head halo. Seeing her like this, I never would have made her out to be either a Harvard MBA or the first African-American senior executive at Quest Security. She was light-skinned—half black and half white—and except for her skin color and the bravura of her hair, with her high cheekbones, green eyes, and slender sloped nose she resembled her Eastern European grandparents, the Steins, as much as her African forebears.

"Wow! What a *surprise*."

"Is Mac here?"

"What?"

"I'm looking for *Mac*. Have you *seen him*? Is he *here*? *With you?*" My voice shook more with every word and I felt as if I was going to hyperventilate.

A bell sounded from somewhere inside the house.

"Come in." She stood aside.

Her living room was a cool and welcome contrast to the humidity outdoors. I followed her through a dining room with pale pink walls, into a large, well-appointed kitchen with white cabinetry, marble countertops, and lots of stainless steel. She went straight to her oven and opened it to let loose a blast of heat and remove four cake layers which she set on racks that had been laid out in advance. An industrial Mixmaster sat on the counter along with parchment sheets of sugar rosettes in different colors and a pastry bag that looked hastily abandoned.

"I just had to do that," she said, crossing the kitchen to face me at close range. "What's going on, Karin?"

"I'm looking for—"

"Okay." Her left hand flew up, stopping me. I noticed that she was wearing a diamond engagement ring and my heart turned over in its grave. "Two questions pop to mind. One, why would you look for Mac here? Two, why would you look for him at all?"

All my suspicions about Deidre being the *other woman* deflated in that instant.

"I'm sorry."

"Don't apologize; I can see you're really upset."

I showed her the photograph. "They never found him. He might not actually be dead."

"He does look a lot like Mac." She looked more closely at the photograph. "But I haven't seen him since I left

Quest. And that *definitely* isn't me in the picture. I've never even stepped foot in the Collins."

Ten minutes later we were parked at her kitchen island, drinking cups of the tea she brewed from whole leaves, telling each other our stories.

She had sold her co-op apartment in Manhattan, trading in a compact one-bedroom for this spacious three-bedroom house just blocks from the ocean and not far from her parents' home. Her fiancé was Bo, a man she'd known since high school, and other than starting her own business catering cakes for parties—a Plan B career she planned to grow into a bona fide business—and planning her September wedding, she occasionally spoke to the lawyer who was defending her against Quest's "absurd allegations."

"Mac never believed you did any of it," I told her.

"And *he* didn't do anything wrong, either. This is office politics gone really awry. I can't tell you how happy I am to have left all that behind. For me, despite all the heartache— and believe me, there's been heartache—I'm happier now than I've ever been. I'll *never* go back to New York."

"I don't know why I thought this could be you." I touched the woman in photo, which lay between us on the counter.

"Of course you thought it was me. Why wouldn't you? Given everything you've told me, I would have drawn the same conclusion. In fact, I kind of wish it was me so I could turn him over to you!"

We laughed.

"But really," she said, "Mac? Having an affair? Ditching you and Ben? I just don't see it. You guys were his life."

That really made my eyes water because I knew in my heart it was true. But I had to make sense of all this; *without a body* . . . well, it was the drumbeat in my mind that wouldn't quit. No body, and now this photo . . .

Deidre fed me a lunch of salad and cake and hugged me at her front door. I drove out of Rio Vista feeling both relieved and dismayed.

What now?

I picked up an iced coffee at a café on Collins Avenue and strolled back to my hotel, unable to fully take any of this in. Sunshine. Palm trees. Summer in wintertime. I was a single woman in vacation heaven, but not knowing whether Mac was dead or alive, whether he had loved us to the end or abandoned us heartlessly, made it impossible to *be here now*. There was no here and there was no now. No center of gravity. There was just me, alone in Florida, tilting at windmills.

Was I delusional? Had I concocted something out of nothing? Back in my room, I took another long look at the photograph. At this point, I had looked at it so long, so hard, and so often that I couldn't recognize or not-recognize Mac anymore. I remembered when I'd realized the memory of Jackson's face was fading; it had taken a year. It had been only four months since I'd last seen Mac in person. With my third husband, would I forget him as soon as he walked out the door? But that was irrelevant because I would *never* marry again.

I carried the photograph in my purse all afternoon but didn't bring it out to show anyone. Raul was still posted at the front of the restaurant and Tara still tended the desk with the rest of the day shift. I felt their eyes stay on me a moment too long whenever I passed through the lobby, monitoring that crazy, desperate woman who believed her dead husband was still alive.

But then in the late afternoon there was a shift change and I couldn't help trying one more time at the restaurant and front desk. No luck. The bar was getting busy and so I found an empty stool, ordered a drink, and waited for one of the two bartenders—a sinewy black guy with short spiky dreads and earrings in both ears, name tag reading *Roy*—to pause long enough to catch his eye.

"Another drink?"

"Sure. And a question." Out came the photograph. "Have you ever seen this man?"

"Looks like the new owner of the hotel."

"He *bought* this place?"

"She. Ana Maria something-or-other. I only met her once."

"Isn't her name on your paycheck?"

"It's a corporate name, Riviera Inc. or something like that." Evidently Roy was not good with names.

A young man in a tuxedo who was sitting on a stool beside me twisted around, paying indiscreet attention to our conversation. He was strikingly handsome, but something about him looked older than his years; I put him at twenty-five. His hair was dyed black and gelled down and he wore eyeliner. My niece Lindsay had once given me a run-through of what she'd called "modern styles" (acknowledging my ancient status), and I recognized this one as emo, short for emotional and meaning hyperemotional or oversensitive, I guessed.

"Soliz Riviera Enterprises." The young guy burped: sour whiskey. I held my breath until the smell passed.

Roy half nodded and began to move away but then my tipsy neighbor pushed his empty glass across the bar. Roy seemed to hesitate, then took the glass and brought the man a fresh drink, delivering it with a whispered reminder: "You're on in an hour so this is the last one."

"Isn't it sweet how they care about me?"

Roy's back was turned but you could tell by the quality of his stillness—the way his neck tightened and how he paused before moving on to his next customer—that he'd heard the remark.

"Why are you looking for him?" The photograph was still on the bar, and now he was looking at it, pulling it closer, holding it up for a better look. "I'm Ethan, by the way."

"Karin. Do you work here or something?"

"I'm the entertainment."

His tuxedo and makeup suddenly made sense. There was a baby grand in a mirrored corner across the lounge.

"You're the piano player—"

"*Pianist*." He took a long drink from his glass. "No, I'm a piano player. You're right."

"I didn't mean it as an insult."

"Why are you looking for him?"

"He's my husband."

"So he's *married*." Ethan nodded slowly, as if something now made sense.

"Why do you say that?"

He shrugged. "She always seems pissed at him, like he can never give her what she really wants."

A fizzle restarted in my blood. Bubbling heat.

"Why didn't anyone else recognize them here?"

"She's a new owner. She only shows up at night and I guess she hasn't met the day staff yet."

"Do they live in the hotel?" I felt myself almost levitate off my seat. Because if they lived here, if they only came out at night, then any minute now they could make their appearance.

"She lives in Mexico, just came to survey her holdings." He drained his whiskey and set his glass down hard on the bar, attracting both bartenders' attention. Roy whispered something to the other one and they both ignored him.

"They hate me."

"Where in Mexico, do you know?"

"Playa del Carmen, it's south of Cancun. Unlike *Roy*," he said loudly, "I actually read my paycheck. She's building another hotel down there—Riviera Maya Palace."

"You know a lot about her."

"Sometimes I Google stuff when I'm bored."

"So what do you know about him?" I touched the man in the photo.

"Nothing, really. Seemed like he went back with her because when she was gone, so was he." He yawned and looked at his watch. "I should catch a nap before the first set. Good luck finding Dylan," he said as he got down from his stool with more grace than I would have imagined him capable of in his condition.

"Dylan?"

"Your husband."

"My husband's name is Mac."

"Oh. Well, I guess it *isn't* him." And then he gave me the same kind of suspicious look Raul the maître d' had treated me to this morning: *Don't you know what your own husband looks like?* But Ethan didn't come right out and say it, and for that I was grateful.

"This has been really confusing for me." My emotions transformed themselves again and quickly, continuing the roller-coaster ride of the past twenty-four hours. Anger turning to bewilderment to determination to disappointment to sorrow. Mac *was* dead, wasn't he?

"You'll find him."

"No, I won't."

"I always kind of worried that there was someone else out there who looked exactly like me." Ethan's expression clamped with genuine angst.

I took a breath, stopped tears. "I shouldn't be here."

"I know the feeling."

"Ethan, can I be frank?"

"You can be whoever you want. I'm open." He smiled, and charm now shimmered off him, vanquishing the existential anxiety that had briefly altered his mood.

"You should stop drinking and get out of here. Go study the piano for real someplace that isn't—"

"Florida," he finished my sentence, half smiling and half nodding in dubious agreement.

"I mean it. Be a real pianist if that's what you want." On impulse, I took a pen from my purse and jotted my phone number on a napkin. "Come to New York, and call me when you get there."

Now it was Ethan who was on the verge of tears. He folded the napkin and slipped it into his jacket pocket. "Good luck finding your husband."

I looked straight at his face and saw past the black tuxedo and black hair and black eyeliner and looked into eyes that were tender brown and flecked with yellow. "He's dead."

Ethan didn't respond. And that was it: the final confirmation.

I watched him weave across the lounge and into the lobby, disappearing in the direction of the elevators. I had run a fool's errand; it was time to go home. I paid for my drinks and made my way out of the bar feeling overwhelmed by exhaustion.

When I reached the elevators I was surprised to catch a glimpse of Ethan in the one that was just about to leave. In contrast to his inebriated wooziness of a few minutes ago he seemed energized, almost sober, in heated argument with another man. I couldn't hear a word of what they were saying but their voices were loud and the other man, a Mexican with thick eyebrows and a squarish face, struck me as the aggressor, though you couldn't be sure. And then, just before the doors closed, the other man looked right at me with black eyes, *enraged* eyes. He wore a low-buttoned shirt that revealed a small tattoo of a lavender dahlia just below his left collarbone.

I blinked. Opened my eyes to the blank canvas of a departed elevator. Waited for the next one.

As soon as I stepped into my fourth-floor room I threw my suitcase onto the bed, wrested it open, and hastily packed my things, trying to shake all the ghosts out of my head. How many drinks had I had exactly? Two or three or four. It was one thing to be intoxicated, another to start hallucinating. Mac's face really belonged to someone called Dylan. Deidre's back actually belonged to a woman named Ana Maria. And now it wasn't just faces and bodies but little tattoos that were appearing before my eyes. When would I start hearing voices, too?

I had to get out of here. Get back home where life was real. Back to Ben and back to my mother.

I had bought an open-ended ticket but when I called my airline, I learned that no flights were available until morning; it was high vacation season and Sunday nights booked up far in advance. So I scheduled a morning flight, ordered up dinner, called my mother, told her I'd be back the next day by mid-afternoon, and went to sleep.

In the morning I checked out early and then stopped at the hotel restaurant for the continental breakfast that came with the room. Halfway through a bagel and a cup of coffee, a commotion in the lobby seized everyone's attention. The dining room fell silent and we all watched as a steady stream of uniformed police poured into the hotel.

Whispers erupted followed by raised voices, and then I thought I heard someone say something about a murder. My gaze followed a man who had gotten up to check the lobby and was just then returning to his nearby table.

"Someone was killed," I heard him tell his wife.

"When?"

"They say last night."

"Maybe we should leave. Find another hotel."

"What for? It already happened. Look at all those police—we're probably safer here than anywhere else in Miami."

I abandoned what was left of my breakfast, grabbed my suitcase, and rolled it behind me. Cops were stationed in the lobby and some were waiting by the elevators. A man arrived who I assumed was the detective who'd caught the case because he wasn't in uniform, yet he quickly found the stairwell door and headed upstairs on foot, and the uniforms at the elevator promptly followed.

I approached one of the cops in the lobby, and said, "Detective Karin Schaeffer, Maplewood, New Jersey. I'm on vacation. What happened?" Exaggerations strung on a thread of truth.

"A maid found a body in a utility closet."

"Time of death?"

"Sometime last night."

"Do we know who the victim was?"

"Lounge musician. He didn't show up at work last night. Who did you say you were again?"

"Sorry, I have to catch a flight."

I hurried out of the hotel, dragging my suitcase, my mind reeling: Ethan could have been murdered any time between six-thirty or so, when I saw him arguing with the man in the elevator, and this morning when his body was found. I should have stayed and given the officer a more accurate description of who I really was. I should have told him about Ethan's argument with the man in the elevator. But Ethan—*poor Ethan*—was already dead.

Mac's parents.

Then Mac.

Now Ethan.

And the man in the elevator, his ferocity . . . his tattoo.

A dahlia under his left collarbone. Just like Mac's.

That tattoo came into vivid focus of my memory of last night. I had assumed I'd imagined it, but now wondered. Had Ethan been killed for talking to me—the woman who had been pounding the pavement, looking for the owner of the hotel and her boyfriend? My recollection of the Mexican's eyes, the way he glared at me, told me my guess could very well be right.

Something was really wrong here. I didn't know what it was, but all of a sudden I knew that if Mac *was* alive, he was in danger. And if he *had* left me it wouldn't have been to run away from me or our life together, but from something else—the danger was that great.

At the airport I changed my route and now, instead of traveling home to New York, I booked myself on the next flight to Cancun. While I waited I bought Internet time at a computer café and got right to work.

Ethan had told me that Ana Maria, the woman in the photo with the man called Dylan—the man I now believed *could* be Mac, under an assumed name—owned a company called Soliz Riviera Enterprises based in Playa del Carmen. The town was described on one travel site as "an ex-pat backwater that has flourished as a tourist center off a highway of mega-hotels hastily developed over the last decade."

During the nearly two-hour flight, I closed my eyes and tried to nap but kept seeing Ethan and that final smile that had broken through his drunken artifice. I had wanted him to run away and become a *pianist* the way a mother wants her child to talk. I had wanted to wipe off his hair gel and his makeup and I had *wanted* him to call me in New York. And now he never would. Because he was dead. I teetered between heartbroken and numb thinking about that young man. *Who was dead.*

So much death. I couldn't stop thinking about that. It just didn't make any sense.

It was no use trying to nap so I looked out the window instead and watched as we descended over the southeast tip of Mexico, a green and purple and brown puzzle of land until, as we came closer, you could make out an abundance of palm trees. I had never been to Mexico before but could already see that it was rougher and wilder here than in Florida. And when I stepped out of the airport, after clearing customs, I learned that it was also hotter and muggier.

If Florida in January had been summer in June, this was sultry August. I dragged my suitcase into the blistering heat and was immediately confronted by a cluster of men wearing identical black slacks and white shirts.

"Taxi? Taxi?" each one chanted, hoping to score a customer.

One in particular seemed to try harder—"Taxi, lady? You need a ride? Where you going?"—so I chose him, or he chose me. I didn't matter. I wanted out of this heat *and I wanted to find Mac*.

"Playa del Carmen."

"Follow me."

The man led me farther along the pavement into a parking lot and to a waiting car.

"You go," he told me. Apparently he wasn't the driver, but an agent of the driver. He walked briskly around to say something to the man behind the wheel, presumably giving him my destination.

"Thank you." I handed him two American dollars. He nodded and returned to the fray.

I slid into the back of the blissfully air-conditioned car and repeated my destination: "Playa del Carmen, please." He nodded and off we went.

I gazed past the back of the driver's head at a heat-wavering landscape of burned grass and cartoonishly gigantic hotel entrances. The sea must have been to the left because nearly all the hotels were off in that direction. The Web site I'd consulted had said that Playa del Carmen was forty-two miles south of Cancun, a straight shot down Highway 307, which was the thoroughfare into the Riviera Maya, so I expected the trip to take around an hour.

The closer we got, the stronger my feelings became—if Mac was alive, if he was Dylan, I was on the path to him now. I could almost see him and almost feel him and almost smell him: the delicious scent of the pine soap he'd used when we first fell in love; the musky smell of sweat that last morning we were together in bed.

Fifteen minutes into the ride, the car exited off the highway, riveting my attention.

"We're going to Playa del Carmen," I reminded the driver.

He didn't answer, just kept driving along a suddenly unpaved road that kicked up dirt the faster he drove.

"*Playa del Carmen.*" The name of the town was the same in English and Spanish, so what didn't he understand?

As the highway vanished behind us, a cord of panic tightened inside me.

"Turn around!"

He jammed on the brakes and the car skidded, its back end spinning before coming all the way to a halt in a storm of dirt.

"*What the hell are you doing?*"

He twisted around and for the first time I saw his face. *That face.* And recognized him: the dark enraged eyes of the square-faced Mexican from the hotel elevator. The man who had seemed to threaten Ethan—*who probably killed him.*

Sweat dripped down his temples despite the frigidity of

the air-conditioning. Only now did I realize that I was also sweating profusely.

"What do you want?" I tried to keep terror out of my voice. In cop school, they trained you to talk to the bad guy if you were caught in a tough situation, to *attempt negotiation*, because talking, sometimes, had a humanizing effect on them. It was a relief when it worked. And awful when it didn't.

He shifted forward and I saw it on his collarbone: the dahlia tattoo. But before I could say or demand or beseech anything else, before I could make a plea for my life, his hand rose from behind the seat and showed me his gun.

My heart stopped.

He lurched forward and pressed the cold hard ring of the gun's muzzle into the center of my forehead.

My brain stopped.

At impossibly close range I watched as the flesh on his finger fattened around the steel lick of the trigger.

I closed my eyes. And waited.

PART II

PART II

CHAPTER 9

I came awake with a start, my face itchy yet strangely numb.

When I tried to scratch my cheek, I couldn't.

My eyes refused to open.

Even my mouth was sealed shut.

An illogical sensation of well-being gave way to the steady ballooning of claustrophobia. And then a burst of panic as I realized I was hog-tied, bound and gagged, alone on my side in some kind of cave—the smell of damp and mold made me want to retch. But if I retched I would suffocate so I held back the almost irrepressible impulse. *Almost*. That was my loophole: If I mastered that one sliver of control, my ability to breathe through my nose, I might yet survive.

I had no idea where I was, other than someplace in Mexico in the vicinity of Cancun, or why the driver had put me here. All I knew was that I was still alive, which exceeded my expectations the moment I'd seen that gun. A moment I recalled now with crystal clarity: the pure fear of being confronted with senseless death by a stranger.

He hadn't killed me, which told me something: He wasn't his own boss. But that didn't surprise me. He'd had the dahlia tattoo, just like Mac. Whoever they worked for wanted me alive. For now.

I had to get out of here.

I pulled against my restraints. Rocked frantically on the dirt floor. It was airless and hot and the more I rocked, the more a slick coating of sweat accumulated on my skin. I tried to use it to slip out of the bindings but they were too tight, there was no give. After a few minutes of futile effort I lay back, to the extent that I could, and tried to breathe deeply.

Where was I?

With every breath I could feel mold spores lodge themselves in my lungs. As my mind raced:

Was it day? Night?

How long had I been here?

What had I stumbled into at the Hotel Collins?

Had Ethan, the pianist, been killed for talking to me?

What did someone not want me to know?

Who did someone not want me to find?

How did Mac fit into all this—or did he?

But the dahlia tattoos: The killer had one, Mac had one.

So *yes*, he fit into it. Somehow.

But why kill Ethan?

Why abduct me?

And why keep me alive?

My brain whirred like a ruined hard drive unable to find a stopping place, building speed toward an inevitable crash. As if I believed I could think my way out of here, which I knew perfectly well I couldn't.

The worst part of my mistake, my *tragic mistake,* was that if I didn't make it out of here—and I wouldn't; how could I?—if they killed me, *when* they killed me . . .

Ben would be an orphan.

He had my mother, but she was old. Would she live long enough to raise him?

Jon and Andrea could raise him, along with their own children. Ben would be their bonus sibling . . . who would never know, or even remember, his real parents.

I couldn't stop tears from filling my eyes and seeping into the blindfold. Soon my nasal passages were swelling, closing. And I learned something new and dreadful: that suffocation came upon you like a rising tide, a gradual overtaking, and it took a moment for you to understand that you were losing your final foothold. That the desire to survive and the ability to survive were not the same thing.

My head jerked backward and I felt a sharp stinging as the tape was yanked off my mouth. My jaw fell open reflexively as damp moldy air spilled into my lungs, triggering in my imagination the dawning of a blue sky like a curtain pulled aside to reveal a glorious day. As I was pushed forward and someone pulled at the knots binding my wrists behind my back, I became aware of a voice. A whisper.

"Quickly."

A man. Who was he talking to? I waited but only one voice spoke.

The rope snaked off, inciting a rush of blood to my wrists. I tried to flex my fingers and move my hands but they were still numb. Next he untied my feet and it was just the same: a surge of warmth followed by numb tingling.

"Try moving."

He was talking to me, not someone else. It was just the two of us here. Terror gushed through my blood, limbs, brain, waking me.

"Try getting up."

He spoke English. Without a Spanish accent. *And I knew that voice.*

Shaking, I sat up and pulled off the blindfold. Sunlight from an open hatch above us seared my eyes. I blinked uncontrollably—and then saw him.

Tan, lean Dylan hovered over me, saying, "Quickly. Get up."

My brain felt muddled. I shook my head, banishing cobwebs.

"Mac?"

"Hurry."

"I'm so confused."

"Come on, let's go." His tone was urgent and I started to move.

But first I needed an answer: Was he Mac, the man I had trusted, or Dylan, the doppelgänger I recognized but didn't know?

"Who *are* you?"

He hoisted me onto my feet and maneuvered me up and out of the hatch, pushing me onto the ground outside before climbing out himself. It was a burning hot day and the sun was brilliant, blinding. As he kicked shut the hatch I realized I had been in an underground pit. Stowed away for later regardless of my chances for survival. Buried alive.

I breathed the fresh salty air that smelled of unfettered, delicious oxygen. A quick glance around told me that we were on an unpaved dead-end road that looked as if it had been carved out of Mayan wilderness: burned, untamed brush, towering palms, sand, and a hut cobbled together with planks of wood and topped with a thatched roof.

He grabbed my arm and tried to pull me toward a rusty white car.

"I don't even know who you are!"

"Not now, Karin!" He ground his jaw in a way I had never seen him do before—*because this was Mac; I was sure now: It was Mac*—and glanced behind him at the hut.

Sweat poured off his tanned face. He was a stranger. And yet I *knew* him.

I wrenched my arm out of his grip. "Tell me what's going on!"

He reached for me again, trying to hustle me forward. "*Not now*."

"Yes *now*."

"Listen to me—"

I reared back and slapped his face so hard my hand stung. The sound rang into the quiet like a shot. It felt liberating—*he was alive; he had left me*—and I slapped him again and stood there watching half his face turn red.

"I told myself if I found you I would kill you, but I didn't really believe you were alive. I didn't *believe* you would leave me—*us*. I loved you."

"Karin—"

"You broke my heart!"

A gust of wind blasted sand into my eyes and stuck to my clammy skin. I turned and ran away from him—*from all of it*. There had to be a main road off this dead end. There had to be a way out.

I ran, aware of him running behind me, pleading, "Karin! What you're doing is *dangerous*. We have to get in the car!"

His earnest tone compelled me to turn and look: He was gaining speed, determined to reach me. Behind him, a man stepped out of the hut, digging into his pocket for something. Before I could see what it was, Mac overtook me, lifted me over his shoulder, and rushed us both toward the car. He threw me into the back and jumped into the driver's seat. Started the engine. Reversed and redirected in a hurry and drove fast along the narrow road.

Glancing behind us I saw that the man was talking on his cell phone. He wasn't making a move to follow us, which worried me. He was calling someone. In moments the result of his call flew in our faces.

A car raced toward us, braking suddenly. Behind that car another sped to a stop.

Mac jumped out of the car, shouting, "Run!"

I leaped out and ran after him into the woods.

But there were four of them and two of us, and they had weapons—the incessant rapidity of the shots that chased us told me that at least one of them had an automatic rifle. Bullets pursued us through the woods, past acacias and mimosas and the striated trunks of palms, until Mac fell at the base of a giant cypress tree. The certainty that I couldn't just leave him came over me with powerful force. How could I abandon him now, after following him this far? How many times could I watch him die and come back to life and die again?

"*Mac*." I fell over him.

"I tripped."

"You sure you weren't shot?"

Behind us, footsteps skidded to a stop. Above us, triggers clicked. He could answer me yes or no but in a moment it wouldn't matter: We would both be dead. I kissed him tenderly, and again more fiercely.

"Why did you leave me?"

He raised a trembling hand to my face. "They won't kill us."

"What's happening?"

"I'm *sorry*, Karin. I made a terrible mistake."

The men forced us to our feet before Mac could tell me what his terrible mistake had been. What could he possibly have done to land us both here, at gunpoint, in the Yucatan?

They put Mac in one car, me in the other.

I sat in the back, with the man in the front passenger seat twisted to point his automatic rifle at me as a reminder that they had captured me, lest I forget. My mind ticked, my heart hammered, my eyes frantically searched beyond the windows of the moving car . . . driving along the wooded dirt road felt like freefall . . . nothing made any sense. The one thing I latched on to, the only thing that was really clear, was that they hadn't killed us when they had the chance. This was a job. I was cargo someone had hired them to deliver.

"I'll pay you whatever you want if you let me go," I said. "More than you're getting paid now. How much do you want? Dollars or pesos—name your price."

The one holding the rifle on me glanced at the driver, who I realized was avoiding the highway, taking winding back roads that were paved randomly and then suddenly unpaved, rattling the car and us. His jet-black hair curled over a dense brown neck that remained still; he kept driving, looking forward, without any indication that he'd heard or understood me. Though I suspected he had and wasn't budging. So if money wouldn't work, maybe something else would.

"My name is Karin," I said. "What are your names? Did you grow up around here? I'm from America, New Jersey, but now I live in New York City, in Brooklyn. Do you know anyone in Brooklyn?"

"Sunset Park," the gunman said. "Cousin."

"Shut up," the driver said without turning to look at him.

The gunman's eyes glazed and stuck to me like glue. When we entered a shantytown he kept his weapon on me in plain sight. My eyes darted along both sides of the road, waiting for someone to see us—the *turista* held hostage in the backseat—hoping someone would call the police. The gunman seemed to read my mind, to see that I not only hoped for help but expected it. He grinned and pushed the rifle a few inches closer to my face.

A man sitting on a plastic crate tipped his broken straw hat at the driver, who nodded back. A thin scabbed woman in dirty jeans and a Yankees T-shirt smiled and waved. The gunman waved the rifle in greeting. Two young children, twin boys with dirty faces, jumped up and down, gleefully calling *hola* when they saw our car.

And then we passed the one small building that wasn't decrepit, a whitewashed stucco storefront with *La Policia* painted in blue above the front window. The driver slowed down and an officer in uniform, leaning against the outside wall, watched us come and go without flinching. No *hola*s, no smiles, no waves; but it wasn't necessary to underscore the implicit friendliness with which the cop observed our passing. He simply watched. In all my experiences as a police officer, a detective and a victim, this one ranked as the most surreal. Not just my captors and the townspeople but the police, too, were all under the same thumb. I knew, in that moment, that no one was going to help me.

Despite the heat—which seemed to grow denser the longer we drove through the seemingly endless village, this ramshackle collection of shacks—chills began to shiver through me. I ran my hands up and down my bare arms, trying to warm myself; and that was when I felt something hard on the inside of my left elbow. I turned my arm over and looked down at an angry sore that was half scab, half festering abscess. At its center was a puncturelike hole that looked raw and open, as if something had burrowed into my skin, dragging in a heap of infection. I spit into the palm of my opposite hand and tried to rub away the damage, erase the growing comprehension of how it got there.

I understood now: how time had slipped by in the hole;

my itchy face; the cloudy almost-nice sensation that had given way to panic. The gang of thugs. I had never been a drug user and certainly had never taken heroin, but I had seen enough junkies in my time on the police force to spot one. I closed my eyes and held down an urge to throw up as the car slid off pavement and bumped along a dirt road.

We pulled to a stop in front of a yellow stucco mansion fronted by a shaded portico. Huge potted hibiscus trees stood in the sun at the edge of the shade, their open-fisted red flowers drinking the livid heat. Together the gunman and driver hustled me out of the car and stood me beside a windowless black van that was parked off to the side. In the distance behind the mansion—newly built to look venerable, as if it had sat there for hundreds of years—you could hear the roar of the ocean, smell the salt air, feel the sharp snap of a commanding wind.

The second car pulled up behind ours and Mac was dragged out as roughly as I had been. He spoke to the men in Spanish, addressing them by name.

A young man in jeans and a white shirt stepped out of the house. He also had the tattoo on his neck, a bit larger than the others and in a brighter shade of violet, and he wore a large gold crucifix. But unlike the other men, all of whom possessed some variation of the squat, muscle-bound stature of their Mayan forbears, this one was taller, leaner, and lighter, with brown hair that was not quite as dark as his cohorts, and blue eyes. It was not his looks, though, as much as his confidence and tone that made his authority so clear; *he*, I was sure of it, was the lord of this mansion—and beyond.

"Felix!" he snapped at one of the men, rattling off something in Spanish that specified Dylan.

"*Sí*, Diego," Felix answered, grabbing Mac's arm and tugging him forward.

So here, to these people, Mac *was* Dylan.

At the same moment my gunman grabbed and tugged me.

Mac defiantly pulled his arm away and walked straight over to me. He took my hand in his, causing my gunman to bristle but that was it. None of them made a move to stop Mac from joining me. They all had guns, even the leader, Diego—or, as I was starting to suspect, the kingpin—had a gun stuck into the belt of his jeans, yet they allowed Mac surprising latitude. It was the strangest thing: as if the closer we got to the house, and more profoundly with each step as we entered the white marble foyer and were enveloped by its shadowy coolness, Mac seemed to gain power over the men. Just a minute ago I had been convinced that Diego was the big boss here. Now I was starting to wonder.

CHAPTER 10

In the center of the mansion's foyer was a gleaming wood table inlaid with mother-of-pearl, and on the table sat a vase holding dozens of peacock feathers. As we passed, Mac surprised everyone by plucking a feather from the vase. Diego glanced sharply at him but didn't object. The other men took his lead, bristling but doing nothing. Mac held the feather loosely in his hand as we were taken through a door at the back of the foyer and led down a wide staircase, Diego in front with two henchmen, then me and Mac, with the last two thugs and the rifle at our back. Small shelves holding Mayan artifacts staggered downward along one wall. The staircase turned twice, landing us in an unlit hallway with a door on the far right that appeared to lead out of the house and another directly in front of us on which Diego knocked, listened, knocked again, and finally opened.

He said something in Spanish to Mac, who nodded and followed him in, pulling me along by the hand. The other men stayed outside in the hall.

It was a large room, whitewashed from the floorboards to the ceiling, furnished and decorated in rainbow colors: a mix of traditional Mexican weavings, more artifacts, and blatantly modern, expensive pieces. Someone collected glass candlesticks; they were everywhere. A wood desk with ornately carved legs stood in front of a huge window overlooking a private beach (not a single sunbather on such a summery day) and beyond it, the ocean. A hint of cinnamon hung in the air.

Diego pulled a cell phone out of the back pocket of his jeans and speed-dialed a call. He spoke in rapid, excited Spanish, listened, and hung up. He then issued an order to Mac and left us alone in the room. The door locked from the outside and it was unnecessary to ask if the cadre of armed guards were standing in the hall; you could hear them shuffling restlessly around.

Mac and I turned to each other simultaneously. He reached for me. I stepped back; what I needed now was answers.

"Why are we here?"

"It's such a long story."

"Just start *anywhere*."

"Okay." He took two quick steps toward me and forced me into a hug. Then he whispered: "I'll start at the end.

No: almost the end. These are the people who killed my parents, but there's no proof, and it's more complicated than—"

I interrupted: "These very people?"

"She's got cells, these little groups of them, all through Mexico and the States."

"She?"

"Ana."

Ana Maria Soliz. Soliz Enterprises. Of course.

I pushed him away so I could see him. "The woman in the photo with you."

"Photo?" But as he asked, he seemed to know the answer; he knew I would have turned every possible stone to find him.

I moved closer to the window—away from him, whoever he was—and sat on a narrow ledge. "How do you know she had your parents killed?"

"It's what she does."

I looked at him, waiting for him to explain. It all sounded so fantastical: a spider woman with far-reaching deadly webs . . . and then I thought of Ethan, confronted in the elevator by the same man who had held a gun to my forehead.

"I knew her a long time ago," Mac began, looking at me from across the room, allowing me my distance. "She found me when she read the *Times* article about my promotion. She contacted me, wanted me to come here, and when I didn't . . ." If he had been anyone but Mac, tears would have filled his eyes; instead, sadness stilled his face, a nearly invisible emotional shift you could only read when you knew him well.

"Your parents?"

He nodded. "My parents were murdered. Danny was in jail. Rosie and I were fighting. Everything was falling apart."

"Why the fake suicide? Why didn't you just tell me you had to go?"

"The flowers that came to the house that day?"

"The dahlias."

"They weren't from me; they were from Ana—a threat. And I got the message. What she had done to my parents, she wouldn't hesitate doing to you and Ben. I wanted you to think I was dead so you wouldn't try to find me; I thought you'd be safer that way. She had shown me how serious she was, though she wasn't always dangerous. I never would have—"

Just then, the lock turned. Diego flung open the door and walked in followed by Felix, the rifle strapped over his shoulder, and the woman I recognized from the photograph taken at the Collins Bar.

In person, Ana Maria Soliz was quite beautiful. She was slender, with shoulders that were broad and open like wings, accentuating an appearance of strength. She was barefoot in a tight-fitting white dress, her long black hair pushed together over one shoulder, just as it had been in the photo, allowing me to see the gold chain at the back of her neck. She was wearing a gold necklace now: a simple lariat whose longer end dangled a diamond crucifix into her cleavage. She was gorgeous in a way that intoxicated men and made women suspicious. Everything about her, from the way she looked to how she moved to the intensity of her black eyes when they appraised you—and she was looking right at me, her attention staking itself into me as she entered the room and stopped in front of me and Mac—*everything* about her reeked of power.

Without saying a word, she answered the question of who was in charge. It wasn't Mac. And it wasn't Diego. The longer she looked at me, boring into me with her dark eyes, the more I understood something crucial, and terrifying, about her: Beneath the heat her body and face would obviously generate in men, she was all icy calculation.

She said something in Spanish that made Diego and Felix laugh and Mac clench his jaw.

"You are not a beautiful woman," she said to me in a soft but steel-edged voice, "and yet you inspire such love in Dylan."

"What do you want?"

"Ah! Right to the point."

"Karin," Mac said in a tone soaked with warning, "don't say anything."

Ana's eyes slid to Mac. "What could she possibly say that would interest me?"

Mac glanced at Diego and Felix, then back at me, and didn't answer.

"Go ahead," Ana said to Mac. "Talk to your wife. The truth of why you're here. If I like what you say"—she shrugged—"I'll let you decide which one of you will die first."

Mac hesitated, appeared to decide something, and then held the peacock feather toward Ana. "You remember the first time we met?"

"Don't even try. I'm no longer such a fool."

"You were never a fool, Ana. But you remember."

A slight smile lit her face for just a moment before vanishing. "I sold you a feather. You sold me a lie."

"I told you you were more beautiful than a peacock feather. And it was true."

She approached him with the smoothness of silk, almost floating, plucked the feather lightly from his hand, and ran its lustrous soft eye along the side of his face.

"But not anymore," he said. "You changed."

She stopped, her eyes hardening. "*You* changed me. *You* are responsible for this." Holding the long stalk of the feather with both hands, she snapped it in half.

"Whatever you have against me, you've blown it way out of proportion."

"You think I loved you?"

"I don't know what to think. You've become a stalker and a killer."

My heart nearly exploded when he said those things to her; it was so unlike him to take that kind of risk with an obvious psychopath who would be happy, to say the least, to strike back.

Ana laughed, her eyes flashing at me. "Dylan knows I like it rough."

"Why does she keep calling you Dylan?"

"Tell her, *Mac*." Ana walked across the room, toward Diego and the other man, dropping both halves of the feather onto the floor. "Felix, let me."

He handed her the rifle, which she strapped over her shoulder. She kept her finger looped inside the trigger and crossed the room, stopping right in front of me, close enough to smell her spicy perfume.

"Come, be close with your wife while you tell her *everything*. And then we will see."

Jealousy: She reeked of it. *Rage. Vengeance. Greed.* She wanted everything, not just material wealth and power but *everything*, including every thought and feeling Mac could scrape out of his depths. Having summoned him to her wasn't enough; she wanted him to regurgitate his soul upon her order. Why? Watching him struggle to find the right place to start—and this time, I knew it had to be from the beginning—I felt the onslaught of his dread as his confidence wavered.

She pointed the rifle at Mac, directing him across the room with it as if he was her puppet. The sight of her controlling him was sickening. And yet she controlled me, too; I was terrified of her and how she controlled us all with the tip of a gun. No, not a gun: her willingness, her *desire*, to use it.

Mac stood beside me and gently took my hand.

"No touching!" Ana said. "This is not the scene of a reunion. This is a moment of truth."

"Ana"—Mac looked at her—"what's the point of this?"

"Turn around." She released the rifle's safety with a small but ominous *click*. "Face the ocean. And talk."

Mac turned and instead of looking at me, as I knew he wanted to, gazed through the glass toward an ocean that broke wavy line after line of foam onto a blackboard of packed wet sand. I shifted to share his view—in the distant horizon, a blur of land—and listened.

"When I was eighteen, a couple months before high school graduation, I came to Mexico, to Cancun, for spring vacation. It was a big deal: A group of us worked for a year to save up for it. I met Ana on the beach. She was selling peacock feathers, but really she was selling drugs."

"What kind of drugs?" I reflexively covered the battered inside of my right elbow.

"Mostly loose joints, that was the big seller to foreigners like us. She wasn't the only one working the beaches; but she was the one who found us."

"She became your dealer over vacation."

Mac nodded, looking ashamed of his teenage self. "Well, I was an eighteen-year-old boy, and I was never much into getting high—other things were more compelling to me."

Sex. I could imagine Ana as a teenager, trolling the beaches for *turistas* to buy drugs, how her sexual charisma would have been her best selling point. I could *see* them, Mac and Ana, twenty-five years ago, teenagers ready to conquer the world, facing each other in a glimmer of heat.

"You bought one of her peacock feathers, and you and your friends bought some joints."

"We invited her to share one with us, and that was how it started." He breathed deeply, closed his eyes, continued. "Back then, I didn't know the difference between sex and love. Ana was thrilling—all of it was: Ana, Mexico, being away from my family, the idea that they couldn't reach me because I was so far away. Without thinking, kind of as a joke to amuse my friends, I introduced myself as Dylan. Bob Dylan was our hero; we listened to his early stuff all the time. So I told her I was Dylan, bought the feather, the joints . . . and the rest of it just rolled from there."

It sounded like a standard bout of teenage lust mixed with teenage idiocy; you couldn't hold that against anyone. Didn't we all have embarrassing memories from those years that we'd prefer never to revisit? For the duration of one spring break when he was a teenager, Mac had been a jerk; it was an experiment he had certainly outgrown.

So far, nothing he had said struck me as reason for the severity of Ana's retribution.

"How long were you here?" I asked. "Those breaks last a week, don't they?"

"They do. But when my friends left for the airport to go home, I headed in the opposite direction—I came here, to Playa, to be with Ana."

I glanced at him, sensed Ana shift behind me with her gun, and returned my gaze to the window: In the distance a boat was passing, and scalloped waves broke in quick sequence on the shore.

"My parents had a plan for me that I didn't want: I was supposed to go to college, not end up working in the store. It was very important to them. Therefore, I defied them. But of course I didn't see it that way at the time. There were seven weeks left before graduation—and I decided to just ditch the whole thing and stay here because *here* I felt, you know, *alive*."

He paused to breathe heavily in and heavily out, releasing a puff of anger at his inner teenager.

"It felt beautiful, even glorious, at the time." Did he mean that or was it diplomacy—a gift for Ana? "It was like this dream we were living together. We shared the room she rented in town, just a bed and a dresser and a hot plate, but to an American kid it was, I'm embarrassed to say it, *romantic*. Now I understand it differently: Ana was only sixteen, she was poor, she was alone, she was doing what she had to do to survive in a town without much of an economy except for the tourism that back then was mostly up in Cancun."

Behind us, I read Ana's silence as agreement, or at least a lack of disagreement. I wondered if it meant anything to hear him talk this way, or if she had heard it all before. In the past five months, what kind of conversations had they had? Had they been lovers again? Or had he been her prisoner? Or something in between? Lucky Herman had photographed them together at the Collins Bar, I reminded myself, and my gut did a flip.

"We worked the beaches together. She made money in different currencies, but the big buyers were Americans. I knew where all the money was stashed, mostly in our room. *Ana—I'm sorry.*"

"I don't want to hear that now! Go on, tell her what kind of a man you really are."

"About three weeks into it, I realized I was making a big mistake. I was starting to imagine what was going through my parents' minds after I didn't return with my friends and they had no idea where I was. I was living under a fake name. The police had come looking and Ana got rid of them pretty easily; she told them she hadn't seen me for two weeks, and she tipped them. It was easy to buy them off. So no one was really looking for me here anymore, and I started to get scared. I needed to get home in time to graduate if I still could. I needed to get to college. I needed to make my parents proud of me. So, when Ana was out one day, I took my passport and my ticket . . . and all of Ana's American money . . . and left for the airport."

"You took *all* her money?"

"Just the American."

"Which was most of it, you already said."

He nodded, ashamed. "She had saved about two thousand dollars. And I took it."

"Why?"

"I had the cheapest ticket and I'd missed the flight; I didn't know if it was still any good. I didn't know how much a new one would cost buying it at the airport. I was a stupid kid."

I had to absorb all that. It was one thing to think he'd fallen in love with a beautiful girl on a tropical beach, and wholly another thing to have robbed her of her earnings, regardless of whether those earnings had been illegal. It was *her* money. I'd be pissed, too.

"I left her a note, explaining. I promised to repay her."

"And did you?"

"I could never figure out how to do it without tipping her off about my real name or where I was. I was already learning to be afraid of her, three weeks into it. She was powerful, even then. I didn't want her to find me."

Behind us, another *click*.

"Go on," Ana said.

"That's the whole story."

"No, it isn't."

"How many times do I need to admit that I stole your money? How many times do I have to offer to pay you back however much you want?"

"You're still a fool. Can't you see it's too late to repay me with money?"

That sent a shiver through me.

"Tell me what you want, Ana. *Please*. I've been asking for months—*tell me*."

"And for months I've been deciding: What do I want from Dylan? From *Mac*? You're not the boy I loved back then, just as I'm not the girl you thought you loved. At our age, now, we understand that, yes?"

"Of course."

"With the passage of time, memories are distorted. Values change. We grow."

Mac nodded.

"And yet, looking back, we can so clearly remember what we believed at the time. Your story to your wife proves that, doesn't it? You can look back and remember why you did the things you did, right or wrong—really *why* you did them."

Behind us, I heard her pace. She was upset, breathing heavily. Mac's evocation of their brief past together had stirred something in her.

"*Mac*—you remember the price of real estate twenty-five years ago in Playa del Carmen?"

"It was dirt cheap."

"Three thousand of your dollars to buy an inn, to get started in business, to stop selling drugs. It was all I wanted and I was so close . . . until you took most of what I had."

"What I did was wrong."

"It was worse than wrong. You have no idea."

"Ana, did I force you to keep selling? You told me yourself that you'd earned that money in less than a year. You were the biggest earner of all the dealers, and the market was just getting better. *You* told me that."

"Yes! *But who buys drugs from a pregnant girl?*"

It landed like a bomb. An explosion of voices and shuffling behind us. Ana ordered her men: "*Silencio!*"

I couldn't help turning around. Mac also turned now, looking shocked. I was sure of it: He hadn't known.

"Pregnant?" he asked.

Please, I prayed, *don't ask if she's sure it was yours*. It was the kind of question that made any woman want to kill a man, and I could only imagine how Ana would take it. She had been sixteen. A girl. Left pregnant by a callous thieving gringo boyfriend whose real name she didn't even know. My heart broke for that girl.

"I didn't . . . Ana . . . I . . ." Reduced to stammering, there was nothing Mac could say.

"Only a coward runs."

"How could I run from something I didn't know?"

"I was going to tell you that night, when I came back

and found your note. I followed you to the airport—there I was, pathetic girl, hoping you might have changed your mind about me. I sat in that airport for hours, first waiting, then thinking: What was I to do? In spite of how you saw me—the drugs, the sex—I was a Catholic, and in my world a girl with child marries the father."

"But I didn't *know*."

"No! *I* didn't know. I didn't know *who* you really were. I didn't know *where* to find you. Well, it was you who taught me my most important lesson in life: I would always be on my own."

He stared at her, obviously afraid to ask the next question. So I did.

"You had a child?"

She turned to look at me, her eyes full of hatred. "Your husband has *two* sons."

"I don't believe this," Mac whispered, struggling to come to terms with something too huge to digest quickly.

"You don't *believe*?" Ana wheeled toward him, enraged.

"It's not what I meant."

"But it's what you said. You are a man who says what he doesn't *mean*. What don't you *believe*? You don't *believe* your son is as real as the money you stole from me?" Her gaze turned toward Diego and Felix, both of whom stood in front of the door looking astonished. Suddenly Diego's physical differences from the other men came into sharp focus: his taller stature, lighter skin, brown hair, blue eyes—and for the first time now I noticed he had a cleft chin exactly like Mac's. He was half American, as he appeared to be. Half Mac.

"He is my father?" Diego asked.

"If you can call him a *father*. He abandoned us. He left us to become what we are: We are wealthy, we are powerful, but we are outlaws. He is why every day is a fight for our lives."

She picked up a glass candlestick from her desk and threw it against the window. Both shattered. A gust of wind from the ocean rushed into the room.

"The papers, they call me a *queenpin*, they say I am helping to run this country into the ground—but whose fault is that? I was sixteen, left alone with a baby. Disgraced. No one would hire me. What was I supposed to do but return to what I already knew to survive?"

"Ana, I—" Mac said.

"No! There's nothing you can tell me to change my mind. I've held this secret in my hand all these months, wondering when and how and if I would tell either one of you. I've tried threatening you. I've tried bringing you into my business. I've tried loving you. Now I see it makes no difference. What's done is done. History cannot be unmade." She looked at Diego, her son, and her tone softened. "But I look at you, and how can I regret anything?"

"So my father was not killed by Medina's people?"

"Ruben Medina would take everything I have if he could, *everything*. But no . . . I'm sorry."

Diego's handsome features darkened. As he stared at his mother for a long, thoughtful moment—reprocessing everything she had ever told him about his parentage in a brand-new context, doing the math—I took him in: the beauty he shared with her, melded into a masculinity so similar, I saw now, to Mac's; his surprise at his mother's announcement. I could hardly fathom what was going through the young man's mind now. And who was Ruben Medina? Assumedly another Mexican drug lord jockeying for power.

"I can't stand seeing you in pain," Ana told her son. "It is too much for me. This was a mistake."

"Another mistake you cannot undo," Diego muttered.

"You were not the mistake, *mi amor*. Bringing this stranger here was the mistake. We must send them away." Ana turned to Felix. "Bring me the visitor's tray."

"*Sí*." He left the room.

"Are you sure?" Diego asked her.

"What choice do we have?"

Felix returned with a red lacquered tray holding a fancier, cleaner version of the works I'd seen at drug busts when I was on the beat: syringe, spoon, lighter, and the kind of rubber lariat nurses used to prepare a vein for injection. She had called it the visitor's tray but I knew she didn't plan to treat us to a friendly little high.

She was sending us away. And it would be to the farthest possible place she could send us: death.

I reflexively reached for Mac, held him, and whispered, "What about Ben?"

Mac pulled me close as Ana, who had heard, leveled her answer: "*Why should your son have a father when mine did not?*"

It was her answer not just for this, but for all of it. And implicit in her answer was another question, addressed to me: *Why should your son have a mother, either, now that you are here?* I had delivered myself stupidly, blindly, directly into Mac's fate. And delivered Ben to something worse, and lonelier, than Diego's.

CHAPTER 11

Felix set the tray on Ana's desk, which was covered in shattered glass, then stood back with his hands in his pockets.

"Murder the parents, I always say." I spoke before thinking but didn't regret it; if I was going to die, I wanted to hear the truth from its source. Wanted to hear her say, out loud, that she had been responsible for Hugh and Aileen's brutal murders. Wanted her to reveal herself, in plain words, for what she really was.

Her eyes snapped to me and a grin ignited ripples from her eyes across her cheeks, betraying her age, consuming some of her prettiness. "I don't think about family lineage when I decide how to . . . restructure."

"You *only* think about lineage. You're obsessed by it. It's why you brought Mac here. It's why you need to punish him. It's why you think you have to get rid of us now."

Mac stared at me, silently beseeching me to *be quiet*, stop angering her further. If he thought we had a way out of this, he was delusional. There was nothing to lose by speaking my mind or asking questions. This close to death, risk no longer frightened me.

She laughed, but it was hollow. "You think too much."

"*Why* did you kill Mac's parents? What exactly did that accomplish? Couldn't you think of a more subtle way to get Mac's attention?"

"*I* did not kill them."

"You *had* them killed."

"So I did." A cold confession; though with her witnesses soon dead, it meant little. "But *you* are lucky. For you I will wave a magic wand that won't be so . . . messy." She picked up the syringe. "Would you like to do the honors?" she asked Diego in a cloying tone that made it clear refusal would be a disgrace.

Diego unplanted himself from the spot where he had stood like an old tree, enduring the winds of his mother's revelations. A grin spread across his face with the studied poise and cunning of his mentor; as if "doing the honors" had been his own idea and nothing made more sense than to get right to it. They were so alike it was terrifying. But of course she would have groomed him in every way; it was what a tyrant always did. Their greatness and power was enhanced by their offspring. In time Diego would inherit everything she had so painstakingly built, and at such great sacrifice. He would inherit, broaden, and improve upon her accomplishments.

But Diego was part Mac; didn't that count for something? They said that morality was partly learned, and partly given.

Who, though, was Mac *really*? And what aspects of him had his first son inherited? The impulse to break the law and ruin others, or to uphold the law and support others? I had only ever known the second Mac, the *good* one, while Ana was all too well acquainted with the first. Where did Diego fit in; which genes had surfaced in his makeup? He appeared to be all Ana and the first Mac as I watched him cross to the desk, tip white powder from a glass vial into the spoon, hold it in the air, and light a flame beneath it. When it had melted to a clear liquid, he angled in the tip of the needle and drew the drug into the syringe. Holding it upright, he tapped out the air bubbles, just like any street junkie—and that was when I knew that Diego Soliz was no better than his mother, if not worse.

"Who first?" Ana said, letting him decide.

Diego looked from me to Mac, where his gaze lingered a moment. I could see him thinking, *This is my father*, and wondered what that felt like to him, after all these years. *This is my father and I am going to take his life*.

He held the syringe between his teeth, picked up the rubber lariat, and turned to Ana.

"What are you doing?" she asked.

"This one is for you, to give you the courage to let me do this in my own way."

She appeared interested but not aghast . . . which told me that she partook, at least occasionally, of her own merchandise. But then any good proprietor should know exactly what they were selling.

"I am not afraid to watch them drift into oblivion," she said. "Are you?"

"It disgusts me to think of them floating away on a cloud." His hand caressed the air as he said this, conducting the melody of the ridiculous idea that Mac and I might enjoy our final moments in a stupor of heroin.

"What do you want, Diego?"

"I want my father to suffer at my own hand, as I have suffered at his."

Nodding, Ana both understood and granted her son permission to destroy us in his own way. "Put it down. I am strong enough for whatever you decide. Your father, your vengeance."

Diego set the filled syringe on the tray. From across the room, Felix stared at it hungrily. "I am going to take the van for a ride," Diego said. And then he reached out to his mother, as if to bid her good-bye, but instead slipped the rifle's strap off her shoulder.

We drove for what felt like hours but could have been any length of time, tied on our sides in the back of a windowless van that rattled with rakes, spades, buckets, and loops of hose. Diego drove and Felix sat beside him in the passenger seat, holding the rifle. They had gagged us so we couldn't speak, and had left our eyes free to see but put us back to back so we couldn't see each other.

Mac's back, pressed against mine, felt warm and familiar. I concentrated on taking deep breaths in the hope that this might calm him—that he might sense my forgiveness. I understood now why he had left us: He had been trying to save our lives. The one remaining question I wanted answered, though, was why he hadn't gone to the police instead. Wouldn't that have been the logical reaction to receiving a threat from a drug lord exercising a powerful personal grudge? But the more I thought about that, the more I appreciated Mac's effort to handle it himself, to just slip away and appease the nemesis he hadn't even realized was lurking out there, ready to pounce on first sight. After all, for twenty years he had himself been the police, and he knew how hard it was to protect someone from even a garden-variety stalker, let alone one with overwhelming power and superhuman reach. He would have returned to us eventually, I told myself. I wouldn't have lost him forever. And I shouldn't have come here; my sudden appearance had shifted whatever balance Mac had managed to accomplish with Ana, shattering the groundwork of the escape route he was certainly building with his typical patience and care. Mac was a man who saw the whole picture, who worked steadily and patiently toward his goal; he had been looking for a way back to us. But now we were both going to die.

I tried to stop my imagination from wandering to all the possible methods Diego might use to kill us; the nightly news had schooled us on the near-daily discoveries of Mexico's gruesome drug war murders: tortured bodies lined up at the side of the road, execution-style killings, amputations, even beheadings. We would be just two more bodies to tally up in the overall count. I heaved at the thought of it, and in response felt Mac's back breathe deeply, talking to me, telling me to *quit thinking*. He had once told me that my imagination got me into too much trouble, that eighty percent of what I actively tried to solve would solve itself in time. He had told me I was too impatient. He was right, of course; but I couldn't help myself. It had made me a good detective, back when I was on the force, despite the implicit dangers.

Through a small blurry window separating the front seats from the cargo area, I could see the backs of our captors' heads and a tiny bit of road in front of us, but that was all. Gradually day began to fade until finally, in a blue twilight, we stopped driving.

The van's weight shifted as Diego and Felix got out, slamming their doors behind them. A moment later the rear doors opened.

"Get them," Diego ordered.

Felix hopped into the van. His hands shook as he roughly untied my feet. I suspected he was an addict and needed a fix, and that worried me as much as Diego's blood thirst. Felix pushed me to my feet so that, crouching, I could shuffle out. I jumped out of the van and stood on numb, tingling legs, yearning to walk, to run, but not wanting to take the chance before Mac was untied.

While I waited, I cautiously assessed our surroundings: We were at the side of a narrow but paved road in what appeared to be the middle of nowhere, a tangle of low-lying bramble and palm trees that suggested we weren't far from the ocean. A vast darkening sky loomed above us. Our bodies could be buried among the weeds, or dumped in the sea, or simply left right here. I wondered how far it was to the main road. If we made a run for it, how long would it take before we reached the relative safety of a highway? It would be perilous but there was no point not trying.

Mac's legs must have been more rubbery than mine because when he reached the outside edge of the van he tumbled to the ground. Diego laughed, and so did Felix, taking his boss's cue. Both men had a handgun tucked into their belts; they had left the automatic rifle in the car. *It would be a simple execution.* Mac rolled onto his side, hands still tied behind his back, and scrambled to his feet. It would take a couple of minutes for his legs to gain mobility. Did we have that much time?

"We do it here, boss?" Felix pulled his gun out of his belt, hands still shaking. I saw Diego noticing this and the disgust that crossed his face.

"Just a minute."

Mac and I stood four feet apart, our eyes trying frantically to communicate. Mine attempted to impart the necessity of running, just going for it. What was *he* thinking? Mac was as careful as I was impulsive. But what other choice did we have right now?

Without removing his gun, Diego walked over to Mac and ripped the tape off his mouth. Felix, likewise, ripped off mine. It stung with such ferocity I felt my skin had come off, but Mac's hadn't, so neither, I assumed, had mine.

"What are you doing?" Diego barked at Felix.

"I thought—"

"Did I tell you to think?"

"*Lo siento.*" Felix attempted to replace my tape, his dirty, trembling fingers pressing into my skin. "It won't stick."

"Just forget it."

The tape fell to the ground at my feet.

Diego wasn't interested in Felix or in me. He stood in front of Mac and looked at him intently. "All these months . . . Why didn't we know our bond?"

"I wish we had," Mac said. "It would have meant a lot to me. We could have—"

"What's done is done."

"If I had known about you, I never would have left."

I wondered if Mac meant that; either way, it was the right thing to say. He was going to try and negotiate our way out of this instead of inviting bullets to our running backs. As usual, he was taking the smart route, which carried its own set of risks.

"You had no real interest in my mother."

"That's not true. I was an eighteen-year-old boy, younger than you are now—I was immature, but not heartless."

Diego seemed to consider that a moment. And then he grimaced and spat on the dusty ground.

"Kneel," he told Mac, and then me, "You too."

"Diego," Mac said softly, paternally. "Please think this through. Think about how absolute this will be. You'll never be able to change your mind."

"*Kneel*. Felix, help them!"

Felix seemed to take pleasure in kicking the backs of my legs, buckling me down. My knees crashed onto the hard earth, sending bolts of pain straight to my head. Terror spiraled through me and I felt breathless, weightless. I sensed I was going to faint but somehow hung on to the edge of consciousness enough to hear Mac crash down beside me.

"Heads down!" Diego told us.

Felix kicked me forward so that my forehead hit the ground, and then kicked Mac, who pivoted forward beside me.

"Who first?" Felix asked Diego.

"No, I will do it. This is *my* vengeance."

There was a click as Diego cocked his gun.

And then . . . *and then* . . . came the first shot.

He had made his decision: who to kill first; who most deserved his animosity.

And had chosen his father.

My mind lost consciousness as my body floated away, flying upward into the bruised sky, in pursuit of my beloved.

CHAPTER 12

My brain shuffled frantically between consciousness and dream: Mac and I, hand in hand, run into the untamed countryside of the Yucatan. Palm fronds are vibrant green. The sky is sheer, vivid blue. The air is light and warm. We are naked, our skin is cool. We *know* in the way that you know something in a dream that Ben is safe on the other side of the road, awaiting us. And the rest of it, starting with Hugh and Aileen's murders to Danny's arrest to Mac's disappearance and suicide . . . the rest of it has been a terrible nightmare from which we have finally awoken.

We run.

Together.

Escaping the nightmare.

And then my mind careened to consciousness, back to the grievous reality of Mac's body collapsed beside me. The reality that Mac was dead. I had come all the way to

Mexico to find out if he might possibly still be alive—and now *he was dead*. His body lay in the dust, proof positive. I had satisfied my stubborn quest by fulfilling the worst possible end of my nightmare.

The mental anguish was unbearable.

But it would be over soon. Any moment.

Because I was next.

I closed my eyes and waited, forehead pressed into the ground, close enough to smell the elemental characteristics of the earth: eons of compounded minerals. Dust to dust. A return to nothingness.

Hurry. Please. Get it over with. End this.

Footsteps shuffled a cloud of dust into my face. Someone crouched beside me. I felt my wrists being untied.

"Get up," Diego said.

My mind defied his order but my body obeyed. I stood there, blinking. Mac was crouched forward in exactly the same position I'd just been in. He was perfectly still. I couldn't see any blood but assumed it was because I didn't want to see it. I knew about trauma: how your mind played tricks. I imagined I saw his back rise and fall with breath.

Diego squatted and began to pull apart the ties at Mac's wrists.

The acrid stench of fresh blood drew my attention behind me. I turned around. And there was Felix, lying on his back in a spreading pool of blood that seeped from his head, half of which had been blown away.

As soon as Mac's wrists were untied he sat up, flexing his fingers. His forehead was covered in dirt.

My mind spun in every direction.

Mac was alive.

I was imagining this.

It was real.

"Get up," Diego said. "Hurry."

Mac brought one leg forward, planting his foot on the ground, then followed it with the other foot and stood laboriously. He took a deep breath. Looked at Diego.

"I thought you'd come around," he said with the durable patience a father affords a child; his words forged in forgiveness.

"I never had a father." Diego's bravado had diminished to something close to humility. Suddenly he had shrunk from an angry god bent on revenge to a confused young man aching for elusive fulfillment.

"I never had you, either. But I can try to be your father now."

"My entire life," Diego said, "I've dreamed of you, but you never had a face. Now I know how to picture you."

Mac smiled and tentatively reached out a hand. But Diego kept his distance, not ready, it seemed, to risk too much trust. Then, suddenly, he reached into the pocket of his jeans, pulled something out, and thrust it into Mac's hand. We both stared: It was Aileen's engagement ring, crusted with dried blood.

Mac's shaking fingers closed to a fist around his mother's ring. In the darkness I could see the silver glint of his eyes watering, the draining of color from his face.

"*Go*." Diego glanced at Felix's body, which had attracted a swarm of flies. "I am going to bury him as you, and return to my mother."

"You don't have to," Mac said. "You can come with us."

Diego shook his head. "If I don't return, it will be worse than if I do."

Neither Mac nor I could argue with that: We had experienced the determination of Ana's wrath. Diego would have to work up close with her to maintain her trust because without it he would be as endangered as Mac and I were. *Heaven has no Rage like love to hatred turned, Nor hell a fury like a woman scorned*, William Congreve wrote in *The Mourning Bride*, a play an unusually lyrical professor had had us read last year in a course called Psychology of Madness. Well, if anyone was a bride in constant mourning, it was Ana to her first love, and it would be Ana to her son if she lost him, too.

"*Run*," Diego said. "If I need you, I will find you."

He went to the gaping van, hopped in, and rooted around for tools. He would need a spade to bury Felix. It would be easy enough to explain away Felix's disappearance: He was a lackey and a junkie, not reliable on either count.

I reached for Mac's hand and tugged him forward. "Let's go."

He glanced at Diego. I could tell he was confused, that he didn't want to leave the young man. But I also knew that this brand-new son, for all his good intentions at the moment, could just as easily retreat to the brutality he knew best. He was taking an enormous risk on many levels by giving Mac the ring and letting us go. An insane risk, if you really thought about it. But there was no time to think. We had to get moving.

I tugged Mac's hand again. "Come on," I whispered. "He could change his mind."

Mac nodded; he knew that anything was possible.

We ran together up the road as fast as we could. It was getting darker and the sounds of nighttime were gathering around us. My legs felt weak from having been tightly bound, now twice, and I felt a kind of exhaustion I hadn't known existed. But as I ran, I imagined light, strength, and speed surging through my limbs. I pumped my arms to ratchet myself forward. My heart beat like a machine, thumping hard in my chest. Sweat poured down my face in the cool humidity. I was aware of Mac's labored breathing beside me as he also pushed himself to his limit, propelling his body and mind forward—away from danger. And in his case, away from a child, a future he had detoured from once before without knowing it. The difference this time was that he knew he was leaving behind a son. I felt for him. But he was also running toward a son, *our* son . . . and a resolution to his parents' murders. Now that I had found Mac, now that we had survived against the odds, I was determined not to let him slip away again.

When we had run for nearly a mile and had reached the main road, we both keeled over. We were drenched, panting.

"She'll kill him," Mac said when he caught his breath.

"You don't know that."

"She'll give an order, it'll trip down a chain of command, and someone who doesn't know what he's doing will kill him. That's how it works. That's why she's so dangerous."

"He seems smart, Mac. And he knows her much better than you do. *And he's her child, she loves him.* He'll handle her."

"I hope you're right."

Suddenly I was overcome with powerful emotion, and I started to weep. "How did we get here?"

Mac pulled me into his arms and held me so tightly I could hardly breathe. We kissed deeply, passionately.

"I love you," he said, crying now himself.

"I had so much trouble letting you go."

"*Never* let me go." He kissed me again.

Holding hands, we started walking along the edge of the road. Occasionally a car sped past, but not many.

"I've always had a good instinct," I said. "I didn't see

you as a man who would bolt. And I didn't see you as a suicide. Your story wasn't, you know, *believable*, at least not to me."

"I was a little worried about that. And I was right to worry. You shouldn't have come here, Karin. For Ben's sake. We were both nearly killed."

"In twenty-twenty hindsight, I'd have to agree with you."

"How is our baby?"

"Great. Ben's great. He stopped asking for you after a while, it was terrible, but it was for the best."

"I feel so awful about all of this, you have no idea."

"I know you do."

We picked up our pace. The road was intermittently lit and in the far distance I could barely make out a road sign, but not its color.

"Where do you think we are?" I asked.

"Don't know." He squinted at the sign. "I'm hoping we're somewhere near the border."

We walked and walked as the air grew cold. I shivered and Mac pulled me close, slowing us down but making me happy. *Here we were, together.* I still could hardly believe it. As we continued onward and the moon arced higher overhead, I began to think we would never arrive anywhere. It was the strangest sensation. And that sign seemed to get farther away the closer we got, as if it was nothing but a mirage.

"I'm so thirsty," I said.

"You're dehydrated. They had you in that hole for about thirty hours. I got there as fast as I could . . ."

He didn't finish the thought: . . . *and if you hadn't made such a fuss, we might have gotten away by car and been across the border by now, minus one harrowing close call.* We also wouldn't have learned about Diego. I wondered if Mac felt he'd be better off not knowing, or if it was worth what we'd been through. He probably didn't know how he felt yet; it was all happening so fast.

Far ahead, a pair of red taillights flicked on. Only now did I realize that a car had been parked near the sign. The taillights began to move, red ovals swerving onto the road. The car stopped, and then began moving backward.

"Do you see that?" I squinted in the darkness.

"I see it."

We stopped walking a moment to watch. The car was now driving in reverse at accelerating speed.

"What the hell is going on?" Mac grabbed my hand.

"I don't like this."

"Neither do I."

We both started to run.

CHAPTER 13

The car moved faster and faster. We stepped off the side of the road to put some distance between it and us, skidding down a sloped embankment.

At two hundred feet, still driving in reverse, the car angled in our direction with such specificity and intent, my bad feeling exploded into certainty: It was definitely gunning for us.

At a hundred feet, the car headed down the embankment.

We ran as fast as we could, letting go of each other's hands, taking flight in opposite directions.

But the car kept coming, aiming for the center space between us.

And then, suddenly, it spun around and drove straight at Mac.

Insanely, I followed it—I couldn't help myself. I picked up a rock and flung it at the rear window. It bounced off.

I found a larger, sharper rock and heaved it with all my strength, and this time it made real impact. A web of cracks exploded across the back windshield.

The car skidded to a stop.

Both front doors flung open.

It was dark, I was frantic, and at first I couldn't see who they were but there were two of them. From the passenger side came someone who was tall and loped forward with a masculine stride—a man. From the driver's side came someone smaller and more slender, moving with a feminine blend of determination and grace.

The man headed for me.

The woman for Mac.

"Karin!" the man shouted. "*Karin!*"

The woman meanwhile called to Mac; her voice sounded familiar: "Hold it! Stop running!"

I heard Mac grind to a halt. Heard him panting for breath.

"What the— Are you out of your mind?" Mac yelled.

"You blew it!" the woman screamed at him. "We lost her!"

"I had no choice! Karin showed up! What was I supposed to do?"

"I don't know, man, but you don't ditch a job—*ever.*"

Her voice . . . *it sounded just like Jasmine*. What on earth would *she* be doing here? I slowed down, feeling dizzy. They were talking as if they knew each other. But Mac didn't know Jasmine, and Jasmine did not know Mac. I met her *after* he disappeared.

"Whoa!" The tall man jumped in front of me, holding out his hands to catch my shoulders. "Hold on there!"

The headlights of the stopped car blazed in the opposite direction, creating a fog of illumination in which a man with curly blond hair and a thick trimmed beard stood, facing me.

"Who are you?"

"Come on." He reached out a hand.

Off to the side, Mac and Jasmine were still arguing.

I backed away, turned, and started walking. Whatever this was, it didn't feel right.

He grabbed my arm and stopped me. "We came to help you; we'll talk in the car."

"No," I said, "we'll talk now."

His smile was a flash of white in the darkness, almost friendly, but his tone was all business. "I hear you, but you're not the only one risking your life." He grabbed my arm and pulled me, resisting all the way, to the car. Then he pushed me into the backseat and slammed the door. I felt a weird combination of safe and confused. As my brain slowed a bit, I began to realize that *Jasmine* was here. They had to be on our side. They had to have come to help us. But that was about the only thing that made any sense.

Mac stalked to the car, fending off more recrimination from Jasmine I could hear only parts of:

"We were *this close* to closing the deal."

". . . pull the thread on Soliz you pull the thread on a web . . . thousand miles . . ."

"When are we gonna get someone like you in there again? *Never.*"

What was she talking about?

And then Mac stopped her tirade by digging into his pocket and handing her Aileen's ring. "Here. See? Don't tell me that's *nothing*."

My mind took that in first like a wife, then like a cop.

Mac had just handed Jasmine the ring. *Why?*

The ring would put Ana Maria Soliz away for murder, thereby also disabling her cartel. A double whammy. Two cases for the price of one.

I stared at Mac as he slid in beside me, wondering anew who he really was. He stared back and took my hand. I pulled it away.

"Close the deal on what?"

His hand followed mine and this time squeezed. "I didn't lie to you, I just didn't finish the story. Obviously, in front of Ana, there was only so much I could say."

"Can you say it now? Or is this also not what it seems? Not that I have any idea what's going on here." The longer I talked, the angrier my tone grew; but the sound of my voice betrayed only a fraction of the depth of bafflement roiling inside me.

Jasmine slipped into the driver's seat and cranked the

engine. The man got in next to her. They glanced at each other, and before driving she paused to dig into her purse, nestled between the two front seats. She pulled out a pink billfold with an illustration of a kitten wearing a tiara, flipped it open, and flashed an ID card with her photograph sandwiched between a header, *U.S. Special Agent*, and a footer, *Drug Enforcement Administration*.

My mouth dropped open.

"What?"

The man then showed us *his* DEA ID: Special Agent Fred Miller.

"What's going on here?" I asked. "How did you find us?"

"It's an hour to the Merida airport," Jasmine said. "Let's get there and then we'll talk."

"Can I ask one question?"

"You already did. Matter of fact, you asked two." She stepped on the gas, the engine roared, and we drove up the embankment onto the road.

"Are you DEA, too?" I asked Mac.

He looked at me, shadows dancing across his face. He didn't nod yes. But he didn't shake his head no, either.

Fifty-seven minutes later we drove up to a guard station at the Merida airport and Jasmine flashed her ID again. In seconds we were cleared to bypass customs and go directly to a small plane waiting on the closest runway.

The staircase was rolled away as soon as we were inside—it was a six-seater with a quartet of cream leather armchairs facing each other over two small tables and an area in the back crammed with surveillance equipment. It looked like someone's luxury plaything that had been customized for surveillance, which fit the bill based on what I knew about the Feds and their covert operations; this was not a group that sought logo identification and so they tended to buy private planes and reinvent them on the inside.

The hatch was sealed and as we hurriedly buckled up, the engine whirred almost silently into action. The two pilots had us up in the air before I even realized we'd left the ground.

I sat in my window seat, watching the arteries connecting to the airport diminish to a spindly map of veins and then vanish altogether beneath cloud cover. Mac sat across the aisle, looking through his window. Jasmine and Fred sat facing us, ignoring the view, though I bet they had taken notice on their way in when their minds were wandering, figuring out how and where and when and in what condition they were going to find us. How *had* they found us? I didn't know—but the amount of equipment packed into the back of the plane suggested they could find just about anyone they wanted to.

"Nice plane," I said to Jasmine. "Is it yours?"

"I wish."

"What am I thinking? Yours would be pink with gold-plated accessories."

"Now you're talking." Refusing to take my bait, she smiled like the old Jasmine. Only she wasn't the old Jasmine. She was someone I didn't know.

Questions fired through my brain. And anger. The insult of having been duped by my husband and friend really stung.

"So, what—are you two partners?"

"Not exactly. Mine got reassigned and I was put on Fred's case to work undercover, what"—she looked at Fred—"about a year ago?"

He nodded. "Just about."

"What else am I wondering right now?" My tone hardened; I didn't care. "Let's see: Were you really just divorced? Are you really from Maine?"

"Listen, Karin—" Jasmine stopped herself with a huff of frustration, then tried again. "Everything we did together and everything I said was for real, just with some missing pieces. You've got to understand that we couldn't tell you about this while it was happening."

"There were serious security issues," Fred added.

"That's right," Jasmine said. "Mac's life was on the line."

Mac looked at me, his exhausted eyes somber but alert. "You don't know how hard it was not telling you."

"As hard as it was thinking you were dead?"

"Actually"—his tone rose—"*yes*. If not harder. Karin, I

feel awful about this in ways you might not even be able to imagine. It's been a nightmare."

The depth of his tone, the sadness of his face, pulled at my heart.

"Please, Mac"—I reached for his hand—"tell me *everything*. All of it. No more secrets."

He undid his seat belt and swiveled to face me. "Do you remember back in August, that morning at home when you read me the article about my promotion?"

"When you were in the bathroom?"

"That's right. And a little while later, the phone rang."

I thought back: Mac had answered a call, said hello a couple of times, and the "unknown caller" had hung up. "I remember."

"That was Ana calling from the Hotel Collins."

"Ana." It took a moment to sink in.

"That's when she made herself known."

"What did she say—*exactly*?"

"She said, 'Dylan—I've been waiting a long time for you to repay me.' And she told me where to find her in Miami. She had picked up a copy of the *New York Times* that morning, just by chance."

"And you said nothing."

"That's right. I just hung up."

"That's it? You hung up on her? And she had your parents murdered?"

"No. She called me again later at the office. She told me

I had a choice: I could meet her in Miami that day or Playa two days later. I told her to give me her address and I'd mail her the money I'd borrowed, with interest."

I'd met Ana and knew that that was not the answer she'd been looking for.

"You didn't borrow it, Mac."

"Stole. The money I *stole*."

"And she said?"

"She said I had to come in person, *or else*—that kind of thing."

"What exactly did she say?" I needed to *hear* it, to *see* it unfold as it happened; I needed to banish all those months of wondering.

"Okay. She said, 'You broke my heart.' I said, 'Ana, that was over twenty years ago.' She said, 'Some wounds don't heal.' It was like one of those soap operas. I didn't really take it seriously. I wanted to repay her the money, since she'd found me, and I was uncomfortable that she'd found me, but . . ."

I got it. "You didn't expect it to go that far."

"Of course not. I told her I couldn't come see her—"

"*Couldn't* or *wouldn't*?"

He thought a moment. "I think I said *wouldn't*."

Jasmine and I glanced at each other. She rolled her eyes. Plain refusal to a woman like Ana was never a good bet.

"She told me I'd regret it, but to me it sounded like more bad dialogue."

"My *abuela* is addicted to those *novelas* on TV," Jasmine said. "The badder the dialogue, the better the passion."

"A woman like that tells you to come to her," Fred said, "man, you tell her you're on your way and you hightail it in the opposite direction."

Jasmine sent him a sharp look. He shrugged his shoulders.

"Later that night," Mac continued, "when you found me at the bar with Billy and told me what happened to my parents . . . only then did I understand how serious the situation was. I called Billy the next day—after you went back home to get Ben and your mom—and told him about Ana and our past, and he made a couple calls. Turned out the Feds had something going on."

"And that's when I came into it, and the rest is history," Jasmine said.

"You went to Bronxville," I asked Jasmine, "when they were planning the funeral?"

"We deliver."

I looked at Mac and thought of his brother, Danny, who was sitting in jail that very moment, accused of a double homicide everyone here knew he didn't commit.

"Danny and Detective Pawtusky—are they in on it, too?" I asked.

Mac shook his head. "We had to make it as credible as possible. Rosie made that easy."

"What are you going to tell them when we get back?"

"And the charges are dropped? Knowing Danny, he'll

have been so drunk he won't be sure if he *did* kill Mom and Dad. He'll be happy to be free. Rosie, she'll welcome me back from the grave. And she'll thank me for getting Danny sober."

I could see it. Despite everything, the MacLearys really loved each other. I didn't doubt that they'd consider Mac's reappearance a miracle and forget the rest.

"Your job at the bookstore?" I asked Jasmine. "What was with that?"

"I needed to get close to you. I sat in on a couple of your classes at John Jay but you never showed up. Had to find another way."

"You went to my school?"

"The Psychopath in Criminology and Drama. I had to stop myself from laughing a coupla times. Like they say, *If you can't do, teach*."

I couldn't help a little smile. Having been on the job myself, I knew just what she was talking about.

"I heard you had a stubborn streak," Jasmine said, "and we decided it was a good idea to get close and make sure you didn't go rogue. Which you did anyway. But whatever."

I almost resented the admission that they'd been keeping such a close eye on me, but I did have a reputation for thinking for myself back when I was a detective, and beyond.

"Why you? Why not just let Billy keep tabs? He already knew me. You took a bigger risk doing it yourself." My mind was ticking, rewriting their strategy to make it better.

"I decided to keep him for myself." Jasmine flashed a coy smile. "But really: It had to be a woman, someone who could blend in, make a close friendship with you. And most of these special agents—white dudes in aviators?" She rolled her eyes. "Couldn't pass for human, if you know what I mean. No offense to you personally, Fred."

"None taken."

The truth was Jasmine had blended in perfectly, played her part to a T. She must have been a very good agent.

"So what was the job?" I asked Mac. "You went undercover for . . ." Fill in the blank: for what purpose exactly; for how long?

"Until they got something to incriminate Ana directly. It had to be good enough to stick. They wanted her off the street for so long her enterprise would go into disarray and hopefully implode."

"Did you know she had an heir?" I asked Jasmine.

"Oh yeah. We had our eye on Diego."

"Did you know he was Mac's son?"

Jasmine's eyes popped at that, and so did Fred's.

"*This* you didn't tell us," Jasmine said.

And Fred to Mac: "You got to be kidding me, buddy."

"It was news to me, too," Mac said in a gentle, pained tone that succeeded in getting them both to back off. "Even Diego didn't know. Ana kind of let that missile loose by accident."

"That's right," I said. "But it saved our lives."

"Diego got Ana's permission to take us away and execute us. Then he killed his partner and let us go. *He* gave me the ring—and you know as well as I do that with the ring, you've got a solid case to put her away. If not for him, you would have found us, but in a ditch. And you'd be no closer to pulling the plug on Ana."

"You trying to cut a deal for your kid already?" Jasmine asked. At first I thought she was half joking but her straight face told me she meant it.

"Maybe." Mac stared back at her a moment before looking away.

"Diego's in it up to his ears," Jasmine said.

"He's my son."

"You get a DNA test on that? Or are you banking on what Ana Maria Soliz, the Wicked Witch of the West, South, East, and North told you in the strictest of confidence?" Jasmine's tone hardened in a way I had never heard it before. Her identity warp was starting to come a little bit clearer to me: She was the Jasmine I knew *and* she was a federal agent. It was going to take some getting used to.

"He has Mac's eyes," I told her, "and Mac's chin."

"I'll take a test," Mac said. "In the meantime, I believe her. All the balls are in her court. Why would she lie?"

Jasmine slipped out of her shoes and crossed her legs, one bare foot dangling a pretty purple manicure. "She know you were a plant?"

"I don't think so."

"What about Diego? Think he followed you after he let you go? Think he might've seen *us*?"

Mac and I looked at each other.

"He told us to go," Mac said. "He wanted us to get away. He seemed sincere."

"He stayed back to bury the body," I added. "We didn't see him again after that. He said he was heading back to his mother to face the heat."

"Nice guy, huh, doing all that for you."

"Hey, this isn't an interrogation," Fred said. "Cut these guys some slack; we're on the same team."

"Just asking a couple questions."

"Everything was going well." Mac leaned forward. "I was getting closer all the time, scratching away, hoping to finally get the one big thing on her. I was prepared to wait as long as it took. I was risking my life by the minute and I would have done it forever if it kept Ana's people away from my family. But when Karin showed up, the game changed. I didn't have to think about where my priorities were."

Jasmine's pretty almond eyes slid to me and hovered there while she seemed to think something over. Then she sighed. "Yeah. Whatever."

"You know what?" Fred said. "Here you are, alive and well, both of you. And now we've got that ring, so once we extradite Ana Soliz we'll be able to put her in jail, choke off her network. We'll get so much junk off the streets it isn't funny."

"Won't another cartel just take over her territory?" I asked.

"Maybe, maybe not," Fred said. "The Mexican cops will have a chance to get in there now."

"I got the impression the cops were all bought off."

"They are," Mac agreed.

"Still, I'd say we can call it a win." Fred tapped his fingers on his knees and I noticed that the backs of his hands were covered in freckles.

"Thing is," Jasmine said, "it's not like they won't be coming after you now, Mac. Ring or no ring, that bitch *hates* you. I wouldn't bet she's planning to lay low—who knows how scared she really is right now? She *knows* the Feds have got some negotiating to do to seal the deal before Mexico extradites her for murdering your parents. She *knows* the people in her pocket might not go for it." She wiggled into a cozy position and shut her eyes as if to close the conversation because right now, right at this moment, it was a good time for a nap. Unless Ana had surface-to-air missiles, it was probably safe to take a break from the job up here in the sky.

I had never known Jasmine was so cynical. But then I corrected my thinking once again: Pretty much everyone who worked in law enforcement was cynical to one degree or another.

"Diego's telling her we're dead," Mac said, "so she won't be coming after us."

"Oh yeah?" Jasmine yawned.

"I believe him."

"You're a nice guy, Mac, aren't you."

It wasn't a question and no one disagreed. But it sent a chill through me. All four of us had at some point in our lives put ourselves on the line for the law. We had all faced down some *really bad* bad guys (who were sometimes women). And we all knew that, when it came to winning the sordid games we had to play to defeat them, the nicest guys lost the quickest and in the worst ways.

PART III

CHAPTER 14

The pallid sky, the spindly naked trees whose branches were etched in white, and the graying slush of a recent snow greeted our return home to Brooklyn. It was the dullest, bitterest time of year and yet I had never been happier for the cold embrace of a frigid New York winter afternoon. It was four o'clock and the late afternoon pall of half light had settled on the neighborhood; the quiet hour when schoolchildren were safely home and rush hour had yet to disgorge itself via the subways and buses onto the local streets, when kitchens were dark and books were opened. The quiet hour of pause. Four o'clock was when Ben was calmest and, having woken from his long nap and finished a bottle or a cup of milk, was just embarking on an avenue of play.

The car slowed as it neared our building, and then eased to a stop.

"You want company?" Jasmine, who sat to my right in the backseat, asked with a hint of humor in her voice.

I lifted my head off Mac's shoulder, yawning. "Oh, sure, I think we'll throw a party tonight."

Mac looked out the window at the brownstone façade of our home. The parlor floor lights were on, two long golden rectangles, beckoning. He put his hand on the door handle. "Give a call if you or they or whoever needs to know anything else." But his tone was deadpan. We had just spent two hours being debriefed at DEA headquarters in Manhattan. Mac had told them everything he had learned about Ana Maria Soliz and her drug trafficking operations, giving them names, dates, and locations that were sure to spawn new investigations in two countries. And I had told them everything of the little I knew. They had a lot on her and her people now, including a glittering piece of hard evidence. Unfortunately, she had vanished into hiding; before she could be arrested or extradited, she had to be found.

I kissed Jasmine's cheek. "Thank you."

"You don't hate me?"

"I'm too tired to hate anyone." I reached forward to the front passenger's side; twisting around, Fred offered his hand and we shook. "Thanks for the rescue."

"Next time you need to save someone, call us first, okay?"

"I promise."

"You lie." Jasmine chuckled. She was the kind of person who liked you more if you gave her a run for her money. And she was turning out to be a truly interesting friend.

"Thanks for the lift."

Special Agent Hyo Park—Fred's affable partner who had participated in the debriefing and insisted on driving the car even though having three agents escort us home seemed like serious overkill—turned around and winked. "It's the least we can do."

"We're really sorry for all the pain and suffering this whole deal has caused you, Karin," Jasmine said.

"We couldn't see a better way to do it," Fred said. "The good news is you're both safe."

"And the bad news?" I asked, not actually expecting any.

"If Ana surfaces, if there's trouble, we might have to move you."

"Move us where?"

"It would be for your protection."

"How much warning will we get?"

Fred and Jasmine glanced at each other. Hyo stared straight ahead through the windshield. No one answered.

Mac got out first. I followed, slammed the door shut, and watched the car slowly drive away. Then we crossed the sidewalk to our house.

The front stoop was coated with ice and so we went to the downstairs door. Stroller tracks in the frozen snow told me that my mother had been coming and going this way. Inside, the house was warm and we could hear Mom singing to Ben as she moved around the kitchen clanking something, preparing an early dinner. And then we heard Ben's voice.

"Gamma gimme bang-bang poon!" He wanted Grandma to give him a spoon for a drumstick.

Mac's eyes widened, and he said, "He speaks in sentences now."

I nodded, my face screwing up; I had missed my Ben these past days. And I had missed Mac unspeakably—*and now he was here, back in our home*—and it felt almost unreal. We turned to hold each other; our breath came into sync. And then there was a pause, footsteps above us nearing the top of the stairs, and my mother's voice calling down, "Hello?"

Unable to contain myself, I went running up the stairs.

"Mom, *he's home*."

"I was *so* worried about you both." Mom opened her arms and as we embraced I noticed that the parlor floor was mostly unlit except for a single lamp in the kitchen, which seemed odd since the lights had just been on. There was a sound of something falling and Ben tottered quickly toward the top of the stairs, grinning from ear to ear. Mac came jogging up the stairs, patted Mom's shoulder in passing, and swung his little boy off the floor into an aerial spin—Ben screamed in delight—and Mac held him fiercely, restraining tears.

And then the lights flicked on to a cheer of "*Welcome home!*" in a chorus of voices, and a loud *pop* heralded the opening of champagne. Before I knew what was happening, my brother Jon was putting a glass into my hand, filling it and kissing my cheek, seemingly all at once. I recognized the bottle I'd bought for Mac's and my abandoned anniversary celebration, five whole months ago. Had it been sitting in the fridge all that time? (The cake had long since been defrosted and eaten.)

Soon everyone was talking, hugging, laughing, drinking: Mom; Rosie and Larry and their kids; Jon, his wife Andrea, and their children, Susanna and David (who had flown all the way from Los Angeles); and Danny, who I couldn't help noticing forwent champagne for orange juice. Danny, *sober*, was tearfully smiling, beaming at his big brother. If he was angry about having sat in jail when Mac knew who had murdered their parents, it didn't show.

Finally, light-headed from exhaustion and champagne, Mac and I retreated to the couch. Ben snuggled on his daddy's lap and the family gathered around us, inspiring an immediate and elemental sensation of renewal.

"Smile!" Mom's camera flashed before I realized she was standing there, aiming her lens.

Squinting, I raised a hand to cover my eyes. Mac, however, complied with a smile so effortful my mother released the camera to dangle from a wrist cord.

"I'm sorry," she said. "I'm just so thrilled to see you two home."

"I looked through your photo album," Jon said to Mom as he slung his arm around my shoulders. "Wow."

"It tells the story of our wait," Mom said, patting Mac's knee.

I sniffed back tears, trying not to cry. "I can't believe you guys came all the way from California."

"Are you really such an idiot?"

He succeeded: I laughed.

"Mom called everyone last night as soon as she heard you were both safely out of Mexico."

"Jasmine e-mailed me from the plane," Mom said, "and I got right on the phone."

Mom had pulled up a chair and sat beside Rosie, who was on the floor with John, her five-year-old, plunked in her lap. Danny sat cross-legged beside Rosie, and Dave, her eldest, sat beside Danny. The other children—Lindsay, Alice, Susanna, and little David—filled the floor space, wiggling in excitement. Jon's wife, Andrea, was on the couch beside Mac, her hand rubbing his back in steady circles. I sat there, amazed and grateful, trying not to think about how many times in the last forty-eight hours I had been convinced I would never see any of them again.

"So what was it like, Uncle Mac?" Lindsay asked. "They said you were, like, held *prisoner* in a *dungeon* by some evil lady!"

"*Lindsay*." Larry shut down his tween daughter's outsized enthusiasm with a stern tone.

"But *Dad*—"

"You smell!" five-year-old John shouted.

"*John*."

I sniffed my armpit and made a face. "Ew! He's right."

"Karin, Mac, I apologize for them," Rosie said, breaking into a smile; it was no secret that she encouraged her children to be spirited. "They're spoiled little cretins."

"I think they're very smart," Mac said. "And we *do* stink. We could both use a shower and a change of clothes." He stood up, trembling, and kissed my mother's cheek. "Thank you for everything." He edged through the seated group, stopping to place a hand on his brother's shoulder. "Danny, listen . . . I don't know how to tell you I'm sorry."

"For what? In the end, it was better than rehab, you know? Not that I want a repeat performance."

"Actually," Rosie said, "*I'm* sorry. I'm the one who drove in the nail. I gave that detective reason to doubt you."

"But I could have pulled the nail out at any time," Mac said, "and I didn't."

"Both of you," Danny said, "I mean it: I love you. All that's in the past, okay?"

"Okay." But Mac's voice was barely a whisper. And Rosie fell silent. None of them would forget what had happened for a long, long time; but at least they were being civil about it. It was a start.

I felt everyone watching us as we headed down to our bedroom and bathroom. When we reached the bottom of the stairs and were out of sight, Mac stopped suddenly and buckled over, cradling his face in his hands, silently weeping. Snippets of conversation floated down:

"They look great!" Andrea.

"They look *terrible*." Dave.

"I meant *considering*."

"They're *alive*." Rosie. "Kids, get cracking: There's a table to set." And a flutter of footsteps that told us life would inevitably go back to normal.

The days drifted by as we settled back into our life together, feeling bruised and weary, but adjusting and happy in the way you are when you wake up from a nightmare and realize that everything is actually okay. The thing that loomed behind us, that terrible sequence of close calls, was over; and yet it wasn't. Ana was still out there . . . we had escaped, and yet we hadn't. Mac jumped every time the doorbell rang. And I kept having the same disturbing dream:

They are together on a beach in the rain—Mac and Ana—making love with languid pleasure, carefree and relaxed, as if they are not engulfed in a storm. They are not young; they are middle-aged. The bubble of their delight comes from the fulfillment of a circle that has closed. It is the celebration of a reunion. She reaches up to touch his face and he turns to lick water off her fingers. Her neck arches, her head burrowing a nest in the sand, as his back straightens and his shoulders open . . . and they fuse, becoming a single organism, a huge bird that rises off the sand as the rain stops and all the wetness instantly evaporates. They soar into a vivid purple sky as a black crow appears and follows them. The crow's feeling of hopelessness becomes *my* feeling and the crow becomes *me*, a bird with my face and then my body who suddenly can't fly and spirals down out of the sky . . .

Which was always the moment when I woke up, startled awake by a sensation of freefall. It had happened three or four times since arriving home from Mexico. The first night we slept deeply with Ben between us, delirious with exhaustion. But on the second night, the dream arrived and kept arriving thereafter.

I had never been jealous before but now every time I looked at Mac I thought: *Did they sleep together again? Did he enjoy it?* Whenever I thought we had settled onto firm enough ground to delve into such risky territory, so many questions swirled through my mind that I couldn't decide where to begin. I kept waiting for the right moment and it kept not coming, until finally I realized it would never appear on its own; I would have to create it.

"Mac?"

He folded down a corner of the newspaper to acknowledge me.

"Did you and Ana sleep together?"

He laid the paper on his lap but didn't answer.

"Not that it matters." I pulled my robe together, warding off the chilly air in the living room. "But I think I want to know."

Mac put the folded paper beside him on the couch and scooted forward to its edge. Clasped his hands between his knees and looked at me intently. He was wearing plaid pajama bottoms and an old T-shirt whose neckline sagged below his collarbone, revealing the top of his faded tattoo and half a dozen hard white scars.

"Are you sure you want to know?"

"I've been thinking it over, and I wasn't going to ask, but I keep having a dream about it and I want it to stop. So just tell me."

"You sure?"

"Yes."

"Okay. I already told you the beginning: how when I found her in Playa at first she acted like we were old friends, we had dinner, she gave me a room, and the next day she told me I was going to work in her so-called business again."

" 'Like old times.' "

"That's right. And I refused, stupidly, so she shot me up and threw me in the hole, just like they did to you."

I shivered recalling its dank mildewy darkness; and then

later, realizing I'd been drugged. Mac had already told me about his time in the hole. "She left you in there for two days."

"That's right."

"And then she had you brought back to her—"

Like a piece of tenderized meat.

"—and she asked me to go to bed with her."

This was new information. I folded my arms over my belly and listened.

"I knew that if I refused, there would be consequences."

"I understand."

"And I would have failed in my mandate from the Feds to do whatever I had to, to get in as deep as I could." He visibly cringed at the metaphor. "I'm sorry, you know what I meant."

"So did you?"

"I followed her to her bedroom—up on the second floor of the house, a room with red walls and windows all around, curtains billowing when there was a breeze. Very dramatic. Very Ana. We had a few drinks, talked. It started getting dark and she lit candles everywhere."

He raked his hands through his hair and stood up. It was a Sunday, early afternoon, and we had been in our pajamas all day. Mac started to pace and I worried that his footsteps would wake Ben, who was napping downstairs.

"*Shh.*"

He stopped and faced me at a distance of a dozen feet.

"But don't stop talking."

"She put on music. She's a seductress, Karin. It's what she *does*. It's what drug trafficking is about: creating desire, feeding off it."

"How many times?"

He looked at me as if the question confused him.

"How many times did you have sex?"

"She unbuttoned my shirt. I was out of it, hungry, terrified. All I could think about was that she'd had my parents murdered, and if I didn't do what she wanted this time . . . I didn't think she'd just toss me back into the hole, you know?"

I nodded.

"In my mind, if I didn't play along, she would make a phone call and in an hour you and Ben would be dead."

"You said she unbuttoned your shirt. What happened next?"

"She saw the scars. She kind of froze and got this awful look on her face. The mood changed and she told me to leave. That was the last time she tried. After that she put me to work, mostly supervising the men who worked in her house, and I went along—surviving, scraping for evidence, keeping her away from you. I hope you can forgive me."

"Forgive you for what?"

"I don't know what would have happened if I didn't have the scars. I feel like I betrayed you."

"You would have done whatever you had to do to

survive. I shouldn't have asked about you and Ana, it was selfish; I thought I needed to know, but I didn't."

"I needed you to ask me because I knew what you were thinking. I could see it in your eyes."

We kissed. And just like that, my nightmare stopped.

But it wasn't really over.

As our first week home came to a close, Mac's own nightmares grew darker, and his ghosts threw longer shadows. He seemed so tired in the days that I suspected he wasn't sleeping much, though he denied it. Then one night I woke up just before three A.M. and found he wasn't in our bed. Standing at the bottom of the stairwell, I could see a light on the parlor floor. I crept quietly up the stairs.

"Mac?" I whispered. "Where are you?"

I heard a shuffle in the kitchen, followed by a reluctant answer: "In here."

He was sitting at the table, a crumb-covered plate pushed aside, an open magazine in front of him, and on top of that a pad of lined paper and a list I had apparently interrupted as he was writing it. He covered it with a hand.

"How long have you been up here?"

"Awhile."

"You can't sleep?"

"Well, if I could, I wouldn't be—"

"Okay, *ask a stupid question* . . . What's that?" I indicated the list.

"Nothing. Just some stuff I need to do."

I sat down. "What kind of stuff?" It wasn't as if he had been doing much of anything lately. Mac's days had mostly consisted of reading the newspaper and trips to the playground with Ben. It didn't bother me; he needed a good, long rest and I knew he'd get back on his feet eventually.

"Nothing that concerns you, Karin."

"What doesn't concern me?"

He pushed the list toward me, saying, "I can't sleep anymore."

The list was titled *Diego*. Beneath that was an inventory of places in and around Playa del Carmen: residences, businesses, clubs, restaurants, shops, beaches.

"What is this?"

Mac's sigh sounded like a collapse, as if he had given in to a dread that had infected him in Mexico. It was awful. Instinctively I put my hand on his arm, but he shook it off.

"What's going on?"

"I have to help Diego."

"What?"

"I knew you wouldn't understand."

"That's not fair!"

As he stared at me his pupils visibly shrank. He started to sweat.

"Are you okay?"

"I need some air."

He got up from the table, opened the kitchen door, and

went out onto the deck that overlooked our garden, which at this time of year was a gray patch of dry, frozen weeds. Through the kitchen window I watched him pace the deck a moment before joining him.

"I'm going to make an appointment for you to talk to Joyce."

"Karin, we can't have the same therapist."

"I don't see her anymore."

"Even so."

"Will you talk to someone else?"

He paused a moment before answering, "I guess so."

"There's nothing wrong with needing help."

He nodded, but unconvincingly.

"Mac, I think you might be suffering from post-traumatic stress disorder."

"That's occurred to me, too."

"Okay, so we're on the same page. That's good."

"The thing is, Karin." He stopped pacing to look at me. Behind him, across the length of two adjoined backyards, a window lit up: another insomniac raiding his refrigerator. "The thing is, all the therapy in the world won't make Diego safe."

"Diego again."

"*My other son.*"

He said it with such force that a fog of frozen breath gathered in front of him. And the way he said it: owning the idea of the relationship. He must have given it an enormous amount of thought; but then why wouldn't he, having learned he had a grown son he hadn't even known existed until just over a week ago? Standing in the freezing night, I closed my eyes a moment and imagined myself in the same position. It was difficult; a woman generally grew her children inside her body, gave birth to them, nurturing a connection you couldn't deny. How *would* it feel to suddenly, one day, find out you had created a child a quarter of a century ago?

"What would make Diego safe, Mac?"

"That's what I'm trying to figure out."

"He's Ana's son, too. Which makes him either very safe or very unsafe."

"I just can't stop thinking that right now he's on the *very unsafe* side of that equation."

"She wouldn't hurt him. He's her child. She loves him."

"Karin, she doesn't love people the way you and I or most other people do. She isn't capable of it."

"I got the feeling she loved you, way back when."

"She possessed me. It wasn't love."

"So what's the solution?" The window across the yard went dark. And I felt my heart drop.

"I have to go."

"How can you? After what we've already been through."

"I *know*, but Karin, I *have* to."

"What about Ben? He's only two. If you leave him and you don't come back, he'll never know you, either."

"I'll come back."

"*Maybe. Or maybe not.*"

"Don't be hysterical."

"Don't be *insane*. She'll kill you if you go near her *or* Diego. You *know* that."

I turned to leave, disgusted by the suggestion that he might abandon us again. But Mac came at me so fast he knocked over a summer chair, its metal edge clanking against the iron deck, ringing into the quiet. He grabbed my wrist, stopping me from storming back into the house.

"*Listen to me.* Diego risked his life letting us go and giving me the ring. The more I think about it, the more I realize that *his* life is in danger now. Ana isn't stupid; she probably knows exactly what he did. So how can I *not* go back? Think about that: How can I *not go*?"

"But Ben—"

"Someday Ben's going to know about this—all of it, including Diego. What will he think of me when he finds out I left his older brother to . . . to . . ." The word was *die* but he couldn't say it, it was as if he was choking on it. I felt so bad for him. I understood his conflict, but Ben was my son. I couldn't stand back and let him lose his father.

"Don't decide tonight," I said. "That's all I ask."

Mac exhaled another frozen breath. "Okay. I can agree to that."

We went back inside together. Locked the door. Cleared his list and plate off the table. And went to bed. Tomorrow

I would find him a therapist who would talk some sense into him. I waited until he had fallen asleep and then, listening to his slow, heavy breathing, allowed myself to drift off until morning, having convinced myself that Mac could never bring himself to leave us again.

The next thing I knew, a doorbell was ringing, integrating itself into an already incoherent dream.

And Mac was getting up, going upstairs to the front door.

And Ben, suddenly, was crying.

I shook off the dream, hauled myself out bed, and went to Ben's room. He was in the act of climbing out of his crib; it was the third time I'd found him doing that.

"Hold it, little man!" I hurried to catch him before he fell.

"Oongry, wanna ee na!" He was hungry, wanted to eat now.

"Okay, let's go up and have some breakfast."

I set him down and he ran his wobbly run out of the room. I caught up with him at the foot of the stairs and walked up behind him in case he fell. On the parlor floor he veered straight to the kitchen and I was about to follow when I saw Mac.

Bright morning sun flooded the front hall, blanching the color out of his skin. He was standing in front of the mail table beside our front door, having just lifted the top off a flower box, and reached in to lift out an armful of purple dahlias.

CHAPTER 15

Mac dropped the bouquet, scattering long purple petals across the floor, and dug through the box searching for a note. I knelt beside the bouquet and with trembling fingers found a small envelope tied to the white ribbon gathered around the stalks. I pulled out the card and read aloud:

"*Imagine this: Best wishes to the memory of your son.*"

He grabbed the card out of my hands and read it again, silently. Then he crumpled it and threw it down among the petals. "What the hell does that mean?"

"Which son?"

We looked at each other.

"She wants it to be confusing." Mac rushed into the kitchen, got the phone, and dialed from memory. "Jasmine?" A pause, followed by a torrent. "*Yes*, it's early, I'm sorry. But listen: *Ana sent dahlias again*. Just now. I don't know who left them. The doorbell rang and the box was on the stoop when I opened the door."

I poured Ben a sippy cup of milk, then set about preparing his favorite breakfast of cream of wheat topped with thin slices of banana. He took the cup and stood there watching his father heatedly talk on the phone. I didn't want to watch and I didn't want to listen anymore. It felt so sudden and so intense: You could almost hear the force of the air *whoosh*ing out of our lives.

The rest happened quickly.

In what seemed like moments, Jasmine and Billy were at our door, having been roused from sleep with a single call to Jasmine's cell (answering the lingering question about the state of their coupledom, and providing another dose of reassurance that some of the elements of herself she had shown me were genuine).

"All right, so here's what we got on the flowers." Jasmine parked her BlackBerry between her teeth long enough to shed her coat and then, standing in the front hall on a cluster of petals, finished her thought. "They came from Downtown Florists on Bridge Street, but the order originated at a public phone at a bodega in La Huacana in southwest Mexico." She flung her coat into Billy's arms and headed through the living room into the kitchen. "You got any coffee?"

After hanging the coats on pegs by the front door, Billy and I joined Mac in the living room while Jasmine took it upon herself to start a pot of coffee. Before we could say much of anything, the phone rang.

I remembered what Fred had said when they dropped us off at home last week: We would hear from them if there was "trouble" and we would then be "moved." I didn't want to answer it. Apparently neither did Mac. We sat there, letting the phone ring, our minds racing in opposite directions: mine looking for answers as to how I could keep my family safe on the run; Mac assumedly figuring out how he could get to Diego now. I tamped down an impulse to tell him, *Stop thinking about that, you're not leaving us again*. If we had been alone, if Jasmine and Billy hadn't been there forcing us to stay on task—the flowers, the threat, *right now*—I would have succumbed to pure emotion.

Jasmine crossed the kitchen and took the call. After a brief conversation, she hung up and told us, "That was Fred. Start packing, people."

"I had a feeling."

"Where's your mother?"

"Sleeping."

"Wake her up and tell her to pack herself a suitcase."

I thought of what had happened to Mac's parents and felt ill.

"A car's coming in an hour. Better hurry."

"Where are we going?"

"You know I can't tell you that." She crossed back to

the coffeepot, which hadn't finished dripping, and pulled out the glass carafe to intercept two full mugs' worth. She handed both to me.

"But I'm going to find out when we get there."

"Honey, it's for your own safety. Come on, there isn't much time."

We stared at each other, two steel wills colliding.

"Can you at least tell me what kind of weather to pack for? Or do I need to bring everything we own?"

She hesitated, then offered one word: "Cold."

In less than an hour, Mac and Billy were hauling four suitcases and Ben's stroller into the trunk of a pale blue sedan. It was all of seven-fifteen in the morning and people were just starting to emerge from brownstones, adults dressed for a day at the office, parents pulling children toward school buses, teenagers with book bags strapped to their backs.

My mother, who had packed just one small suitcase and wore a worried expression but so far hadn't asked many questions, helped buckle Ben into his car seat and then slid in beside him. I got into the back, and Mac slammed shut the door. For a split second my heart raced; I thought he was going to leave us as we traveled to destinations unknown. But then he walked around to the front passenger seat and got in, turning to look at me as if he had read my mind. I thought I saw resentment flash across his face but wasn't sure and in any case this wasn't the time; I pushed it away, we were all under stress, no one liked what was happening.

The driver got out of the car and Jasmine slipped behind the wheel. Billy knocked on her window and she rolled it down.

"All set?" He leaned in to kiss her.

"Call you later."

"Don't drive like a maniac."

She grinned. "Who, me?"

By early afternoon we were crossing the Sagamore Bridge onto the archipelago of Cape Cod and the islands and siphoning off a rotary onto Route 6, a two-lane road that snaked across the summer resort island that in winter was bright, gray, and lonely. After another hour we turned into the long driveway of a gated community whose sign announced itself as *Shore Haven, Brewster, Massachusetts*. A security guard emerged from his station to clear our entry.

Jasmine got out of the car to greet him. She showed him her identification and then brought him around to meet us. When Mac opened his window, frigid air swept into the car, waking Ben from a truncated nap.

"Kids," Jasmine said, "this is Mike."

Mac shook his hand, but before he could introduce himself, Jasmine cut in.

"And these are the Peltries—Sam and Joan; their son,

Timmy; and Joan's mother, Cornelia, but you can call her Corny. We all do."

We sat there in stunned silence, digesting what must have been our new aliases. Of course. They wouldn't sequester you from the world under your own name.

"Nice to meet you." Mac, or Sam, shook Mike's hand.

I nodded. "Hi, Mike."

Mom just smiled.

"You need anything, the guard station's extension zero on your phone."

"Easy to remember," Mac said.

"That's the whole point." Mike noticed a man walking nearby and waved him over. "That's Doug, our groundskeeper—you'll want to meet him, too."

Doug wore dirty blue jeans, a black down jacket, and work boots with untied laces. He had thick snowy hair, a grizzled face, and a smile that revealed a broken front tooth. We were put through the same introductions, at the end of which Doug fixed his attention on Ben.

"Looks like I might have a customer for the old carousel."

"I'll point it out to them on the way up," Jasmine said.

"Catch me around one of these days, I'll unlock it, give you people the grand tour." Then Doug stood away from the car so Mac could bring the window up and we could drive away.

"*Peltrie?*" I snorted.

"Names come out of the hat." Jasmine shrugged. "Comes

with social security numbers, a credit card, anything you'd need to stay awhile."

"*Cornelia*," Mom tested her new name. "When I was a girl, I used to wish for a fancier name. *Corny. Cornelia.*"

"You got one now," Jasmine said.

"But would a woman named Cornelia name her daughter Joan?" I asked.

"I think so," Mom said. "Growing up with a fancy name, she would want the opposite for her daughter, something easier, don't you think?"

"I don't know what to think."

"Then don't," Jasmine said, earning a grin from Mac.

Half a mile along the wooded drive we came to a vast clearing of dead grass that in summer would have been a green vista undulating toward a mansion that was now a sort of manor house to the condo development and in summer doubled as a hotel. As we drove through the nearly deserted grounds we passed covered swimming pools and signs pointing to beaches, a golf course, playgrounds, restaurants.

"There." Jasmine slowed the car and pointed at the gray-brown distance.

"What a lovely gazebo," Mom said.

"No, behind it to the right. See that big shed thing?"

"Looks out of place there," Mac said, "like a gardener's outbuilding."

"That's the carousel Doug was talking about. It's

an antique and the management put some money into
restoring it. They cover it in winter."

"Does it work?" I asked as Jasmine picked up speed,
driving us away from the development's center.

"I think so, but I never saw it in action. Place mostly
shuts down for winter." She pulled the car to a stop in
the driveway of a small two-story building at the end of
a staggered row of identical attached condos. "The Feds
own this unit, use it off season."

Mom unbuckled Ben and passed him to me, and together
we got out of the car. We followed Jasmine down a short
curved path to the front door, which she unlocked with
a key she then handed to me as if I was the proud new
owner.

"Thanks," I said, sparing no enthusiasm. But what was
the point pretending I was actually thankful to be here?
Running and hiding were bitter pills you took because you
had to. You sucked it up. Moved forward. When I was a
kid my father's army career sent us from place to place
to place (until we were finally able to settle down in my
grandparents' big old house in Montclair, New Jersey)
and so this was really nothing new. My mother and I had
experience setting up house on the fly.

I walked all the way in and put the key on the white
counter of a white galley kitchen that shared space with a
white dining/living room. A white staircase led up to what
I predicted would be a white upstairs. Through the living

room's picture window was a barren, icy landscape that we could banish by closing the white drapes. I wondered how long we'd be here, if it would be worth the investment in a colorful throw for the beige couch and maybe a few bright posters for the walls, which at the moment were decorated with bland seascapes that did little to enliven the place. I wasn't a fussy decorator or much of a housekeeper, but even I had my limits. Though we'd arrived only moments ago, I knew we could be here a long time; like it or not, for now we'd have to make this our home.

"Three bedrooms," Jasmine said, "and they brought in a crib so you're all set. There's food in the fridge so you can lay low before we clear you to go out—when and where, we'll let you know."

Mac came in, lugging suitcases, and set them down at the foot of the stairs with a heavy *thunk*. "Not bad," he said, glancing around.

"I'll be in touch." Jasmine headed to the door.

"You're leaving?" Without meaning to, I'd sounded like a disgruntled child, which earned a disappointed glance from my mother. I was tired and angry and scared . . . but so was everyone. "I'm sorry."

"Maybe we can get Ben back into his nap." Mac put his arm around me and his warmth infiltrated the jacket I had yet to remove. "And take a nap ourselves."

"That's a good idea," Mom agreed, opening the fridge, peering in to inspect its contents.

"You're taking the car?" Mac asked Jasmine.

"You won't need it. In a couple days someone will come by with a car if we decide it's okay. Meanwhile there's a book over there about Shore Haven"—she pointed to a blue three-ring binder on the counter—"telling you about amenities and whatnot." She had been here and done this before, that was clear.

While Mom took Ben upstairs to get him acquainted with his new room and hopefully lull him back to sleep—I heard her singsong voice as she placed his favorite stuffed animals and toys around their "new home"—Mac and I found the master bedroom suite. More white: sheets, duvet, rugs, curtains, sinks, tiles, towels. It was certainly clean here, there was no doubting that. We kicked off our shoes, stripped off our pants, and got under the covers to warm each other up.

"What just happened?" I whispered. "My head's still spinning."

"Ana and her damned purple dahlias." Mac rolled onto his back and rubbed at his tattoo. "I swear, as soon as this is over, I'm going to have this thing removed."

"Now that I know its origin, I'm surprised you haven't already."

He turned onto his side to face me. "I got used to it. It stopped having anything to do with her until last summer. All her guys have the same tattoo."

"I noticed."

Mac shook his head. "Talk about youthful folly. There was this Dutch tattoo guy in Playa, I'm talking twenty-five years ago when it was a backwater town, and this guy—I can't remember his name—was doing tattoos for five bucks. I chose a dahlia because it was Ana's favorite flower and it was the national flower of Mexico. What an idiot. I was so busy rebelling I didn't even think about how permanent a tattoo was."

"Why right here?" I touched the faded lavender dahlia.

"Ana chose that spot."

"But why?"

"Who knows? She was sixteen."

"Mac, you won't go back there, will you?"

A shadow seemed to darken his face; but the shades were drawn on our bedroom window and if the sun had shifted, we didn't see it.

"I love you," I said, my finger tracing its way from his collarbone up his throat to land on his lips.

He kissed my fingertip. "I love you, too."

After that we held each other in silence and gradually drifted off to sleep.

Mac and my mother cooked dinner together, moving like shifting puzzle pieces in the galley kitchen, while I hung out in the living area with Ben. Seated on the floor with a big pad of paper and fat washable markers scattered atop the coffee table, I drew stick figures in various poses and

Ben scribbled in what I called creative background but was really just filling in empty space. After we stuck our two favorites to the fridge with magnets, I began to see how what I had already started calling the White Palace would incrementally become disordered enough to feel like home.

Whoever had prepared the condo for us had been thorough enough to have provided not just the crib but a high chair. Ben loved the little white sheep dancing across the blue background of the cushioned seat and kept twisting to get a better look, thereby dripping bits of mashed potatoes onto the rug.

"Oh, he's making a mess," Mom fussed, a guest in a stranger's home.

"At least it's white," I said.

Mac laughed. "Maybe we should stick to an all-white diet so we don't stain anything."

"Let's see," Mom thought aloud, "potatoes, cauliflower, egg whites, cream of wheat, oatmeal—"

"Vanilla ice cream," I added. "Marshmallows, whipped cream, milk, rice, cheese."

"White bread," Mac jumped in, "fish, mayonnaise, scallops, tofu, yogurt."

"It could be done," Mom said, glancing around. "But let's not."

"I think we could just go on and on here at the White Palace, couldn't we?" I reached for Mac's hand across the table. "It would be kind of simple."

Mac smiled, but it was forced. "Ben's going to grow up; he'll have to go to school."

"We could homeschool."

"Karin, you're too impatient," Mom said. "I can't imagine you educating a child hour by hour, day by day, month by month. It isn't realistic."

"But if we had to—"

"They're going to find Ana," Mac said, "and put an end to this. Don't worry. *They will*." He was trying so hard to convince himself that he sent a tremor of uncertainty through me.

"She could elude the DEA and the Mexican police for years." Mom looked from me to Mac. "Couldn't she? It's been done before."

That was true: Ana was tough and wily. "She has a vast support system," I said.

"But that's her weakness," Mac argued. "There's so much money involved, and drugs, and people more addicted to those drugs than they are to serving Ana. Someone's going to turn her in—it's just a matter of who and when."

"As long as it isn't *you*," I said, squeezing his hand.

He squeezed my hand in return, and any uncertainty I felt about him vanished. Ana was the wild card, not Mac; he would have to be crazy to return to that perilous place, even for the sake of his child. Diego was an adult, after all, and he had grown up in his mother's world; he would know how to defend himself. The more I considered it, carrying the thought with me that night as I lay in bed (unable to sleep thanks to our midday nap), the more confident I became that if Diego was half the man his father was, and if he possessed half the cunning of his mother, he would be just fine.

Eventually, lulled by the sound of Mac's rhythmic breathing beside me and the sensation that we were at last together and if not safe then safe enough, I fell deeply, contentedly asleep.

And I dreamed of them: Mac and Diego, father and son, as they might have been twenty years ago had they known of each other's existence. A white man of Irish descent and his half-Mexican little boy, walking hand in hand on a beach that morphed into a carousel that morphed into a classroom, into a tree house, into a canoe, into a swim in the shallow water of the beach where it all began—talking, laughing, playing the way any father and son did just because they were pleased to be together.

Then the man and the boy rested together on a towel on the sand.

The man kissed the boy on his forehead, wishing him sweet dreams.

And I felt the kiss on my own forehead, and heard the man faintly whisper, "Good-bye."

CHAPTER 16

I woke up with a start, my heart pounding, my skin clammy, and kicked off the thick duvet. The room was pitch dark. A glance at the clock told me that it was just past five A.M. Breathing deeply, calming myself, I looked around and saw that Mac wasn't there. He must have gotten up to nurse his conflict about Diego again; as I pulled on my robe and found my slippers, I knew that's why I had been dreaming about them: Mac had not completely made up his mind.

As I came down the stairs I saw him stretched out on the couch, huddled under a blanket. But as I got closer, something was different; the body shape was wrong, too curvy, and I was sure Mac had never worn a pair of fuchsia socks in his life.

I grabbed the bottom edge of the blanket and flung it off.

"Karin . . . what time is it?" Jasmine was suddenly awake and disoriented.

"What are you doing here?"

She rubbed her eyes. Took a breath. "He didn't tell you?"

"Where is he?"

She looked at her watch. "By now he's halfway to Mexico."

"Fuck!"

"You wanna wake your kid and your mother with that?"

"Why are you here?"

"Diego called him—"

"When? I didn't hear his phone ring."

"Late afternoon. Maybe he had his phone on vibrate or something. He got a message from Diego saying he was in deep shit and when he tried to call back, he couldn't get through. Then he called me. He needed the car."

My brain turned over the hours since she had left us here; she should have been back in New York long before we went to bed. Before Mac snuck away.

"So you never left the area? You waited so he could sneak out in the middle of the night?"

She didn't answer, which *was* the answer. Once again they had colluded, dividing our family, sending Mac head-on into danger. I didn't know who I was angrier at.

"Is he working for you guys again?"

"Listen, he was gonna go back to Mexico anyway. I guess when he heard that message it made up his mind. He was really upset, he—"

I picked up a beige and white couch pillow and flung it at her head.

"So now *he'll* get killed! And we're right back where we started!"

"You don't know that."

"It would have been better to send *anyone* other than him! Ana knows him—they all know him."

"Yeah, but they don't know he was working for us."

"You don't think they figured that out by now? She sent flowers again—she threatened us."

She sighed—another nonverbal answer.

"Get out."

"Karin, it's still dark. I don't have a car. I can't—"

"*Get out*." I threw another pillow. This time, she ducked.

"All right."

She got up and shoved her feet into her cowboy boots. Grabbed her coat from where she had flung it over a chair and made it through the front door as a third pillow sailed at her.

Just then, Ben issued his morning cry.

Mom called out from her room, "Karin?"

And my cell phone rang.

Thinking, hoping, it would be Mac—calling to recant his determination to save a grown man he hardly knew; his single-minded, self-destructive impulse to do the right thing at all costs even when the costs were so high—I ran to my purse, dumped its contents onto the living room floor, and rooted for the phone. Flipped it open to see who it was.

Unknown caller. That pitiless cipher.

My mind flashed back to the peaceful summer morning almost six months ago, the innocent beginning of a pivotal day when the phone rang—and an unforeseen door opened onto a realm of terrible danger.

I stared at the phone, still thick-headed from the dream, distraught over Mac's departure, angry at Jasmine and bewildered once again about the true tenor of her friendship. Shaking. Trying to understand exactly what was happening. Who I should talk to. What I should do.

I didn't want to answer it.

But that was not an option.

"Hello?"

"*Karin*—"

"Billy?"

"What the hell?"

"Excuse me?"

"Jazz just called me. Told me you gave her an earful. She's doing her job—you remember what that's like?"

"There are other ways to go about it, Billy. For example: sending someone else to Mexico. For example: *not* colluding with my husband behind my back."

"You've got to understand—"

"That Mac's guilt about Diego was a really good handle to get him back into the game?"

"Not exactly—"

"I'm not stupid; I know how it works."

"He has a unique role—"

"*He's a walking target.*"

"Just the word that he's back is going to draw her out. They'll get her before she can sneeze."

"You're deluded, you know that?"

"You're too emotional, Karin. You always have been."

"Just how well do you think you know me, Billy? I mean, *really*? Because you're close to Mac you think you know me?"

"I know you well enough. I know you think your own way and do what you want."

"As opposed to abandoning my humanity and becoming a job? Like you, Billy? How old are you—forty-five? Single, no kids . . . I've never even seen you with a girlfriend until Jasmine."

"You're hitting below the belt there."

"But you don't understand how much is at stake when someone has a family. When he loves people who love him. When there's a young child whose whole existence, his entire life, will be damaged irreparably because he never knew his father."

"You describing Ben or Diego? Because I'll tell you, in Mac's head, you'd be talking about both of them. He made an impossible choice. He gambled he could slip in and out, help Diego, get back to Ben."

"But it's not Atlantic City—it's Russian roulette with a bullet in more than one chamber. If I never see him again—"

"Cut it out, Karin."

"If I never seen him again I'll hold you and Jasmine—"

"I said cut it out. You want to know what you accomplished just now? You made Jasmine feel like the world's biggest piece of shit—"

"She feels nothing. She's an agent twenty-four/seven—"

"You're wrong. She's a woman with feelings and *I love her*. And now she's on her way to Mexico to get Mac back *for you* because she's even more pigheaded than you are if that's actually possible."

"What do you mean?"

"I mean what I say, Karin. *I mean what I say*."

"Who are you talking to?" Mom came down the stairs, holding Ben in one arm and the banister in her opposite hand. She looked halfway between sleepy and alarmed.

"That was Billy. He hung up on me." The cell phone in my hand felt radioactive. Actually hot. I dropped it into my purse and then item by item put everything else back in, my mind spinning. What had I done?

Mom put Ben down and he tottered over to the television set, on a low stand facing the couch, and pressed every button until it came on. I picked him up and kissed his cheek. Found a cartoon and positioned him on the couch.

"I have to go out," I told my mother, who was standing at the kitchen sink, filling the kettle.

"Now?"

Flipping through the pages of the blue binder on the counter, I found the number for a taxi service. Dialed.

"I need a cab to pick me up at Shore Haven in Brewster as soon as possible," I told the dispatcher.

"Going to?"

"Where's the nearest airport?"

"That'd be Hyannis. Matter of fact, we just ran someone over there from Shore Haven."

Jasmine.

"Can someone come right now?"

"About fifteen minutes."

"I'll be ready."

I hung up the kitchen phone to find Mom staring at me. "Here we go again," she said. "You do realize you have a child?"

"How could you ask me that?"

"Where's Mac?"

"Mexico."

She looked stunned and immediately tears gathered in her eyes. She shook her head and said to herself, "No, I will not." And then to me: "Do what you have to, Karin. Ben and I will be fine."

By the time my taxi pulled around the rotary in front of the small, single-story airport, nearly an hour had been lost since Jasmine left the condo—since I had forced her to leave. Half a dozen cars were parked at meters directly in front of the airport but otherwise the place felt deserted at not yet seven o'clock on a frigid winter morning. I pushed through the glass doors into a large reception area with a few ticketing counters for small airlines, seats clustered together for waiting passengers, and a home-style coffee shop off to the right. The air inside was warmer than outside, but only just.

Two middle-aged women in turtlenecks and navy-blue blazers with airline pins on their lapels chatted behind one of the counters; both were white with short puffy hair, but one's was dyed red while the other had let hers go gray. They were the only people around. I rushed over to them.

"Excuse me, have any flights just left?"

"Where you going, honey?" Gray asked me.

"I'm looking for a friend—" Calling Jasmine my friend felt half truth and half lie, a discrepancy that pained me; I still hardly knew who she was but I was clear on one thing: My vehemence toward her had been a misfire. "— who probably got here about half an hour ago. She's about thirty, Hispanic, with long hair, very pretty."

"Oh, sure—cute gal. Flew out to Boston."

My forehead grew damp despite the cold. "When did she leave?"

"That'd be me," Red said, walking out from behind the counter and positioning herself behind a different airline's counter twenty feet away. She typed daintily on her computer's keyboard and tapped the screen with a long fingernail until she found the flight she sought. "Went out on the six twenty-five to Logan."

I glanced at a digital clock on the wall midway behind both counters: six forty-seven.

"When does it arrive?"

"Seven-forty."

"Is there another flight out to Logan?"

Both women looked it up on their airlines.

"Not until eleven-fifty," Red said.

"That beats me at twelve noon."

"Could you find something out for me, please? On all the airlines flying out of Logan this morning, are there any flights to Mexico?"

"Where?" Gray asked.

I didn't know exactly where La Huacana was but maybe they could help me. "It's a small town in southwest Mexico . . . La Huacana. Can you find out what the major airports are near there?"

Keyboards clacked and then Red answered: "Okay, well, you've got flights out of Logan to Morelia and Guadalajara, but not too many, and nothing direct. Still, there's availability and you *could* get there today if you really wanted to. Maybe not today but tonight—it's a long trip with waits at each connection."

"What I wouldn't give to be in Mexico right now," Gray said.

"You and me both." Red smiled. "If you'd like to book a connecting flight from here to Logan to one of those airports, we can certainly help you."

"I'm not sure—thank you." I offered the ladies a smile, or something I thought was a smile but may have been more of a grimace based on the way Gray's eyebrows shot up. Then I went to sit in the waiting area and think this through.

Jasmine would be landing in less than an hour. By the time I could get to Logan airport, if she was still determined to go to Mexico—and if I was stubborn by the foot, she was stubborn by the yard—she would be long gone. I wasn't even sure if she'd be flying into Morelia or Guadalajara or someplace else. If she connected with one of the DEA surveillance planes, she could land almost anywhere. I took two deep breaths, tried to slow my pulse. And then dialed Fred Miller at the DEA in the hope he started his day very early.

He didn't.

I tried reaching Hyo, Fred's partner, but he also wasn't in yet.

Finally I wandered into the coffee shop where I was one of two customers; the other was a man wearing a blue jumpsuit with *Bill* embroidered under one shoulder. His fingernails were etched in grease and as he drank his coffee and finished his Danish, his eyes kept flitting to his watch.

I sat at a small round table and ordered coffee, eggs, and toast. But I couldn't eat much. I felt disoriented, thwarted. What, exactly, was my plan? My mother's words began to ring in my mind: *You do realize you have a child?*

I had a child, a beloved son, Ben. Just as I once had a beloved daughter, Cece. Having a child was nothing to take for granted; their very existence was a fragile sprout. Cece's had been destroyed so easily. I remembered the last time I saw her, a quick kiss and hug before handing her back to Jackson; how I'd tossed off "See you guys tonight" and then headed out to work, not imagining that I would never see either one of them again.

And this morning, when I ran out to the taxi, I didn't even say good-bye to Ben. "See you guys later," I'd said to my mother. And left.

Sitting there over my cold eggs, soggy toast, and coffee whose steam had already dissipated into the air, I felt queasy.

Was I really planning to chase Jasmine to Boston? Hunt for Mac in Mexico? Fly straight into the heart of darkness? *And risk leaving Ben an orphan?*

How could I?

The longer I considered my options, the more insupportable leaving became.

I tried Fred's and Hyo's numbers every five minutes. At just past eight, Fred answered.

"It's Karin Schaeffer."

"And you're calling about Special Agent Alvarez." He sounded aloof; he was annoyed that I was interfering in agency business, I could tell. But for me it was personal and urgent. And I had never been one to back away from boundaries.

"She's on her way to Mexico," I said.

"Umm hmm."

"I know you're not going to tell me her plans."

"Umm hmm."

"But I was hoping you could tell me how she's getting there."

"I can tell you she isn't walking."

"Is she on a commercial flight?"

Pause. Deliberation. "No."

Which told me everything I needed to know: The moment Jasmine landed at Logan, she would be whisked onto a private surveillance plane and scuttled into the air, beyond any possibility that I could reach her in time to change her mind about going.

But I had already decided not to try, anyway, because of Ben. He was my priority. If I followed another knee-jerk reaction and ended up back in the eye of the storm with Mac and Jasmine, I would be doing exactly what I had warned Mac not to do. I would be abandoning my child. It would make me a hypocrite and worse: a bad mother.

Mac had made his choice. It pained me, and shook my trust in him, but there was nothing I could do to change his mind at this point. I now had to make my own choice, the one that made sense to me.

I had been a soldier.

A cop.

A detective.

Twice a wife; once a widow.

And twice a mother . . . with one child still living. That much I knew for sure.

I was not going to run to Mexico now—even with good cause—and leave my Ben without a mother for a day, a week, or possibly a lifetime.

They said that a bird in hand was better than two in the bush.

I said that a bird in hand was better than anything.

CHAPTER 17

The grounds at Shore Haven seemed to have been designed so that you could stroll or jog or bike and never arrive anywhere. You'd pass something—a café or a shop on a limited schedule, a covered pool, the ice-etched gazebo—but if you didn't actively choose to enter you would instead loop endlessly along a curvy web of paths. That one conceit was the perfect distraction for our stay here: We could walk and walk and walk, letting time ease past us, and always end up back at the White Palace, which we quickly took to calling home.

Before we bundled up and struck out for our first walk, though, we consulted our new bible, the three-ring binder in the kitchen, which delineated security boundaries and everything else. That binder—the more you read it, the more it declared itself as not just the kind of friendly document you'd find at a vacation rental but a security

briefing issued by a federal agency. It had a sheen of
friendliness, but if you picked beneath the words and
between the sentences there was a deeper meaning, and it
always came down to *caution*.

And just as meaning hovered between the words in the
binder, and time formed itself around the curvature of the
development's walkways, we molded ourselves to the
situation. We were neither prisoners nor witnesses but
potential victims being sheltered from a distinct threat.
*Ana was out to get us. And she would, if they didn't get her
first.* It was like a paranoid thought that surfaces in a dream
and, upon waking and contemplating its strangeness, you
discover a poignant seed of truth. Whenever Mom or I
suffered a moment of bewilderment, looked at the other
and said, "What are we doing here?" the coded answer
was always "Mexico." Everything came down to that now.
The dahlias had promised us that it wasn't a matter of *if*
but *when* and *how*. We knew that until Ana was captured
she would be lurking everywhere, aiming for us.

As for my feelings about Mac's decision, his choice,
I swung between resentment and understanding. My
emotions about him felt like the roads of Shore Haven:
looping in every direction, never arriving exactly anywhere.
My mother seemed to understand this instinctively and we
both avoided the subject. We were here, together, sharing
our *situation* and would do the best we could with it.

On our second day without Mac, out walking in the

morning, we ran into Doug, the groundskeeper. He was slowly driving a truck that spewed crystals onto the road. When he saw us, he stopped and got out, smiling. He was dressed exactly as when we'd first met him, in jeans and his puffy black jacket, without a hat to protect against the bitter cold. As before, his work boots were unlaced; it was a wonder they stayed on his feet at all. The tops of his ears were bright red.

"Hello ladies!"

I wondered if he'd forgotten our names, the aliases that felt like ill-fitting clothes, or if he knew we weren't actually Joan, Cornelia, and Timmy.

"Doug," Mom said, "why are you salting the roads? You keep them perfectly dry . . . we must have walked every inch and haven't seen any ice at all."

"It's CMA—calcium magnesium acetate—helps stop new ice before it takes hold. The weather here . . . well, humidity and cold make for the kind of slick ice that brings you down before you see it. How are you ladies holding up?"

Mom and I both shrugged, smiled. What could we say? Doug probably had no idea what we were doing here or who we really were.

"We're having a peaceful week," Mom said, as if we'd be packing up and leaving come Sunday.

"Well." Doug clapped his bare hands into the frozen steam emitted by that single word. "I promised this young man here a look at the carousel, now, didn't I?" He smiled at Ben, who didn't understand why he was suddenly the focus of attention but smiled in return, anyway.

"He'd like that," I said.

We folded the stroller into the back of the truck and crowded into the front with Doug. I held Ben tightly on my lap as we bounced off the road and drove across the rutted frozen ground, passing the gazebo and stopping by the large shed. We got out and followed Doug to a pair of loosely chained front doors. He took a big key ring out of his pocket, found the one he wanted, and unlocked the padlock. The heavy chain rattled as he pulled it out and tossed it to the ground behind us. He dropped the padlock on the metal coil and pulled open the first door and then the next.

We stood there, watching, as darkness spilled out of the shed. Thin winter light penetrated the interior gloom until the carousel materialized, as if magically, complete with horses and sleighs all freshly painted in an eighteenth-century palette—rich cream, sky blue, lemon yellow, earthy green, brown so dark it was almost black.

"It's beautiful," I said.

"Just gorgeous," Mom echoed.

Ben didn't comment; he ran right in.

"Hold it now!" Doug went after him and we followed. I grabbed Ben and lifted him onto my hip. "It's dark in here so you better hang on to him—there isn't a light because this is just a storage shed. We take it down board by board in springtime." He crossed the circular platform, ducked between two horses, and stood in the center of the carousel. "Here we go. Hang on to your hats."

With the turn of a switch, Doug launched the carousel. Cheerful tinny music started with a jolt as the circle turned and some of the horses bobbed up and down on their poles. We stood there, mesmerized, watching horses and sleighs—and now I saw that there was also a cat and a frog—rotate through the shadows. Laughing, Ben struggled to get down.

"Wait," I said, but he fought harder.

"Want."

"Could he have a ride?" I called to Doug.

The carousel whined to a stop. "The question is"—Doug's voice rang through the residual mechanical hum—"how could he *not* have a ride? Choose your horse!"

I settled on the back of a white stallion with a blue mane and flashing black eyes, strapping Ben firmly onto my lap. Mom sat beside us on a stationary horse: pink with green hooves and a white saddle.

"Ready?" Doug called.

"Ready!"

And we were off.

Greedy for amusement, we took five rides and, by the time all was said and done, consumed over an hour of Doug's time. Mom, Ben, and I were all pink-cheeked, a

little breathless, and grateful as we stood back and watched
Doug close the doors, hiding the treasure I suspected
would tempt us—Ben, especially—whenever we walked
this way.

"Thank you." I shook Doug's hand. "That was great."

Mom beamed, and Doug seemed to blush a little bit.

"It was my pleasure," he said, and I believed that it really
had been. "Next time this little guy here wants a ride, find
me."

"We will."

We piled back into the truck and Doug dropped us
off pretty much where he'd found us. We watched him
drive slowly along, dropping CMA on the road, until he
disappeared from sight.

The carousel had been without a doubt our high point,
and the next day when we took our walk we kept a lookout
for Doug but didn't see him. Nor did we see him the day
after that.

When we weren't out walking, we were home playing
games with Ben, or cooking and eating, or trolling the
Internet for news. My searches always started with Ana
Maria Soliz, then expanded to Soliz Enterprises, Diego
Soliz, La Huacana, Playa del Carmen, Cancun, and anything
else I could think of that might net some information about
what was going on down there. I stopped calling Fred
Miller and Hyo Park at the DEA, neither of whom would
tell me anything. Bottom line: I knew that if something

happened, I would somehow find out. So I relied on what I could discover online or through the media, which so far was a big nothing.

Then, on our fourth night at Shore Haven—our third without Mac—as I came down the stairs after putting Ben to bed at just past seven o'clock, Mom stood up from the couch and pointed the DVR's remote control at the set like a magic wand. She had paused a CNN newscaster mid-word and mid-blink; his frozen, hooded eyes and half-opened mouth made him look as if he was yawning.

"Karin, your cell phone rang while you were upstairs. But first, *look at this*."

I stood beside her and she pressed play.

"Earlier today in Mexico's Michoacán state, outside the village of La Huacana, police arrested a real estate mogul believed to be a major queenpin in the drug wars that have gripped that country for some time now."

A photograph filled the screen and my pulse leaped: There was Ana, smiling, dressed in a white sequined gown that hugged her body and had a neckline that plunged almost to her navel.

"Ana Maria Soliz, seen here at a fund-raiser for a Mexican politician, has long eluded international authorities who have sought to curtail her expanding grip on a wide swath of Mexico reaching from Michoacán into the Yucatan peninsula where she was born and where she has been expanding her real estate holdings along the so-called Mayan Riviera. She is believed to use drug money to fuel her real estate empire. While she is thought to be responsible for dozens of drug-related deaths, she was arrested today specifically for murders committed on American soil, which authorities say will complicate her indictment but at the same time offers the best chance of putting her away for a very long time. CNN was unable to confirm whether an indictment will be pursued in Mexico or the United States. Ms. Soliz was arrested along with eleven associates, and more are being sought."

The newscaster moved on to the next story.

My heart was pounding so hard I could hear it.

"Do they mean Hugh and Aileen?" Mom asked.

"I don't know. And they didn't mention Mac or Jasmine."

"Listen to your message."

I found my cell phone; there were two messages, one from Fred and one from Billy.

"Good news, Karin!" Fred. "Ana Maria Soliz was arrested. I thought you'd like to hear it from me."

And from Billy: "They got her! Ana's in custody! No word yet on Mac or Jazz. Call me."

I called Fred first. He answered my first question before I asked it.

"No reports yet on your husband or Special Agent Alvarez."

"What about Diego Soliz?"

"Ana Maria's son." A note of disapproval in Fred's tone.

"And Mac's son."

"No word. But you understand, if he's found, he'll be arrested like his mother. We view him as her partner, almost her equal."

"Of course." But my heart sank, as if my emotions were channeling Mac's.

Mac. Where was he?

"Who found her?" I asked. "How?"

"I'm sorry, but I can't discuss that. The investigation is still ongoing."

That stopped me cold. It meant they had swooped in to get Ana but loose ends were still flapping—significant loose ends. Jasmine was a federal agent and they were not typically abandoned on the job, even if the main goal had been met. Did Mac qualify as a federal agent, or was he a mercenary, the kind of loose end you cut away?

I called Billy immediately after that.

"Miller won't tell me anything about Mac or Jasmine."

"Me neither."

"How did they find Ana?"

"Don't know, but they did, and that's really good news. That means they can start to unwind this. So listen, I was thinking . . . when they give the word that you guys can go home, I'd like to come and get you."

Tears welled up and I wiped them away. We hadn't spoken since our argument on the phone; his offer was not just kind but conciliatory. "Are you sure? It's a long drive."

"Positive."

"That would be nice."

"So let's keep each other posted."

"Will do."

From there the night descended into a muddle of hope and fear.

Ana was caught!

Mac and Jasmine were missing . . .

Ana couldn't get us now!

Mac could be dead . . .

Jasmine could be dead . . .

Had they succeeded or failed? Could death be counted as a measure of success? Not for me. The DEA had scored a major win, and if Mac or Jasmine *had* been killed in the line of duty it would be chalked up as collateral damage. I shook that cold thought out of my head.

We also didn't know if Ana's capture meant we would be free to go home.

Mom and I drank coffee, forcing ourselves to stay up late so we could be ready for anything. News trickled onto the Internet but nothing substantially different from what CNN had reported and no news of Mac, Jasmine, or Diego. It was a terrible silence filled with echoes that no amount of caffeinated vigilance could drive away. I kept my phone in my pocket, set to loud *and* vibrate so I wouldn't miss an important call. *The* important call that didn't come and didn't come and didn't come . . .

I must have fallen asleep on the couch because there I was, sprawled out with one leg hanging off, when my phone came alive. My eyes opened to a living room bright with morning. I pulled my phone out of my pocket and saw that Fred Miller was calling. Seeing his name triggered a frisson of dread.

"Any news?" was my hello.

"No. But I know you'll be wondering if you're cleared to go home."

"Are we?"

"Not yet. I'm sorry."

"Why not?"

"We're picking up some chatter. Better safe than sorry."

It was all he said.

Five more days passed; we had now spent a week and a half at the White Palace. We still hadn't been cleared to leave the grounds, but we'd started to receive mail under our new names, mostly catalogs and sales flyers marketed to a generic American family. Nothing I wanted. Still, each piece of mail felt oddly significant, like a small transition inching us toward the possibility that we could be here indefinitely. That we might actually be forgotten and hover for months or even years in our strange white bubble. I realized we were settling in when I went online and ordered a bed railing for Ben, having decided that it was time to transition him into a twin bed since he now routinely fell in the act of climbing out of his crib. I also ordered a new hat for my mother to match her green scarf, and a two pairs of warm socks for myself. A few days later, a phone call from Mike notified me that something had arrived.

"You've got a package, Mrs. Peltrie," he said before we lost the connection, which I had been told happened here occasionally when the temperatures were very low.

Mom had just maneuvered Ben into his jacket, boots, hat, and mittens—the whole winter ensemble whose confinement my son resisted—and was buckling him into the stroller.

"Something came," I told Mom. "I hope it's the bed railing. Mind if I go down to the guard station and see?"

"Why don't you catch up with us when you're done?" She zipped up her jacket. "I don't want to go through all that again."

"See you in a few minutes."

She headed out the door and I slipped into my boots and coat. I saw them stroll off in the direction of the carousel—Mom singing, Ben kicking his feet. Always, now, we started our walks in the hope that today would be our lucky day even if that only meant a ride on the carousel, not what we truly hoped for: the return of Mac and the end of our time at Shore Haven. Every day you hoped today was the day, and took what you got.

I headed the opposite way, toward the guard station. After a few minutes I was alone on the long wooded road, puffs of icy breath preceding me as I walked and walked. It was so quiet that every sound was amplified: my steps crunching on twigs, dead leaves, and pebbles that had strayed onto the road. My breath moving through my body. Even my thoughts seemed louder: of Mac, whether we would ever see each other again; of the isolation of this place, its stern beauty and loneliness; of the bed railing that would allow Ben a new measure of freedom and me a new measure of both worry and relief. Time moved. Things changed. You changed with them because you had little choice.

I heard something and stopped walking. Listened: music in the distance behind me. I pulled my hat off one ear and leaned into the sound. It was the carousel. My heart swelled with the knowledge that Mom and Ben had stumbled into Doug.

Now I walked faster, wanting to reach the guard station, get the package, and make my way to the carousel before they finished. If it *was* the railing, and the box was too big for me to handle alone, then Doug could drive us down, put the box into his truck, and take us home.

Through the web of bare trees I saw the hulking brown UPS truck drive slowly up an alternate road used for commercial deliveries to Shore Haven. One of the staff must have ordered something, too.

A large box was sitting on the ground just outside the door of the guard station.

"Mike, I'm here!"

He didn't respond. I stopped to look at the box: There was no return address. And something seemed odd about the way the address was written. It wasn't just the strangeness of seeing myself addressed as Joan Peltrie; it was something else. The box was the wrong shape for a bed railing, but I hadn't ordered anything else that was large. There was no UPS label, and none of the scrawls or stamps that indicated it had gone through the standard delivery process. And the handwriting itself . . . I stooped to get a closer look . . . *It looked just like Mac's.*

"Mike?"

The quiet suddenly felt thick, heavy. I stepped into the booth that was large enough for two people and a desk. It was empty. Through the small side window, I saw something that looked like the toe of a shoe.

I hurried outside and around to the other side of the booth.

It was a black shoe, double-tied, at the end of a leg that was Mike's . . . and there was Mike, flopped on his side. I crouched beside him. He looked at me with panic-bright eyes.

"What happened?" I asked him.

His eyes dulled, seemed to freeze, and his pupils dilated to large dark saucers. It was a sign I recognized from too many crime scenes, too many corpses; I had looked into dead eyes before, but no one's life had ever drained away in front of me.

"*Mike*," I whispered.

And then I saw the blood oozing from a wound behind his right ear.

I twisted around and closed my eyes, forcing back an impulse to vomit. Swallowing, I stood up and reached into my pocket for my cell phone: It wasn't there; I must have left it at the condo. There was a phone in the guard station I could use to call 911.

But as soon as I stepped around the guard station, I saw the box and remembered the UPS truck snaking its way up the alternate road.

And then I heard the music from the carousel.

A map appeared in my mind: how the other road was a shortcut to the part of the grounds where most of the development's commercial and social life took place—the restaurant, the café, the pools, the gazebo.

The carousel.

The music now seemed to saw through the cold air, slicing open a path for me to follow. Revealing an imperative. Because I knew . . .

. . . that the person who had delivered the box had also killed Mike.

. . . that this person was now driving into Shore Haven.

. . . and that he wanted access for a reason.

. . . a purpose.

. . . a goal.

. . . a target.

I needed to call 911.

And I needed to open the box.

But mostly I needed to get to the carousel.

CHAPTER 18

I cut through the woods, hacking branches with my arms as I raced toward the steady trill of the music. The drumbeat of my heart grew louder and faster as I ran until I could hardly hear the music anymore. The sharp rasps of my breath, the banging of my pulse was deafening. I couldn't run fast enough; as in a nightmare, I seemed to move backward, unable to gain any ground.

And then a branch swung back at me after I'd pushed it aside, smacking me hard in the face. Pain fountained from my nose, flooded my brain. I fell backward onto the ground, my head pounding. Salty blood trickled into my mouth. I got up and ducked under the branch and kept going.

And going.

And going.

Until finally I emerged onto the alternate road.

I raced across the road and up a slope of hard earth

at the crest of which I stopped. My nose throbbed with excruciating pain. With the back of my arm I wiped blood off my face.

Down the slope, in the distance, beside the gazebo, sat the big brown truck.

The doors to the carousel's shed were open, spilling music.

I ran, building downhill speed to accelerate myself as the land flattened. As I got closer I saw Ben's stroller sitting empty in a shadow that fell from the gaping mouth of the shed.

Closer still, I saw other things:

The rear door of the UPS truck was slightly open.

The end of my mother's bright green scarf trailed through the cracked-open doors.

One of Doug's muddy work boots lay on its side between the shed and the truck.

I reached the truck first. Whoever had shut the door had meant to lock it but failed; the latch had closed on the outside, instead. I swung open the door. Nestled among disarranged boxes were Mom and Doug, bound and gagged, laid back to back in a manner that was sickeningly familiar: it was just how Diego and Felix had situated me and Mac in the back of the truck in Mexico as they drove us to what was supposed to have been our deaths.

I jumped into the truck and pulled the tape off Mom's mouth.

"Are you okay?"

Her voice shook with urgency: "He has Ben—the carousel!"

I pulled out the knot binding her wrists and then flew out of the truck, propelling myself to the shed where I was swallowed by a shadowy darkness that blinded me for a moment.

Blinking, gasping for breath, *frantic to see*, my eyes began to adjust.

The music played steadily as the carousel turned.

And then Ben rotated out of a shadow into a fragment of light.

"Mommy!"

"Ben!"

"*Mommy. Mommy. Mommy.*" His plaintive voice reaching for me. His expression looked horrified, and for a moment I thought it was because he'd seen my battered, swollen, bloody face. But then I thought again.

He came closer and I stepped toward him—he was on the largest horse, an orange stallion with blue eyes—and in that moment of apprehension I saw not just Ben and the horse but the man who rode the horse and held Ben in his lap.

His eyes were almost as blue as the horse's.

His skin a creamy russet brown.

But in that moment it all seemed to fuse together into a single inextricable being: Ben, the horse that slid up and down its pole, Diego.

"Give me my son. That's all I want. *Just give me my son.*"

As the carousel revolved them closer to me, Ben reached and cried. Diego's mouth lifted into a grin. In a wedge of light I saw that one of his hands gripped Ben's middle. The other hand held a gun.

"*Why are you here? What do you want?*"

"I felt it was time to meet my brother."

As the carousel drew them away, Ben disappeared behind Diego's back. The uniform he had stolen was too small and his thighs in the tight pants threatened to rupture around the body of the horse. The horse suddenly looked fragile, as if it would shatter any moment.

I ran alongside the carousel.

"Please. *Please*. Just give me Ben. Hand him to me. And I'll go."

In turning to look at me, Diego kicked the side of the horse and nearly lost his balance.

"Ben!"

"Mommy!"

"He's just a child—*please*."

Diego steadied himself, gripping Ben too tightly. My baby started to cry.

"My life was without a brother or a sister or a father—and now it is without a mother. I am alone. Why should I be alone?"

"You're not alone."

"I have much to share."

"Please give him to me."

"I will share it with my brother—my protégé."

A bundle of cords running from the carousel to the side of the shed caught my foot and I crashed forward, landing facedown on the ground, the impact igniting a blast of pain to my nose. The carousel kept moving at its steady pace; the music, playing. I pushed myself up and hurried forward but the carousel had moved on. Gyrating shadows made it difficult to find the blue and orange horse, the man, my boy.

"Ben?"

"*Mommy.*"

Ben twisted sharply, taking Diego by surprise, and I saw it in slow motion as it started to happen: the whole piece of them, the man-boy unit tilting heavily off the horse, Diego's opposite arm suddenly reaching for the pole.

The gun flying out of his hand. Bouncing off the moving platform. The *thunk* of it landing on hard-packed dirt.

And then it was steady again, the heartless centaur, riding forward.

I dropped to the ground and crawled through a shifting latticework of shadows to find the gun. Hoping I hadn't imagined it falling right . . . *here*.

My hand gripped the handle as, shaking, I got to my feet and shouted, "Stop! Right now! Give him to me!"

"You think you can have everything? The father, the son? Greedy woman—you will have *nothing*."

The hysteria of his voice—powerless, gunless—reached me before the words made sense and before I saw them emerge into a beam of gray light from the open door. It was as if they had stepped into a spotlight: Diego, practically standing astride the horse now, holding Ben high in both hands as if about to throw him.

"No! *Don't!*"

With the gun aimed at Diego's chest, I moved toward them, waiting, *waiting*, until I was close enough to shoot him and catch Ben at the same time.

Aware that in shooting Diego I could be killing Mac's other son.

Aware that, if Mac was still alive, this could end our marriage.

Aware of the risk, of the price, I would pay for my child's life.

And aware that at this moment, there was no chance of compromise.

"*Mommy!*"

Carefully, slowly, maintaining my aim on the moving target of Diego's heart, I edged closer. Erasing the distance between us. Until Ben was close enough. And then I would shoot.

"I'll give you one more chance!" My voice shook. But my hands, my aim, remained steady.

"You—think—you—can—have—*everything*."

Almost close enough now to shoot Diego and catch Ben—*but not yet*.

And then Diego did something I hadn't anticipated, yanking Ben out of the air and pressing my little boy to his chest like a shield.

A voice boomed: "*Now—hit his leg!*"

I squeezed the trigger and a shot roared through the shed. Diego crumpled forward.

And Ben, *my Ben*, dropped like a weight into nothingness.

I was almost close enough to catch him.

But *almost* wasn't good enough to bridge an impossible distance.

I didn't hear him fall.

But he must have fallen; gravity demanded it.

I knew I would live and die in this moment for the rest of my life.

Knew it, as I ran through shadows and light.

I couldn't remember shooting the gun. But obviously I had. I had *seen* Diego move Ben in front of him, I had *known* my strategy would no longer work—and I had pulled the trigger anyway.

Even as I ran to Ben my mind dissected my fatal error: a moment's miscalculation, a body shifted in space, an action occurring before comprehension. And in an instant, everything was over.

A dark blot in a deep shadow drew my eye and I crawled

to it. Fearing Diego would jump off his horse and stop me. Crawling faster.

"Ben? I'm coming."

"*Mommy*."

It was as if his voice awakened me; and I saw him: cradled, on the ground, in his father's arms.

I stopped. Blinked. And still saw them: Ben, safe; Mac, returned.

Pulling Ben away—feeling his warmth, smelling him, my heart opening to the miracle of what we had just survived—I stood and ran to the door, terrified Diego would come after us, worried Mac wasn't real, uncertain exactly what had just happened and was still happening.

"Karin!" Mac called in the same commanding tone that had ordered me to shoot. "You're safe."

My body stopped but my brain kept going; my eyes swept the dim space like a searchlight. Diego was buckled over the horse, gripping the pole so hard his knuckles were white, blood pouring from the front of his thigh.

"He's not going anywhere," Mac said.

Now I really looked and *saw* him: He was a mess. Dirty and bearded with jaundiced bloodshot eyes.

"Karin!" It was my mother's voice, and then I saw her rushing into the shed with Doug.

So many things crashed through my mind all at once:

Mac was alive.

He had escaped the cartel, fled Mexico.

He was here.

Ben was in my arms, alive and well.

Mom was fine. Doug was fine.

I hadn't killed Diego, or my marriage.

"What happened to your face?" Mom asked.

"Tree branch."

Mac was next to me now, taking Ben out of my shaking arms. "That looks bad, Karin. Let's get you to a hospital."

Mom hovered her fingers in the air an inch from what now felt like the ballooned sausage of my nose, not touching me, understanding the pain would be too great. "Can you see? Your eyes are so swollen and your skin— it's turning green."

Outside, sirens blared. Doors opened and slammed shut. Voices called.

"How did you get here?" I asked Mac. Queasiness crept through me, but I had to know.

"Long story."

"Were you in that box—was that your handwriting?"

Nauseous, dizzy; and then the next thing I knew I was strapped to a gurney in an ambulance and Mac was holding an ice pack to my face.

"Where are we going?"

"Hospital. Shh."

"Where's Ben?"

"With your mother. They're fine."

"What happened in Mexico?"

"Like I said, it's a long story."

"It's the only story I want to hear."

"Can't we just deal with your broken nose right now?"

"What makes you so sure it's broken?"

He looked at me. We both laughed. Pain bolted across my face; I winced, and stopped talking.

CHAPTER 19

Keeping his promise to me, Billy Staples drove up from Brooklyn to personally bring us home. Between the time he'd heard the news and I was released from the hospital with my nose in a splint, he had arrived at the White Palace and helped my mother pack up most of our things. Their ambitious plan had been to leave immediately, get out of here, go home—now that both Ana and Diego were in custody, there was no reason to stay. But when everyone saw my bandaged face and woozy eyes, the plan was revised. We would leave tomorrow.

Billy greeted Mac with a big hug. "Oh, man, it is *good* to see you. I hear you flew out of Mexico in a box. You cheap bastard."

"You know me, can't resist a bargain." Mac chuckled, and then his expression darkened. "Actually, we drove. I got to experience what it was like to *be* the drugs getting smuggled in."

"It's incredible you survived." Mom was standing at the counter stirring mayo into tuna, building sandwiches. The kettle was on behind her and she had the teapot out.

"They took me out every so often, gave me some food and water, let me stretch my legs. Then this kid, this teenager they had working for them—a Mexican American, he didn't have an accent, that's why I figured they were bringing me across the border, that's why I felt the tiniest ray of hope—this kid would shoot me up"—his gaze dropped to the floor when he said that, knowing how disturbed we'd all feel to hear it—"and they'd stick me back in the box. What can I say? It was a nightmare. But I'm here. I survived."

"Sounds like they went to some trouble to keep you alive," Billy said.

"More like they went to some trouble to not kill me, to keep me semialive, or alive enough. Diego hadn't decided what to do with me yet."

"That's one scary case of ambivalence."

"You're telling me."

With tears in her eyes, Mom sliced the sandwiches into quarters. I reached over to gently touch my husband's shoulder. I was so thankful he was safely back that all recollection of my anger at his leaving vanished.

"And look at you," Billy said to me, shaking his head.

He pulled out a chair at the table. "Sit down. Think you can eat?"

I shook my head. "Not very hungry."

"It hurts her to talk." Mac sat beside me.

"I can listen." I looked at Mac and he knew what I was after; I had asked enough times: I wanted to know what had happened in Mexico.

He looked from me to Billy to Mom and back to me. "Can't it wait until tomorrow?"

"No." Mom joined us at the table with a plate of quartered sandwiches for them and a yogurt smoothie for me with a straw peeking above the top. "When you get to be my age, and when you go through what we've been through today, you don't put things off. And frankly? I think you'll sleep better if you get it out now."

Mac sighed. "You may be right."

I leaned over the smoothie and managed to sip a little through the straw. The cool, sweet strawberry flavor ignited a tumult of hunger in my stomach. I drank some more. All the curtains were open and the dark winter night beyond the windows created a vacuum, erasing the outside world, time, exhaustion, reluctance, despair. I looked at Mac.

"Talk."

He ate a quarter sandwich in two bites, swallowed, took a deep breath, and began.

"When I landed in Morelia, the first thing I did was call

Oscar, one of Ana's men. We had kind of bonded those months I was in Playa, and whenever we went to Miami Ana always brought Oscar along, too—he was, you know, her strong-arm. He was tough, but he was also basically a drunk, which was how Ana kept him under her thumb. But what she didn't know was that he hated her. I always thought that she didn't realize he was her weakest link. I figured he'd be the easiest to buy off—give him a wad of cash and he'd drink his way to the bank, you know?"

"Sounds right," Billy said.

"So. I call Oscar, and I ask him to be discreet, and I tell him there's five thousand bucks in it for him. I tell him I'll be waiting for him behind the airport, and an hour later, he's there."

"You had the money with you?" Mom asked, always the practical planner.

He nodded. "Jasmine arranged it. I told Oscar that for five thousand dollars, I wanted to know where Diego was. And for another five, I wanted Ana's whereabouts *but I did not want her to know that I was there*. He told me, he said, 'I'll take the ten,' and then I got into his car and off we went."

"Already I don't like the sound of this," Billy said.

"I know, but in Mexico it's quid pro quo. That's how it works."

"So he took you . . . where?" I asked.

"We drove for about twenty minutes. Then he stopped in

front of a kind of a hut—banded logs, thatched roof—and in we went, me expecting to see Diego."

The tea kettle screeched and Mom got up.

"Ana was sitting there in the one comfortable chair in the place, like a queen on a throne. Four or five of her men were with her. When I walked in, I couldn't believe it. I looked at Oscar and I wanted to throttle him. He already had five thousand dollars. But it was too late; I'd lost that bet. Ana stared at me and then she said—calmly—she said, 'I'm disappointed in you.' Very creepy, because of how even her voice was. No feeling at all, not even anger. Then she told me Felix was dead, it was my fault, and it was a good thing Diego hadn't been hurt. I told her I could never hurt my own child, and that was why I came back. She smiled but it was a *ruthless* smile, like she not only didn't believe a word I said but it didn't matter what I said. Then she dropped the real bomb, 'I know you're working for your government.' Just like that: She knew, and I was cooked. She told Oscar to take me to 'the diamond hole' and that was when I found out she had more than one hole—she must have them scattered around the country, just in case."

"I'll never forget being in the hole," I said. That dark, damp pit. But something else flashed into my mind when I heard *diamond*: the necklace I had never found. Who had he given it to? I felt a new pang of jealousy and shooed it away; it was no longer important.

"So Oscar pulled a gun on me and that was the end of the conversation. He and another one of the guys drove me to an abandoned field of diamond mines—Ana had claimed one for her own purposes; the mines were huge pits but this one was relatively small, like a false start—and opened the hatch long enough for me to see that someone was already in there, and to push me inside. The other person down there shoved me away when he felt me come too close, like he was guarding his space. Maybe he was scared. I didn't know what to think." Mac took a deep breath and exhaled. "We didn't talk at first, and then after a while he said something to me in Spanish and I recognized his voice. It was Diego."

"So you found him." Mom passed mugs of tea to Mac and Billy and sat back down to join us again.

"She'd had him beaten. I could smell that one of his wounds was infected. My clothes were a lot cleaner than his so I ripped a sleeve off my shirt and turned it into a bandage for his arm. He was in bad shape—exhausted and disoriented. I had a really strong feeling that he was about to die."

For a split second I wished Mac had let Diego die in that hole. But then I corrected myself, because Mac might have died with him if somehow they hadn't gotten out.

"I wasn't there five minutes before he made it clear that he knew I was an informant. Ana had told him before she threw him away. She wanted him to understand he'd been a fool to free us—a fool to betray her."

"Her own son," Mom said. "Heartless."

"When she threw me into that hole, she was giving me to Diego: He had no choice but to hate me. So now he hated me, and he hated her, and he hated himself for hating us. His loneliness was deep and *sticky*, you know? You could *feel* it. It was really sad."

I wiped my eyes, having suddenly realized they were tearing.

Mac looked at me. "It's okay to feel bad for him. Despite everything, he's human, and he was still . . ."

He couldn't finish but no one needed him to. I took one of his hands between both of mine and warmed its dry, cold surfaces: skin, muscle, bone. Humans were made of only that, and yet through sheer imagination we had concocted the capacity to extend terrible power into the world. Power we could use, abuse, or ignore. Our choices complicated everything.

"I don't know how much time passed," Mac continued. "A day, maybe a night. And then all of a sudden the hatch opened up and there were voices, and it seemed like it was raining. But it wasn't rain. Someone was urinating into the hole, onto us." He sipped his tea, put down his mug, closed his eyes a moment, opened them. "It was Oscar and he was with a woman. They were speaking Spanish, laughing about the gringos and the Americanos; I understood enough to know that she was goading him into peeing on us. He was very drunk, and obviously he'd told her he had a couple of captives and she seemed to find that amusing."

Mac paused, and Billy urged, "Go on."

"I recognized the woman's voice. It was Jasmine."

"Tell me the dude didn't have his gun."

"The dude had his gun. But you know Jasmine; she had a plan, and she was packing, too. I heard her tell him, 'Drop your weapon!' He begged her not to shoot him. And then there was a shot; hers, I think. She told him again, 'Drop it!' and he must have—if I knew Oscar even a little, he was a classic coward—and then she told him, 'Show me where Ana is.' The car started up and they were out of there."

"She didn't wait . . ." Billy said.

"My guess is she didn't want him to get any ideas about finding his gun and shooting us to cover himself. He was in deep water at that moment: us getting away, and then Jasmine with a gun on him, wanting Ana."

"So," Billy muttered, "that was how the Feds found Ana in La Huacana . . . Jasmine. I had a feeling."

"They tracked the signal from her cell phone. She left it near the place where Ana was staying, which tells us Oscar took her there. What happened next—where Jasmine is now—we just don't know."

Billy's expression was muted but his eyes betrayed him: His pupils contracted as if someone had shone a bright light on his face.

"Go on," Billy said.

"I helped Diego climb out of the hole, then I followed. We were standing in that field of abandoned mines, it was really dark. I didn't see him pick up the gun, he just suddenly had it. He used it to knock me out. And here I am. So for us it's over, but I'm worried about Jasmine."

Billy's gaze fell on his clenched hands; he refused to let emotion overflow in front of us.

"I talked to Fred Miller a few hours ago," Mac said, "while we were at the hospital, and told him about the abandoned mines. They checked every single one."

"And?" Billy asked.

"No Jasmine."

Billy stood up so quickly his chair fell behind him. He didn't bother to pick it up before taking his cell phone out of his pocket and dialing Fred Miller. His end of the conversation confirmed everything Mac had just told us, but also added a new bit of information, which he shared the moment he hung up.

"That Oscar dude—they found him off a highway near Ana's hiding place, all cut up, way dead."

"Jasmine?" I asked.

"Nothing yet. Still waiting."

"It's my fault." Tears burned into the wound of my nose. "If I hadn't screamed at her and blamed her for letting you return to Mexico," I said to Mac, "and if she hadn't gone after you—"

"She was working the job," Mac said. "It's *not* your fault."

I still felt it was; but I couldn't regret it. Because if Jasmine hadn't done whatever she did to get Oscar to take her to the diamond mines, Mac would have died in that hole with a presumed son who didn't love him, who didn't want him, who he shouldn't have gone after in the first place.

If Mac hadn't gone back to Mexico, Diego would be dead, he would never have come to terrorize us, and both Mac *and* Jasmine would be here now. An undercurrent of resentment bubbled under my skin; I rubbed my arms, closed my eyes.

If. Wishful thinking: It was toxic. I pushed it away.

CHAPTER 20

The next afternoon, we exited the Brooklyn-Queens Expressway onto Atlantic Avenue. We'd taken two long breaks that had both broken up the journey and prolonged it. Ben was bouncing in his car seat to "On the Road Again." Halfway through Connecticut we had discovered that he was a major Willie Nelson fan and so we listened to dozens of his songs from Billy's iPod; anything to pacify our restless toddler during the long car ride.

We pulled up in front of the brownstone and the car came to a gentle stop. I looked out the window at our home. It was the same as when we'd rushed out a week and a half ago, and yet everything was different—because our ordeal was over, we were safe now, and my face was in excruciating pain.

We unloaded the car, thanked Billy, and said good-bye. He had declined our invitation to join us for a dinner of take-out Chinese food; I suspected he wanted to be alone with his anguish over Jasmine's disappearance. The silence about her whereabouts worried all of us, but it pained Billy in particular. He was in love with her. She had vanished. I knew the feeling and it was awful. Mac and I stood outside on the sidewalk and watched Billy drive away. Then we went into the house and joined my mother and Ben for a quiet family evening. It was the kind of evening you would consider typical, even dull. But for us, the homecoming was magnificent.

Later, after Mom and Ben went to sleep, Mac and I lay in bed talking. Stretched out on his side in his striped pajama bottoms and a clean white T-shirt, facing me with his head propped on one hand, you would never have known what he'd been through. He had showered away the grime and anguish that had coated him so profusely during his week in Mexico. A lavender edge of his tattoo peeked above his collar, enough to remind me of it, though I would have been happy never to see it again.

"So . . . are you going to find out if Diego really is your child?"

"You think he isn't?"

"I think he is, but that's just my opinion. A DNA test would tell you for sure."

In the soft light of the single lamp we had left on, I could see enough of the remorse in his eyes to know how badly he felt about everything: accidentally fathering a child when he was practically still a child himself and the havoc it had wreaked. And how, as a result of all that, he had abandoned us twice . . . and now Jasmine had gone missing.

"I doubt Ana would have put everyone through all this if he wasn't mine. She would know."

"You're probably right, but on the other hand, she's a little off her rocker!"

He barked laughter and rolled onto his back. He was punchy from stress, but nevertheless his levity was contagious and soon we were both smiling.

"So let's count up all the things you missed since August." I raised one finger: "Our anniversary." Second finger: "Thanksgiving." Third: "All the winter holidays." Fourth: "Ben's birthday. Not to mention two of Rosie's kids' birthdays *and* Danny's birthday, which, by the way, he spent in jail thanks to you."

"I have a lot of shopping to do."

"No you don't. You're present enough for all of us."

His eyes moistened and he reached for me. I reached back. And as the clock passed midnight and started a new day, we made love in the quiet safety of our own bedroom, in our own home, on the street in the neighborhood in the city where we had chosen to make our lives together.

We were home.

The next morning I awoke to the purr of breakfast chatter

in the kitchen upstairs. It sounded as if everyone was up but me. I looked at the clock: It was after nine. Mac had let me sleep in, which was sweet of him and way beyond the call of duty. I stretched out and rolled over, and that was when I saw it on his pillow:

A narrow box wrapped in silver paper and tied with a crimson ribbon.

I sat up and pulled an envelope out from under the gift; it had my name on it. Inside was a pretty card showing a detailed illustration of a yellow orchid on a creamy green background. I opened it and saw that it was a blank card filled with Mac's handwriting. He had written the date— September third of last year—in green ink I recognized from a pen that had run out months ago.

Happy Second Anniversary

to my beloved wife

Karin . . .

With love forever

and ever

and ever . . .

From your devoted husband,

Mac

I couldn't help myself: I started crying.

Carefully, as if I would save the wrapping paper when in fact I never did, I pulled apart the seams without ripping anything. Then I pressed open the hinged top of a long black jeweler's box. And there it was, the necklace I'd first learned about months ago on a receipt from a Manhattan store, a slip of paper that had arrived in a box from Mac's office and set off a chain reaction in my imagination: *Diamond and ruby cluster pendant on 18k gold chain*. In my mind's eye I had seen this necklace on Deidre's neck, then on Ana's. It was the totem of disaffection that had sown the doubts that hurled me to Florida and then Mexico. I lifted the delicate gold chain out of its box and looked at the glittering cluster of jewels dangling in mid-air. Then I put the necklace on and got out of bed.

That I had been crying must have shown because when I reached the kitchen, Mom and Mac and even Ben looked at me and froze.

"Oh dear, does your nose hurt a lot?" Mom asked.

"Yes, but that's not it." I unbuttoned the top of my nightgown so Mac could see I was wearing the necklace.

He smiled. "Do you like it?"

"It's beautiful. Thank you."

"Last night, you reminded me. I hid it so well I could hardly find it this morning."

"Where was it?"

"If you think I'm going to reveal my secret hiding

place"—he grinned—"think again."

I poured myself a bowl of cereal while Mac and Mom finished theirs, and Ben sat on the floor with a board book, pretending to read. As soon as Mom left the kitchen to take her shower, I stopped eating, looked at my husband, pulled the necklace out from under my nightgown, and held the cluster of jewels in my hand.

"In a way, this was what propelled me to Mexico."

"But you didn't know about the necklace then."

"Tina sent over your stuff from the office. I found the receipt."

He cringed. "Ouch."

"I searched the house top to bottom. I even called Tina and she looked in the safe at Quest."

"I can imagine what was going through your mind."

"It's funny—my first thought was that it was an anniversary gift. I assumed I just couldn't find it. But when I saw the photo of you sitting at the hotel bar with some woman wearing a necklace, I thought it was *this* necklace, and I got a little . . ." *Jealous*. It felt silly saying it although it was an understatement.

He came around the table and kissed me. "You never need to wonder about me when it comes to other women."

"I know—but what was I supposed to think?"

"I should have tossed out that receipt or hid it with the box. I hate the thought of you thinking about the necklace, and what it might have meant, on top of everything else."

"Except then what would have happened? How long would you have stayed in Mexico? As far as I knew, you were dead."

"I was looking for a way back. I didn't know how long it would take. But I would have found a way."

"But don't you see? At some point, I would have started to really believe you were dead—and then you would have been. To me."

"I was always aware of that. It kept me up nights."

"When I thought I saw you at the airport that time— when I *did* see you—when you'd flown into Miami to meet with Jasmine—"

"I never flew there to meet her. Ana was there and she'd called for me; I knew the consequences if I didn't go."

"But I thought—"

"—that Jasmine and I had arranged to meet?"

"Yes, for the case."

"Never. It would have been too dangerous. She knew I was in Playa del Carmen and that was enough. So that's what you've thought all this time? I didn't even know Jasmine was with you that day, until right now. When I saw you at the airport, spilling that cup of coffee, I was stunned. I was scared you'd make a scene, that Ana would find out—it would have destroyed the safety I was trying to create for you. So I kept walking."

We looked at each other and seemed to have the same thought at the same time.

"Why *was* Jasmine flying to Miami?" I asked. "She said it was to spend her birthday under a palm tree. But now that I think of it, so much of what she said was fiction . . . is her birthday even in November?"

"I have no idea."

"So if she wasn't going to Miami for her birthday or to see you—why was she going?"

I stood up to get the phone, and at the same moment Ben started to cry; he had gotten his finger caught in a cabinet door.

"Call Fred Miller." I handed Mac the phone and went to Ben. "Ask him about Jasmine."

"Don't you think he would have called us if he knew where she was?"

"Not really." I picked up Ben and kissed his finger.

Mac dialed from memory, having learned all the pertinent contact numbers of his DEA handlers before landing in Mexico the first time. I sat down and listened to his end of the conversation: a brief greeting and then a list of questions.

"What's Jasmine's birthday?" Pause to listen to Fred's refusal; frustrated glance at me. "I understand."

"Where did Jasmine grow up?" Pause; frustration. "I understand."

"Where did Jasmine live before she came to Brooklyn?" Pause; frustration. "I understand."

"Just tell me—why would she travel to Florida?" Pause;

frustration. "I understand, I *understand*, but I'm just wondering—"

Then he listened while Fred told him something, after which the conversation, if you could call it that, was over. He blew out a long sigh after hanging up.

"Same as you'd expect: active investigation; can't divulge anything. He made a point of reminding me I'm not a part of it anymore."

"Technically," I said, "that's true. Except Jasmine went missing when she was in Mexico looking for *you*, and not because she was ordered to go."

"I thought you ordered her." He half smiled, but it was unconvincing; we were still too close to all that to make light of it. "The one thing Fred said that didn't sound like a brick wall was that they haven't heard a peep from Jasmine since I was in Mexico. He said it's like she evaporated—that's a quote."

"How much did I tell you about Lucky Herman? The private investigator I hired to find you in Miami."

"Just a little."

"Let's see if he can find any traces of Jasmine in Florida, just out of curiosity . . ."

"Karin, the DEA isn't forgetting about her. They know she fell off the radar. They'll find her sooner or later . . ."

That did it, his *sooner or later*. I wasn't famous for my patience, and before he finished his sentence I was on my way to the front hall for my purse where

I had Lucky Herman's number. Back at the table I dialed the phone and in moments was talking to Lucky himself.

"Hello Karin," he said with a smile in his voice. "Are you calling to say hello or do I have a repeat customer? Between you and me, I hope it's the former."

"Repeat customer," I told him. "How was the Metropolitan Opera?"

"It was beautiful, the best gift my wife ever gave me, and we've been married thirty years. So . . . you still can't find your husband?"

"He's sitting right here with me."

"I won't ask what happened—I've always found that congratulations are enough."

"Thank you, Lucky. Really, *thank you*."

"All I did was take a picture."

"It wasn't just *a* picture, it was *the* picture. It set the wheels in motion for me."

"I think the wheels were in motion before you called me. So what's going on now?"

I told him.

"Jasmine Alvarez," he spoke slowly, writing it down. "You say she's DEA?"

"Yes."

"That'll be tough. Might not even be her real name."

"You're right, it might not be."

"I'll see what I can do. How much detail do you want?"

"As much as you can get. Especially why she might travel to Florida."

"Can you send a picture? Real name or not, if I know her face it's a leg up. No pun intended."

I didn't get it and didn't try because a spasm of frustration was gripping me—why would I have a picture of Jasmine?—and then I thought of my mother's Thanksgiving photos.

"I'll send one right over."

I gave him my credit card information (he hadn't kept it from the first job, which made me trust him even more), and he reminded me once again that he had no idea how long it might take or if he'd be successful. But I knew from experience that he was competent and didn't let his words discourage me.

"Thank you—I wish you luck." When he ended the call just as he had the very first time we spoke, I felt a little lift.

Mom had downloaded her photos onto her laptop. I found a beautiful picture of Jasmine standing in the kitchen wearing the cow-print apron with her arm around my mother, both of them beaming, and e-mailed it to Lucky Herman with a note: *Please just do the best you can.*

While we waited to hear from Lucky Herman or the DEA, *anyone*, our lives rolled forward: Mac went back to work as an independent forensic security consultant, working from home; Mom found a new apartment and organized her move; and I decided to wait until fall before resuming my studies at John Jay so I could spend time with my family before picking up the pace again. Meanwhile Mac and I went into couples counseling together; we were basically okay but we'd been through a lot and there were some marital threads that needed sorting before they turned into knots. One of those threads was about trust (it was hard for it not to fray when your spouse had developed a habit of disappearing). Another thread was Diego. He *was* Mac's son; a DNA test had confirmed that. And based on the evidence the prosecution was building up against him, it looked as if he was going to spend the rest of his life in prison—for the murders of Aileen and Hugh MacLeary—as was his mother. These were murky emotional waters for Mac, to say the least.

Five weeks went by, and then it was the middle of March: Yellow crocuses peeked above the melting snow in our backyard and some days the temperature rose to nearly fifty. Winter was unwinding with a great sigh of relief.

And then one day the doorbell rang. I saw the Federal Express truck through the front windows before opening the door and assumed it was another delivery for Mac, who had been receiving a steady stream as he set up his new business, MacLeary Forensic Security Specialists (the plural in Specialists was more hopeful than anything, as he was working alone). I signed for the envelope and was about to put it down on the front hall table when I noticed that it was addressed to me and then saw the return address—Miami Investigation Services—and my pulse took off like a rocket.

Her given name was Jasmine Baez but she had not changed it to Alvarez for duplicitous reasons; it was the name of her ex-husband. Joe Alvarez was a ski instructor in Maine, just as she'd told us, and she had indeed grown up there. Her birthday *was* November 27. On paper she was pretty much who she'd said she was; good news, as it reality-checked my instincts and made me feel I hadn't been so badly fooled. It also deepened the feeling that when Jasmine vanished, I had lost a real friend.

Paper-clipped beneath her life résumé was a nine-by-twelve manila envelope. Sealed. I thought it was strange that Lucky Herman had done that, which made me afraid to open it. What had he found?

"Mac?"

"Down here!"

I went to the spare room—now Mac's office—where he was at his desk working on something. When he saw the look on my face, he put down his pen.

"What's wrong?"

"This just came." I handed him the sheet of paper.

"So she's who she said she was." He handed it back. "But it doesn't say anything about the DEA—how long she's been doing it, all that."

"Which just tells us she's a good agent."

"True."

"She bought a bungalow in Key West seven years ago."

"Must be her getaway." Mac stood up and stretched. Smiled. "We should do that."

"We should. So . . ." I handed him the envelope. "You want the honors?"

He must have thought what I'd thought because he stared at it before answering. "Okay." And then he tore it open and withdrew a photograph.

It was a picture of a house, a cottage really, painted blue, green, and pink. Attached was a handwritten note from Lucky:

Special Agent Alvarez's Key West neighbors said she mostly visits alone but sometimes with boyfriends or ex-husband. However none of the neighbors have seen her since last winter. There's been no activity at the house since that time. Utilities have been turned off due to nonpayment. Mail is no longer delivered.

(My apologies for the delay in supplying this information. My wife has been ill and my assistant returned to his family in Mumbai. I had hoped to find more for you, but alas . . .)

It read like a eulogy. No wonder Lucky had sealed the envelope.

"So I guess that's it." I slipped the photo and note back

into the envelope and handed it to Mac. He opened a desk drawer and dropped it inside. A powerful feeling of loss blossomed inside my chest. "She's really gone."

"It doesn't look good."

"Why didn't Billy know about the house in Key West?"

"Maybe he hadn't ranked high enough yet."

"Boyfriend-wise?"

Mac nodded.

"So, do we tell him?"

"Nah."

"You're right. What now?"

"We move on."

I kissed Mac and he went back to work. And we did it: We moved on, all the way to summer. When, during the last week of June, as we deep-cleaned our house in preparation to host a Fourth of July barbecue—just like Hugh and Aileen had always done; we would keep that family tradition alive—I lifted the corner of the living room carpet to sweep beneath it and found a surprise: a slip of paper in Jasmine's handwriting.

CHAPTER 21

It was a phone number, scrawled in blue pen on a ripped corner of a white paper—definitely Jasmine's large loopy scrawl—which must have fallen out of her purse when it fell to the floor at Thanksgiving. I recalled the moment as if it was yesterday: I had rushed through the living room to answer Ben's cry and accidentally knocked against the purse, dumping its contents on the floor. I could still see her plane ticket to Florida in my mind's eye; but that was all the detail I could remember other than scooping stuff quickly back into the purse with Jasmine. This paper must have slipped under the edge of the carpet and gone unnoticed.

The area code was 305, which I recognized from my visits to Miami. It was probably nothing, but I was curious anyway. So I went to the couch, picked up the laptop from the coffee table, settled it on my knees, and typed in the

phone number. A page of reverse directories popped up.
I clicked on every link and learned that 305 was also an
area code for Key West, where Jasmine had her cottage,
and that it could be used for either a landline or cell phone.
Every site charged about five dollars in exchange for a
name and address, and I was about to get my credit card
when I had a better idea.

Why not just call the number?

I put down the laptop and stepped over the broom on my
way to the kitchen, where I lifted the phone from its cradle
and dialed. My call was answered quickly.

"Hello?"

"Jasmine, is that you? It's Karin!"

She hung up.

Still, I felt giddy a moment: *She was alive*.

Then my brain cranked into action: Why had she hung
up? And why, if she didn't want to talk to me, had she
answered in the first place?

I remembered that Mac had had our phone number
blocked from caller ID when he returned from Mexico the
first time. He had also had our number unlisted from the
phone book and every online directory he could find that
published our information. Jasmine hadn't realized it was
me calling her just now. But why had she answered at all
if she was being so selective? I recalled what it had been
like to work undercover jobs back when I was a detective:
Hiding in plain sight was tricky business. This cell number

had probably been established specifically for the job; assumedly only certain people were supposed to have it . . .

Just as I was figuring it out, the phone, still in my hand, rang. Unknown caller. I answered immediately.

"Listen—you don't know this number, okay?"

"I understand."

"You gotta promise me, honey, *promise* me. It's not like you're not on their radar. If they find out you have this number, I'm seriously fried."

She must have infiltrated the Soliz cartel, picked up where Mac had left off. That they had never found out she was an undercover agent felt like a miracle. I also assumed that Fred knew the number. Of course he knew all about this; of course he had never let on. It was treacherous work, and you didn't risk anything you didn't have to.

"I'm on board, Jasmine. Don't worry."

"Thanks." I heard the retreat in her tone, her imminent good-bye; but then she asked, "How did you get the number anyway?"

"I was cleaning under the rug. It must have fallen out of your purse at Thanksgiving."

"*You* were cleaning?" She chuckled. And then she hung up.

I smiled at the phone, the piece of plastic that had done a good deed: I now knew for sure that Jasmine was out there, doing her thing. It was all the certainty I required.

Now I could stop lying awake at night worrying about her.

Mac walked into the kitchen, bringing his empty coffee mug for a refill. I told him about the number and the calls.

"That's great!" He leaned against the counter, facing me. "Fred really knows how to keep a poker face, but hey, how many times did we do the same thing when people asked us questions from outside a job?"

"You have to."

"Did she sound nervous?"

"She hung up on me, so I'd say yes."

"I wonder if Fred should know the number's been breached." Mac poured his coffee, lifted it, and inhaled the aroma before taking a sip.

"She'll let him know."

"If she can."

It was true: Working undercover, it was sometimes difficult to find a safe moment to call base. "You want to call him," I said, "or should I?"

"You. I'm right in the middle of something downstairs, and I have a couple of calls to make while it's still quiet." Ben's long mid-afternoon naps served as both breaks and prime work opportunities. Mac made all his work calls on his cell phone, so after he kissed me and went back downstairs to his office, I used the landline to call Fred at work but instead reached Hyo.

"It's Karin Schaeffer," I greeted Fred's partner. "How are you? It's been a while."

"Good, good. You?"

"Fine. Nothing much is happening here."

"Like I always say, no news is good news."

We both laughed. From the point of view of an enforcer of the law, every day on which some horrible crime didn't erupt was a good one. The little stuff, you swatted away.

"Fred around?"

"He just stepped out. Can I help?"

I told him about my phone call with Jasmine. "I'm worried I may have accidentally compromised her safety."

Hyo wrote down the number. "I don't recognize that one. I'll run it by Fred when he gets back."

"Thanks. And just so you guys know, I shredded the paper," I said, ripping it into tiny bits over the garbage can as we spoke, "and I already forgot the number."

"Fat chance." Hyo laughed. "I don't think you forget anything."

"Sometimes I wish I could. But I mean it: I don't want any part of this. I like my life, you know?"

"I hear you, Karin."

We said good-bye and that was that.

I finished sweeping, did a couple of things in the kitchen, and then decided to run some errands before Ben woke up. Grabbed my purse and went downstairs to let Mac know I was going out. After filling the watering can in the tub, I left through the ground-floor door and took a minute to water the red begonias that were starting to fill out the huge blue enamel flowerpot I had recently bought to liven up the front of our house. I tucked the empty watering can inside the vestibule, locked the iron gate, and went on my merry way in the direction of Smith Street.

As a mother, running errands alone was practically a treat, especially on a gorgeous June day like this one. It was going to be a hot summer; you could feel it in the air. Sun shimmered through the dense green foliage of the sycamore trees that lined our block, throwing coins of shimmering light and long, cool shadows across the sidewalk.

I heard shouting and turned around. Far at the other end of the block, a Con Ed truck had barricaded access; the electric company was digging something up, embarked on one of its ubiquitous repair projects. Voices were arguing: A driver I couldn't see was angry because he was unable drive onto the block. The Con Ed guy was shouting back. I tried not to let their agitation infiltrate my mood, but living in the city, constantly bumping up against other people's conflicts, made it a challenge to keep your calm.

Something pinged loudly against the iron fence two feet away from me, and I jumped. I looked around to find out who had thrown what I assumed had been a rock but didn't see anyone on either side of the street. I took a deep breath and resumed walking.

Suddenly I realized that I had forgotten to bring the list

I had made. I remembered many of the items I needed but not all of them, so I turned around and headed home, thinking it was lucky I hadn't made it all the way off the block . . . when to my surprise I saw Billy Staples running toward me.

"Karin!"

"Was that *you* arguing with the Con Ed guy?"

"Get back into your house!" His expression was tight, agitated.

"What's wrong?"

"For once just listen to me!" He grabbed my arm and turned me toward the gate in the iron fence that separated my house from the sidewalk.

"You're scaring me."

He hustled me through the gate into the small bluestone area where we kept our garbage cans and the new blue flowerpot. "What did you do? Calling some phone number you find on the floor!"

The downstairs door opened and Mac stepped out, holding his phone. "Hyo Park just called—" and then he saw Billy. They locked eyes. And I knew something was very wrong.

Billy propelled me toward Mac, who pulled me into the vestibule.

There was another loud ping—*a gunshot*—and the big enamel planter blew apart in an explosion of flying dirt, blue shards, and red petals.

Billy stepped onto the sidewalk, holding his gun with both hands, pivoting his aim back and forth, up and down, frantically searching for his target across the street. "NYPD!" he yelled. "Hold your fire!"

Mac tried to maneuver me into the house—holding me with one hand and dialing 911 with the other—but I couldn't not see. I had to understand what was happening.

My phone call to Jasmine. Her call to me. What had that triggered? And so quickly. How could this be happening from two brief conversations less than an hour ago?

Who was shooting at us?

Or were the shots meant for only me? The first one had come close when I was alone halfway up the block. Missed me by a couple of feet. If not for the trees, that bullet might have found me.

I broke out of Mac's grip and hid behind the latticed ironwork door, hiding and watching.

Billy's body now appeared frozen, his aim steady and high: He had found his target. I shifted for a better view and barely managed to see someone crouched on a rooftop diagonally across the street. The top of a head in some sort of dark hat. The curve of a shoulder and part of a back clothed in dark brown. Bright sun glinted off something metal: the gun. The shooter appeared to be lying facedown atop the roof, allowing himself just enough visibility to aim and fire.

"Billy," I hissed, "what is this?"

"I told you: *Get inside*."

He held his ground, his unswerving aim. As did the shooter: keeping still, the nose of his gun glowing in our direction. Even as a car now raced wrong way up the street, neither Billy nor the shooter shifted.

The dark blue car jerked to a stop. The driver's door swung open and Fred jumped out. He had shaved his beard since I'd last seen him.

"Hyo told me—" Fred cut himself short when he saw Billy, whose face I couldn't see. I could imagine the ferocity of his expression, the mix of rage and terror you felt when you knew you could die any moment. "Up there?" Fred drew his gun.

Billy nodded. A vein of sweat trickled down the back of his neck, disappearing beneath the ribbed edge of his T-shirt, which was soaked straight down the center.

Fred stopped where he was and leveled his aim at the roof. "You try talking to him yet?"

"Therapy never worked for me."

"Funny." Fred didn't laugh. "Federal agent! Don't move!" he shouted at the rooftop figure, a shadow that appeared to recede at the sound of his voice. The hat, the shoulder, the back, the glowing gun: gone.

"I don't see him anymore," Billy said.

Behind me I heard Mac's footsteps coming closer, felt his determination to pull me away. But I was all stubborn conviction to stay where I was, watching this. I would be a witness to whatever happened; when it was time for questions, I could help.

"Mommy."

I glanced over my shoulder to see Mac three feet from me, turning to look at Ben, who was groggily making his way along the hall.

"*Shh*," Mac said, hurrying to our little boy. He picked Ben up and covered his mouth with a hand . . . a gesture that broke my heart. Mac glared at me and whispered, "*Get inside the house. Lock the door.*"

But I couldn't. Or wouldn't. Someone had to see this in case everyone—Billy, Fred, the shooter—ended up dead.

Mac retreated with Ben into our bedroom and shut the door. He had already called 911. It was just a matter of time before they swarmed the block.

Across the street, Mrs. Petrini—the white-haired lady who swept her stoop every single day about this time—appeared at her front door holding her broom. She stepped out and demanded, "What the heck is happening down there?"

Billy and Fred raced across the street and up the stoop.

"Police," I heard Fred say as he pushed Mrs. Petrini aside and ran into the house. Every brownstone had an interior entrance onto the roof, accessed by either a stair or a roof hatch off the top-floor hallway.

The street was eerily quiet now. Just the blue car haphazardly abandoned, facing the wrong direction. And me and Mrs. Petrini staring into otherwise empty space. She cursed aloud and walked slowly down her stoop, not bothering to close her front door. It was a smart move, getting out of there; anyone in their right mind would have been afraid.

I hurried into my house, down the hall, and into the spare room that was now Mac's office. His reading glasses sat on his open appointment book, a pen lay on a pad beside an unfinished sentence, a screensaver photo of Ben laughing flitted across the computer screen. I opened the closet door. Turned on the light. Crouched down, pushed aside some winter boots, and dialed open the safe. Tossing off envelopes and the clipped sheaves of our important documents, I picked up our handgun, inserted the cartridge, and ran back outside.

Across the street.

Up Mrs. Petrini's stoop.

Into her house—a widow's house, sour, dust hovering in darkness—and wove two flights up to her top floor. A narrow doorway at the top of the final flight told me this one led to the roof. Normally these doors were closed and preferably locked. This one, however, hung open onto a rectangle of sweet blue sky and a trio of agitated voices.

CHAPTER 22

I hid behind the door, watching and listening through the crack where it hinged open onto a slice of tar roof and an imperfect but telling view.

Jasmine. Aiming a gun at Billy. Her panicky eyes moved between him and Fred; she knew she was trapped.

My mind spun, disbelieving, reaching for explanations.

It couldn't be true: *Jasmine?*

But there she was. I was looking at her. Other than Billy and Fred (and me), she was the only one on the roof . . . which meant *she* had shot at me down on the street . . . which meant she had *never* gone missing in the line of duty but had been up to something else all along.

Why hadn't it occurred to me that she was in New York? When we'd spoken I'd pictured her in front of her cottage, under a palm tree . . . I had pictured her in Florida. It was a thoughtless assumption. The area code could have been either a landline or a cell phone; she could have been anywhere.

Jasmine's face wore a new mask, or maybe the old one had finally fallen away. Instead of pretty and shrewd and fun she was *malevolent*. I recognized her perfectly from past encounters with sociopaths. I couldn't believe it. And yet I was looking right at her . . . not at the Jasmine I thought I'd known, but at someone else, someone capable of horrible things.

"Why don't you just put the gun down, Jazz?" Billy's voice was tighter than I'd ever heard it. Incredulous. Hurting. "Tell us what's going on. We'll figure it out. There's got to be some kind of misunderstanding." He went on and on, trying to convince himself.

But I couldn't see where the misunderstanding was. She was pointing a gun at him. And she had just tried to shoot me: twice.

"You are *sweet*," she said in a withering tone. Her eyes shifted to Fred.

And then, *and then*, Fred swung his gun toward Billy. "It's game time."

"What the *fuck*?" Billy said.

I could see from behind that he was shaking. His brain, like mine, exploding *Jasmine and Fred, Jasmine and Fred* and trying to figure it out in the split second before they went ahead and killed him. He was dead and he knew it.

It was the coldest place a cop could go, a terror I knew too well: I had been there.

"You're never going to get away with this," Billy tried.

I stepped away from the crack. Peered past the edge of the open door. Got ready.

"Ruben should've already taken care of you," Jasmine said. "You and Karin both."

Ruben? . . . Ruben? . . .

I moved from behind the door in time to see Jasmine's fingers constrict around the gun's handle while her trigger finger squeezed. In time to notice the surprise on her face as she registered my presence, as clouds of outrage and questions and frustration flitted across her eyes.

Fred was closer.

I took aim, saying, "Billy, you do her," as I pulled my trigger and felt the powerful kickback of the gun's discharge rocket from my hand into my shoulder.

There were two shots, only one of them mine. The answer to who had managed to get off the other shot came to me before the question had time to formulate.

The two men fell in what looked like choreography, both bodies jolting simultaneously but enacting different sequences of movement. In reaction to the force of the bullet that passed through his right rib cage, Fred dove leftward, arms flung out as if starting a cartwheel. By the way he bounced and settled when he hit the ground, I guessed I'd killed him. At the same moment that Fred curved sideways, Billy spun, rotating three-quarters of the way around in my direction and looking straight at me in a weird mix of astonishment and capitulation. His left eye—his beautiful brown eye with its soft curled lashes—*saw* me so deeply a quiver ricocheted down my spine. His right eye was gone, replaced by a bloody chaos of sinew and bone. He hit the ground with a dreadful heaviness.

Jasmine and I stared at each other, aimed at each other, calculating. I couldn't stop processing the sight of Billy half blinded, in shock, going down, maybe dying, maybe dead. Cold to my core, I began to shake and ordered myself to *stop. Now. Or she will kill you, too.*

Jasmine's face glowed with determination to be the last one standing in the scorched blue gun-smoke silence. And then, down on the street, sirens blared, cars jammed to a stop, voices gathered. In a few moments we wouldn't be alone; but up here, right now, it was lonely in the most terrible way.

"Ruben Medina," I said, suddenly remembering: He ran another cartel in Mexico; Ana had worried aloud about him taking over her territories. "When did you start working for him? How long before Thanksgiving? How long before Mac got pulled into it? How much did he pay you?" As the questions flew out of my mouth and the layers peeled away, the betrayal at the heart of this grew more and more putrid. "Where's the money he paid you and Fred?"

"Like I'd tell you." Her gun arm stiffened.

Just then Billy moaned and we both glanced at him, realizing he was alive, if barely. Jasmine's eyes narrowed as they looked back at me.

"Let me go. I'll cut you in. Half."

"You are a certified bitch."

"I never said I wasn't." She steadied her aim.

I steadied mine.

Shouting. Footsteps running up the stairway to the roof.

In a fragment of a moment, everything shifted. I didn't need to kill her to stop her anymore. And if she killed me, it would only add murder to her list of crimes.

As her eyes metronomed frantically between me and Billy, I could practically see her tallying up the damage, weighing her options: If he didn't die, she wouldn't have killed anyone. Maybe she could cut a plea in exchange for everything she knew; maybe they'd even send her back to Mexico as a triple agent, working for the Feds she was supposed to have been working for all along. It made me sick to think there was a chance she could pull that off.

"I'll testify against you. I'll talk to the press. I'll blow your cover if they let you keep it." She knew I'd do it.

"Shoot me." That was how badly she didn't want to rot in prison while the government publicly debated when and where and how to execute her for treason.

"I'd love to. But no way."

Cops stormed the roof. Mac was with them and after the briefest mental reckoning with what he saw—

understanding that Jasmine had been the rooftop sniper—
he pointed at her and they flooded in her direction.

I couldn't tell if he was angry or terrified (or both) when
he took the gun out of my hand. With his other hand he
too-tightly gripped my arm, and I knew: *angry*. Because
I had risked my life and our family's future by running
up onto the roof. What he didn't know, what he hadn't
seen was how Jasmine's iota of inattention as she prepared
to shoot Billy, and then saw me, had shifted her aim and
possibly saved his life.

In moments she was handcuffed, read her rights, hustled
off the roof. She avoided looking at us but we watched her
arrest avidly. Loathing her not just for her duplicity toward
us but the toll it had taken on everyone. For blinding Billy
in so many ways.

"I don't believe it," Mac muttered, but unconvincingly;
he'd been a cop for twenty years and thus was primed to
believe anything. Then he looked at me and said, "They
found Hyo Park in Fred's trunk. Apparently Fred killed
him to shut him up."

Vomit rose to my throat. I had given Hyo that phone
number Fred and Jasmine had been so desperate to
suppress, a number that must have linked them to Ruben
Medina. I swallowed the guilty bile, refusing it. This
whole thing was not my fault.

Tears gathered in Mac's eyes when he turned and saw
Billy lying in a spreading pool of blood. A pair of medics

was working on him now. Filling the crater that had been his right eye with wads of sterile gauze that swiftly turned pink then red then purplish black. Stanching the bleeding as best and quickly as they could. Mac and I knelt down close to our friend. We both said his name in case some part of him could hear us. But we couldn't tell. He was so quiet. And so still.

CHAPTER 23

Cops in uniform and plainclothes, patrol cars and ambulances filled our street, which was now blocked off at both ends to civilian traffic. Red lights flashed from everywhere though all the sirens had been turned off. But to me the drone was grating, overwhelming: all the voices, and something inside my brain that wouldn't let me forget the awful stillness of Billy's half-wrecked face as he lay there on the roof.

Behind me I heard a knocking sound and turned around to see Mrs. Petrini standing at the window in my living room, holding Ben, who was crying. I waved and forced a smile I hoped would calm him. As he tried to reach for me through the glass, Mrs. Petrini took hold of his tiny wrist and made him wave back. Revulsion undulated through me: What had I been thinking? What if I hadn't come off the roof alive? What about Ben? I waved and

waved and smiled and smiled until finally he stopped
crying.

A body bag was carried out of Mrs. Petrini's house on
a stretcher and loaded into an ambulance beside which a
television reporter dressed in a pink skirt suit spoke rapidly
into her microphone, facing a camera.

"Breaking news from Brooklyn! Two rogue DEA
special agents who were reputedly working for a Mexican
drug cartel were just captured on a rooftop by NYPD
Detective Billy Staples of the Eighty-fourth Precinct here
in Boerum Hill. What you see behind me is the body of
one of the rogue agents who was killed in gunfire just
minutes ago—Special Agent Fred Miller. The other
fatality is his partner, Hyo Park, whose body was found
in the trunk of a car here at the scene. We're waiting for
details on Special Agent Park's role in all this, but it's
our understanding right now that he is *not* the other rogue
agent. We are told that *that* person is DEA Special Agent
Jasmine Alvarez, who has been arrested and is on her way
to Central Booking where apparently she'll be charged
with a long list of crimes. Detective Staples was wounded
in the gunfire and we're told Emergency Services is still
working on him on the roof. An unidentified person is also
said to have been involved in the capture of the double
agents but we have been unable to confirm that. We'll be
following this story as the details emerge, so stay tuned."

As the ambulance drove away, Mac came across the

street, veering out of the range of the television camera, and joined me on the sidewalk in front of our brownstone. I wove my arm around his waist and pulled him close. I didn't have to ask to know what was running through his mind: ten months ago, Bronxville, standing in front of his parents' red-white-and-blue house, weeping as we watched them being brought out in body bags. I felt a sharp pang of grief for Aileen and Hugh, and squeezed Mac closer. He leaned in to kiss me.

"Karin?"

I felt the warmth of a hand on my shoulder and turned to see my mother's worried face. She must have argued her way onto the sealed-off block.

"Are you all right? What happened? Where's Ben?"

"I'm fine. He's in the house with Mrs. Petrini. We'll be right in."

As she hurried up the stoop and went inside, a youngish man walked over—tall and thin, with black hair in a deliberate, stylish mess and small gold hoops in both earlobes.

"Karin Schaeffer?" He held out a veined hand that betrayed his age and he popped from thirty to forty.

"You know me?" We shook hands.

"Special Agent Rick Latham, FBI, Counterintelligence Division."

"*Counter*intelligence," I repeated. Because if that's who he worked for, it told me Jasmine and Fred had been on the Bureau's radar, that they were being investigated by another agency of the Department of Justice. It almost came as a surprise but shouldn't have.

"You must be Mac." Rick Latham offered his hand, and Mac took it.

"Yup."

"This got ugly," Latham said. "Sorry you people got dragged into it."

"Into what, exactly?" I asked.

"Maybe the less we know the better," Mac said.

"He has a point." Latham glanced between the two of us.

"How long have you known they were double agents?"

"Karin, *please* . . . aren't you tired of this yet? It probably never should have involved us in the first place."

"But it did."

Mac stopped arguing; he knew I was right.

Latham kept quiet, listening, as he dug into his jeans pocket, searching for something. He seemed to find it but didn't take it out, nor did he remove his hand.

"Before Mac left for Mexico the first time?" I asked. "Just tell us that."

He nodded. "Your husband's right: it's over now."

"Was that a yes?"

"I've probably said too much already."

"You haven't said anything."

Latham finally pulled his hand out of his pocket, a tortoiseshell guitar pick pinched between two fingers. He flicked his thumbnail against its edge a few times and then nodded at us. "Thanks."

"For what exactly?" I raised my voice as he walked away, joining the others at the blue car where Hyo's body was waiting to be bagged for the coroner.

"Thank us for what?" I asked Mac, as if he could answer that.

"I guess we'll have to use our imaginations."

"I'm thinking they knew all along."

"I'm thinking so, too."

We waited another fifteen minutes before Billy was finally brought down to the street. He was strapped to a stretcher, threaded with IV tubes, wearing an oxygen mask. Half his head and one eye was mummified in gauze. But he wasn't in a body bag and that was something.

Mac and I hurried over to walk beside his stretcher as it was loaded into an ambulance.

"Can we go along?" Mac asked.

"Just one of you," the chubby medic answered. He had a pencil-line mustache that barely moved when he spoke.

"I'll go." Mac looked at me. "You stay with Ben."

What he really meant was that Billy was his best friend and he loved him. He couldn't *not* go.

"I'll see you later." I kissed him. "Call me from the hospital."

"Don't ask anyone any more questions for now," Mac added with an unmistakable note of exhaustion in his voice; he was advising himself as much as he was advising me. "We have to let this be over."

I smiled and nodded but didn't promise anything. Mac hopped into the back of the ambulance. The medic closed the doors, the engine started, and I stood there watching them drive away into the opposite end of a summer day that had started out so nicely. It had been a truly duplicitous day, promising one thing, delivering another. I realized that Mac was right: We knew everything we needed to know at the moment; our part was over.

And so I did as my husband suggested. I didn't speak with Special Agent Latham again, nor did I seek out anyone else for answers. Instead, I turned around, walked up my front stoop, went through the front door—and closed it behind me.

**Turn the page for an excerpt
from Katia Lief's
*YOU ARE NEXT***

There was something intensely satisfying about digging bare-handed in the dirt. My gardening gloves were soggy so I'd abandoned them on the cracked cement next to the barrel planter I was filling with orange begonias. By late summer these six plants would be triple in size and the pot would overflow with clusters of bright waxy petals. Waiting patiently as they grew and enjoying their beauty was one in a million facets of my therapy, but then everything I did these days was an aspect of recovery. So sayeth Once-a-Week Joyce, as I had secretly dubbed my therapist, recalling as I had a hundred times and with the usual inner tickle how at my initial appointment she had made sure to point out that the word *joy* was embedded in her name. I had smiled for the first time in months, which had been exactly her goal.

I'd been outside doing the back garden all morning

and these front pots would take the last of the dozen trays of spring flowers I'd carted home from the nursery yesterday afternoon. One of the planks on the barrel had rotted over the winter and was sagging out. I wouldn't bother my new landlord with it; next spring I would use my own money to buy another one. I patted down the soil, noticed that every one of my short-bitten fingernails was crusted with black dirt, and wiped my hands on the front of my jeans. It was hot out. I was suddenly thirsty and my mind conjured a tempting image of sweet ice tea over a stack of ice cubes. The cool, shadowy inside of my ground-floor one-bedroom apartment beckoned. I bent down to collect my gloves.

A dented gray sedan stopped in front of the brownstone.

A black guy wearing a red baseball cap turned off a Willie Nelson song and leaned partway out of the driver's window. That was when I saw the police radio on his dashboard and knew he was a cop.

"I'm looking for Detective Karin Schaeffer."

"I'm no longer with the police force."

He left the motor running and got out slowly. Smiled. All I wanted to think about was that I liked his perfect white teeth.

"Billy Staples, detective first class."

I stood there. It wasn't nice to meet him and I wouldn't lie by saying it was. I didn't want him to be here because they didn't show up in person to deliver paperwork, and anyway, my medical discharge had already been signed, sealed, and delivered. They only came in person with bad news.

"I'm kind of busy," I said. Standing there in my dirty jeans. Holding limp gardening gloves and a muddy spade. Looking like a retired old lady with nothing but time on her hands, though I was only thirty-three.

"Listen, Karin, I know you don't want to hear anything from us. I got that. But there's something you have to know."

"How did you find me?" Phone book, Internet white pages . . . I had made an effort to unlist myself in every directory.

"Well, for one thing, you sent the benefits department a change of address."

Of course I had; I needed those disability checks to pay my rent, since the sale of my house hadn't netted any profit.

"Right," I said. "Sorry, I'm just a little tired. Not thinking straight today."

"I understand."

I'd heard that too many times by now: *I understand*. So he knew. Everyone knew. All the world had been informed of Karin Schaeffer's tragedy, and then moved on to the next big bad story . . . except for me, of course, having been abandoned to it.

"You know you have an enemy." It was smart of him not

to have phrased it as a question. Of course I knew I had an enemy.

"Martin Price is behind bars," I told him.

The media had called him the Domino Killer. In the detectives unit we'd called him JPP for Just Plain Psycho. The judge called him the worst threat to innocent people she'd ever encountered and put him away forever, specifically for the murders of Jackson and Cece Schaeffer, my husband and three-year-old daughter. There had been others before that but it was my family's murders that had put JPP away once and for all.

"He escaped last night. Got a call from your old unit in Jersey—asked me to find you. Seems no one answered when they called."

"Well," I said, "thanks for telling me. I guess." I wanted to get inside. Wanted the cool of my own private space. Wanted that sweet ice tea. But Detective Staples wasn't finished.

"The thing is, he left a note for you."

"A note?" Please, no. Not another note from Martin Price.

"Well, kind of a note."

I could already see it. I already knew.

"They found three dominoes laid out on his mattress: three, five, and one."

My address: 351 Pacific Street. Brooklyn, New York. A far cry and a different life from the house in New Jersey

I'd shared with Jackson and Cece. Ours was such a sweet house, green clapboards and a front porch where we used to sit and watch Cece play on the lawn. I could still see her running toward me across the dandelion-speckled grass, bare-legged in a plaid sundress, brown curls bouncing around her cherubic face, calling, "Mommy, chase me!"

"He also left you another message," Billy said in a lower, softer voice that told me he wished he didn't have to deliver this one.

I closed my eyes. Saw the last message he'd left me almost a year ago, written in lipstick on my bathroom mirror: *You Are Next*. Only it wasn't lipstick. It was my daughter's blood.

"It said, 'See you soon.'"

"Whose blood this time?"

"His own. Must have cut himself. Probably had to steal some bandages, so every local pharmacy is getting its security footage looked at right now."

I nodded. It would be the logical first step. But knowing JPP, he'd have disinfected and bandaged his wound and moved on by now. He was scary good at this. JPP's thing was to engineer the toppling of a whole group, to watch an entire family fall one by one by one.

He had already murdered five members of a family, the Aldermans of Maplewood, New Jersey—my old beat. Three murders into it the dominoes JPP left behind started making sense. Their face numbers offered a clue. The problem was deciphering it before he came back for the kill. My department and the FBI had already been working the case for a year before I was put on it.

I was a newly minted detective when I found him pretty much by accident. I never would have thought to look in one of those zillion-gallon chemical tanks off the highway. Never realized any of them sat empty sometimes. We'd had a tip and were canvassing the area and I heard an echo that sounded like it was coming from inside the tank. Climbed the side ladder and there he was, way at the bottom, napping on his side with his fists clenched just like Cece used to do when she was a baby. How he could sleep in that fog of petroleum fumes, I never knew. But there he was, superhuman, inhuman, or both.

Because I had found him, his imagination focused on me, and my family became his next target—though I didn't know it at the time. To anyone else it would have seemed random, but to JPP it made some kind of twisted perfect sense.

Two months after his arrest, he escaped off the prison bus during a transfer to the courthouse to hear the charges read against him, five separate charges of murder in the first degree. He nearly killed two guards with a homemade shiv on his way off the bus. Hid. Traveled, somehow. Found my family, and the rest was history.

Now whenever I pictured our lawn I couldn't help seeing six dominoes sitting in plain view on the grass—

the first three digits of Jackson's and Cece's social security numbers—though in reality the dominoes weren't found until the grass was cut and my husband and child were already dead. JPP had "warned" us, his way of giving us a loophole of escape; in his mind, he had done the right thing before proceeding with the inevitable. He was chillingly efficient in that way, like a corporate functionary, following his own predetermined procedures as he went about his task. My former partner, Mac, tried hard to convince me it wasn't my fault we hadn't found the dominoes in time. They had sunk into the long grass. Jackson and I had run errands all that last weekend, and the lawn had gone uncut. We had missed our loophole, our chance. And then JPP showed up early one morning, after I'd left for work and Jackson and Cece were alone in the house. Mac had tried so hard to convince me that there was no way I could have known the dominoes were there or that JPP had targeted my family as his next set of victims. "You would have had to be as crazy as he is to think that way," Mac had said. But none of his comfort reached me. Jackson was dead. Cece was dead. And it was my fault.

I had come to Brooklyn because it was unlike anywhere I had ever lived. I thought of it as hiding in plain sight; hiding from myself, really, since JPP was locked up and couldn't get to me. Everyone had agreed it was a good idea, safer to lose myself in a crowd than suffer alone in the country somewhere. How did he find me? I had moved here only four months ago and had spent hours online and on the phone erasing any trace of my new location. But the thing about JPP was that if he wanted you, he found a way.

"Come on," Detective Billy Staples said. "I've got orders to bring you in."

I heard it two ways at once: Protecting me was the obvious thing to do, and yet I didn't want to go. I'd been there, done that. The police could do their best to save my skin, but the part that really needed saving— my heart and soul—were very much my own problem. I had been working on them full-time for months now, doing nothing but finding any small way to "recognize pleasure" again, as Joyce would say. She hadn't bothered saying "feel" pleasure or "be happy" because I wasn't nearly that advanced yet. I was trying to hold myself together and I had discovered that I had to do it on my own. If I stepped into a police department right now, or any place filled with the smells and sights and sounds of my old life—the life that had brought this on—I didn't think I could handle it. I needed to stay quiet and stay home, at least for now.

"Don't I have a choice?"

"I'm not sure what other choice you really have right now, you know?"

"I'm going to stay."

"No, Karin, you've got to come with me. It isn't safe for you here."

But safety for me, these days, was in the eye of the beholder. "Detective Staples, I don't believe you have the right to compel me."

He jammed his hands in his pockets and stared at me. He was wearing jeans, too, but his were clean. "Okay," he said. "Have it your way. But we'll be out here, just in case. And I want you to call me the minute you change your mind." He handed me his card, white embossed with shiny blue lettering showing his whereabouts at the NYPD.

"Thanks." I slipped the card into my pocket. "I just want some time to think, and then I'll get in touch."

He paused, then asked, "Do we need to worry about you?"

I knew what he was referring to: Nine months ago I tried to take my own life. "No. You don't need to worry about me. I've dealt with that."

A cloud passed overhead and the sun blasted into his face, revealing a map of lines across his high cheekbones and a few gray hairs at his temples. I had put him at about thirty but saw now that he was older by a decade. He nodded and turned toward his car, then looked back.

"By the way, I almost didn't recognize you. You don't look much like your photo."

No, I didn't. In the head shot they took for my employee ID I had shoulder-length reddish hair and a big smile. The

photographer had been joking around that day, or maybe
he always did so staff photos wouldn't look like mug shots.

"That was taken five years ago," I said.

He nodded, understanding me. "A lifetime."

"Thank you, Detective. I have your number."

He drove away and I went through the locked iron gate
most brownstones had at the ground-floor entry, separating
a small space from an inner door. Between the two doors
there was a cupboard beneath the front stoop that served
as a catch-all for stuff I didn't want to bring into the house,
like the bag of rock salt I'd bought to melt ice from my
entryway in the winter when I'd first moved in, and the
dirty gardening accessories I stashed there now. The inner
door itself had a glass-paneled upper half and a flimsy lock
I rarely bothered turning. I turned it now and stood in my
front hall, knowing that even the best of locks couldn't
keep JPP out if he wanted to get in.

I had tried to make my new home as comfortable as
possible, more like the apartment I'd lived in before
Jackson and I bought a house together and tossed
our eclectic stuff away in favor of the more mature
and dignified stuff of coupledom. I'd sold all our real
furniture with the house and started fresh when I came
here, collecting castoffs from the sidewalk and buying
cheap furniture off Craigslist. I bought what I *liked* and
what I *wanted*. It had been one of Joyce's dictates. *No
shoulds*. Except for one thing: She specifically asked

me to put a mirror near the front door so I could check myself coming in and going out. She wanted me to catch myself if I "zombied-out" again. I'd hung an enormous mirror with an ornate faux-gilt frame on the wall above a shoe caddy. There were four pudgy angels, one at each corner, each aiming an arrow at the image in the mirror, the idea being to make you feel beautiful, chosen by love, when you looked at yourself.

But I didn't feel anything when I looked at myself today. What I experienced was a kind of muted unfeeling I'd gotten used to since after my suicide attempt. It was the best I could do and it was better than despair. I looked at myself, at the long hair I'd colored blond at Joyce's insistence; in the weeks after my family's murder my hair had turned prematurely gray, and Joyce said that, when she met me months later, my faded appearance had shocked her. She said it wasn't good for me to "go around looking like a ghost." Now that I'd dyed my hair, its lack of natural color made me feel like a blank canvas, as if I could be anyone, and in a way I liked that. I wanted nothing more than to be someone else, someplace else, without any of my own memories. I looked at myself. Tall. Thin. Flat. Sinewy limbs like a boy's. Expression a blank wall between memory and feeling. I felt no fear, and I had nothing left to lose.

I knew what I wanted: I wanted him to find me.

Then this could be over, once and for all.